———

The park was not empty, even though dark had settled in. Floodlights illuminated the abandoned tennis courts, spilled on to the swings and monkey bars. A light rain soaked everything. It was just above freezing. Still, a number of kids from the nearby junior high hung out, talking. They barely glanced up from their intense circle as Ginny passed. But she noticed them.

Every sweaty boy, every waft of cheap, teen-aged cologne, every Bonnie Belle faced girl, every flavored lip gloss and sweet shampoo that floated to her, Ginny noticed. Deeper, still, in rising alarm, Ginny could discern cooking odors from their homes, chalk dust from the classrooms, disinfectant one of the boys must have brushed against in the locker room. Deeper still, the musky, mushroomy scent of the boys, in their more private zones—some wearing talc, others clearly unwashed that day. And the girls, the girls! Their intimate aromas almost made Ginny salivate. Shocking, even to herself.

The childhood visits, the unwanted attention from her father, came streaking into her consciousness like errant stars. Had his hunger been this insatiable? Had her scent aroused such fury in him? No! It was intolerable. How often had she become physically ill after hearing about adults who preyed on children? Now, in this very playground, she, she had come here, specifically. She knew the older children would still be out, after dark, knew exactly which area they'd gather in. She had come here, stalking them, even as her father had stalked her!

Rising from the bench at the sandbox edge, Ginny began to run. Faster, faster, not stopping for so much as a backward glance, needing to get away, she ran on, away from the children, out of the park!

All the junior high students noticed was a flash of tan trench coat, the streak of muted gold which was the dancer's hair as it came undone from its braid, the rapid exit of another nameless adult from their intense, young lives.

Immersed, once again, in each other, they were unaware of how close, how close they'd really come . . .

———

On Karen Marie Christa Minns' vampires . . . met again in "Bloodsong"

"**Virago** is full of the power, eroticism, and fear that are so much a part of vampire stories . . . . Minns' novel will surely become a part of the standards by which other vampire stories are judged. Well-developed characters and good plotting make **Virago** one of the most readable vampire novels available." _Jackie Cooper, Lambda Book Report

"**Virago** is a strange and exotic tale. The dark sensuality and underlying fear will leave you breathless." _The Coffee Club

"Anne Rice's vampires are wimps compared to the terrible and terrifying Darsen, perhaps the most frightening female since Elizabeth Bathory." _Jesse Monteagudo, TWN

"Minns has published more erotic fiction in **<u>On Our Backs</u>** than any other author, including **Ginny at Tea** (which established her as a readers' favorite in 1985), **Detention**, **Final Sitting**, **Etudie Erotique** and, most recently, **The Saddlemaker**. Unlike many writers who eschew the notion of lesbian romance, Minns is genuinely gifted at delivering believable lavender prose that tugs at the clit as well as the heart." _Susie Bright, On Our Backs

"Not a usual fan of horror fiction, this reviewer was pleasantly surprised, finding **Virago** a fast paced book which pulls the reader from romance to terror and back. **Virago** will haunt you long after you've devoured the last page." _The Inkblot

Bloodsong

a novel

KAREN MARIE CHRISTA MINNS

Bluestocking Books . Irvine . CA

This is a work of fiction and any resemblance to events or persons living or dead is unintentional and purely coincidental.

The publisher gratefully acknowledges permission from Martin Secker & Warburg Ltd, to include the excerpt from "Way of All the Earth" by Anna Akhmatova, translated by D.M.Thomas, published by Martin Secker & Warburg Ltd, Great Britain, 1979.

Cover art copyright © 1997 Bluestocking Books
Cover design by L. Norman.

Published by
Bluestocking Books,
P.O. Box 50998, Irvine, CA 92619-0998
Phone: 714/857-9043

Library of Congress Catalog Card Number: 97-70611

Library of Congress Cataloging-in-Publication Data:
Minns, Karen Marie Christa 1956-
Bloodsong: a novel / Karen Marie Christa Minns
p. 224   ISBN: 1-887237-08-9

1. Vampires.
2. Vampires fiction.
3. Lesbian vampires fiction.
4. Darsen (Fictitious character).

First Edition, April 1997
10 9 8 7 6 5 4 3 2 1

DEDICATION

To Teresa DeCrescenzo, defender of children.

　　You have always known . . .

ACKNOWLEDGMENTS

Special thanks to Margaret Gillon who called my Muse back from sabbatical; to Jayne and Nancy and Susan and Barbara and Janice and DeAnna—the women who save my life each and every day.

All Love.

But I warn you,
I am living for the last time.
Not as a swallow, not as a maple,
Not as a reed nor as a star,
Not as water from a spring,
Not as bells in a tower —
Shall I return to trouble you . . . .

"Way Of All The Earth" by Anna Akhmatova
translated by D. M. Thomas
published by Martin Secker & Warburg Ltd, Great Britain 1979

PART 1

It was the sound of the geese over the music she felt, as if their haunted syncopation were calling her to mark this time. This time. The first time. Spring rising from the lake with the night mist. Still cold enough to remind them all of the past winter but not so biting as to cool the sweat from the dancers' bodies. The first time she had seen Ginny MacPhearson fill space with her golden presence. Manilla listened to the weird night music of the birds on the water's edge and the African drums that propelled the dancers on the Boathouse floor into a frenzy.

Ginny MacPhearson, the diplomat's daughter, one of the elite of Weston College's senior class: her hair moved as if it were alive, streaming honey and wheat stalks and precious, melted metals; plastered in hot tendrils across her naked back, then released; whirling, a mask, a veil, a shadow; her hair its own entity, riding her, moving her, whipping her on.

Manilla's heart began its own drum solo, the steady pulse building. Watching Ginny and the other senior women in this hundred-year-old rite of spring, at this two-hundred-year-old women's college, made Manilla feel heavy, drugged, very wet.

No professors, no faculty, no staff and definitely no men — this was an Amazonian gathering. Even women who would be horrified at having this fact pointed out to them were lost in the wild revelry. In the morning, they would shower, revert to their common, good-girl forms, attend classes, kiss boyfriends, call home. But, at this outrageous moment they were all, yes, Amazons — abandoned by everything save the lake, the music and each other.

A snaky circle began to form, then melt back, only to reform in a sinuous glide. At its center was the darling of the oldest class, Ginny. Ginny. Dancer, summa cum laude scholar, daughter of Ernest and Olivia MacPhearson, apple of their eyes. She would be leaving the nest of Weston College for — where? Manilla, watching as Ginny rose and fell in the dervish the dance had become, could only guess. Probably to Europe, where her father made constant news as the hottest diplomat the U.S. had seen in recent years. Or Africa — there had been that rumor of an appointment for her father there. Should he receive it, Ginny would follow. Adventure. Culture. Money. All the things Manilla knew only from books — these were Ginny MacPhearson's life. What would Weston be like without its Athena, without the haloed one?

Of course Manilla was in thrall. They all were — Ginny's family had appeared in Time, Newsweek; hell, at the fall of apartheid there had even been a blip in Rolling Stone. In the scholarly, prestigious womb of the college, Ginny was a star-baby — and she was acknowledged as such — much to her chagrin.

In Manilla's life there had been only that which she had fought for — even as she watched the golden-limbed older student, Manilla could smell the rust from her own factory town. Only her art and the scholarships it brought her had allowed her escape. Only her paintings and their brilliant promise, had gained her access to the bookish paradise of Weston. Each day she had to prove herself again. Most of the other women came from old American money or older European roots. Their families had known each other for as long as Weston had been in operation. Upstate New York was the perfect holding tank — too far from the City to cause worry, yet close enough to the Ivy League to insure the old money's daughters ample opportunity for good matches. Weston bred educated ladies in a way that held on to nineteenth century morals but formatted twenty-first century skills. There was no paucity of p.c.'s, no lack of technical laboratories or elite lecturers. Weston was the place you went if you had clout, but couldn't cut Harvard. Only five hundred, hand-picked women made it onto this campus — and Manilla was one of them. Raw nerve (and a gift recognized by the right people early on) had allowed her access. She was among them but not one of them. Never one of them. She had gained access because the aristocracy had always been patrons of the arts. If Manilla was anything, she was an artist. And, in America in the last part of the twentieth century, she filled an unspoken and publicly denied quota. That was all right — as long as she understood the rules. As long as she was given the odds up-front. She knew, going in — after three hard years, she knew it still.

No flying to Aspen for the week-end, no trips to the islands over the winter break; Manilla's fight was merely to be allowed to stay. In dark dorms, in cold studios, she worked on that which had gained her entry into the ivory halls — she worked at her painting. Through vacations, through summers, Manilla stayed on. Nothing would beat her. The promise was slow, recognition slower — but she fought on. Through those endless hours when most of the campus was away, Manilla had crossed paths with Ginny MacPhearson. Ginny, equally alone — was always headed in the opposite direction, to the Dance Studio. As they passed there was often some small spark — recognition, electricity — who knew for sure? Clearly, though, Ginny had her own demons.

Manilla knew who Ginny was, of course. She had even caught Ginny staring at her across the dining hall, once. But to actually speak to the dancer, to initiate more than the casual notice, impossible. Besides, in the small pond of Weston, an "out" lesbian like Manilla (class issues aside) was a risky friend, at best. No, the contact was at a distance. Spark or no spark, Ginny was off limits. Manilla's friends reminded her of that. Often.

Then, one night, cutting across the frozen lawn, head low, ducking snow, Ginny had literally bumped into Manilla.

The roll of canvas Manilla was carrying fell to the icy path. The dancer helped the painter to gather up the material. Briefly, their hands touched.

"I know your work. In the Studio, I've seen it. It, it makes all the others seem so small and pale . . . ."

Then, Ginny was gone.

Manilla felt the burning in her face the rest of the evening. So, Ginny had known her work!

That meant Ginny knew her core . . . . Ginny had seen past the torn denim, the unruly mass of curls, the dark eyes and macha swagger. Ginny had seen the paintings. Ginny had seen her soul.

Weeks passed. A hurriedly scribbled note was left on Manilla's easel in the Art Studio — the invitation to the Boathouse. An invitation to watch Ginny dance! Of course,

Manilla went. Like artists for thousands of years, she went, hoping to spot her muse.

The circle formed and fell back. The drumbeats grew louder, mingling with flutes and rattles, drowning out even the geese. Voices began to rise in constant chant. Feet smashed savagely against the straining floor. The scent of varnish mixed with the scents of rigging and expensive perfume.

Ginny was in the center; some great goddess, Kali or Shiva — she seemed to be stalking the crowd. Then, her gaze found Manilla.

Ginny's look was like a touch — a ripple of heat sending fever chills across Manilla's skin. The painter felt pulled into the dance, past the others, pulled in until she was directly facing Ginny.

Ginny stood, palms touching Manilla's face in scalding benediction.

In unspoken hauntings — Manilla had entered her dreams. Now, like a great river breaking after winter ice, Ginny was breaking.

Ginny believed in Fate, in magic and omens. She had watched Manilla. She had been watched in return.

In front of them all, caring not what anyone would later say, would think, would insinuate, Ginny MacPhearson had made her decision. She pulled Manilla as lightly as if she were plucking a blossom from an apple tree. Manilla came to her, there, in the midst of the heathen dancers. For that moment, in the middle of that hedonistic circle, time stopped; judgment, suspended. Only fire, sweat, hunger mattered. The dancers paid homage to this goddess alone.

Manilla knew who she was; she had always known. Her love for women had been ignited in her first year at Weston.

But Ginny? What did Ginny know? Did Ginny know how this would look, or what rumors were sure to rise — if not this night, then at least by morning? Before Manilla could break the spell, before she could pull back, smile, apologize, melt into the undulating circle and then out of the crowd, away, Ginny pulled her tight.

The dancer smelt of hyacinth — of hyacinth and clean-sweat — and more. It was unmistakable. The hunger was raw, was right on her skin — Manilla knew, then, for the first time. Whatever else would come of it — even if nothing came of it — in this second, Ginny MacPhearson wanted her. Ginny wanted her exactly the way Manilla ached for Ginny.

Manilla's heart rang louder in her ears than even the stamping of the women whirling around them. Ginny's strong embrace pulled the shorter woman tight, the softness of Manilla's tee-shirt betraying the hardening nipples and panting chest. Ginny's hot tongue found its way into the shell of Manilla's ear, causing such an explosive sensation that Manilla felt as if she would go down in a puddle at the dancer's feet.

"Please, please, not here . . . ," Manilla panted, moving only slightly away from Ginny's arms.

"Then let's go — now," Ginny whispered.

The gyrating crowd hardly looked back as Ginny moved Manilla from the Boathouse.

Down the rocking pier, over the beach, past the parking lot and across the mighty expanse of Weston's main lawn, they moved. Every few yards Ginny would slow, touch Manilla maddeningly, then laugh and run on.

Manilla could not remember when she'd been so wet, so open, and yet still able to walk, let alone follow. She wanted to scream, to tackle Ginny, to ravage her there, on the grass, to take her under the giant sycamore outside the dorms — but Ginny was too fast. The dancer was Spirit made flesh. Lithe, tall, so quick she was merely night-shadow, weaving, disappearing and then re-appearing along the edges of the trees, she was always just out of grasp.

Manilla could barely keep up. Then, Ginny waited, enticingly, calling Manilla's name like a soft breeze coming out of the woods. Finally, the pursuit halted just where the forests that lined the college began.

Ginny stopped, breathing hard, pushing Manilla almost roughly against a huge oak. Manilla felt trembly, a little scared. This was, after all, Ginny MacPhearson. Yes, there had been all the synchronicity of their quick meetings, hurried glances, passings these many months. Yes, there had been some direct current, powerful, undeniable, visibly moving between them, and there had even been the invitation to the Boathouse. Ginny had slipped it onto Manilla's easel the week before. But nothing this bold, this overt. Was Ginny just drunk with the debauch of the evening? Was she stoned, toying with another exotic adventure in a life of such encounters? Or was it a cruel joke? For a millisecond all the insecurities of Manilla's past welled up, threatened to spill over. Her eyes began to blur, a lump began to form in her throat. Why would Ginny choose her?

Before she could form the words, the dancer leaned against Manilla. Ginny's form melded with Manilla's, filling each hollow, touching and molding against every soft curve as if Ginny could press beyond flesh, beyond bone — become blood and, in so becoming, flood Manilla with her presence, her energy, her heat.

"Shhh," Ginny crooned, her lips finding Manilla in the deep shadow of the trees, "Shhh."

"Are you sure you want to start this. Are you really sure, Ginny? Because, if we start, I can't go back." Manilla breathed the words into the dancer's neck.

"It's all right. I am sure — very, very sure.

Then, Ginny kissed her, and Manilla filled with different questions.

———

"Thank Maggie for lending the car, okay?" Ginny pushed her shoulder against the Fiat's door. It was hard to move in her low-cut formal.

"Wait, I'll get it." Manilla was half out of the driver's seat when Ginny grabbed her, stopping her short.

"Don't, Manilla! Please. You aren't my servant." Ginny calmed a bit, then took her lover's hand.

"Nor your escort, right? I know. They'll be watching." Manilla settled back behind the wheel.

"You know I don't give a damn who sees what! I just don't want you to go through — I don't know. It's too complicated. It's about seeing him up there, seeing them both at Weston." Ginny's voice broke.

"Oh, Gin, don't go to the dinner — you won't be the first to skip the President's reception — fuck it. They can't stop you from graduating —" Manilla pressed Ginny's palm.

"It's just that this is my place, my turf. He has nothing to do with this place, these people."

"I know, Gin. Hey, I'll wait up for you." Manilla tried a half-smile.

"I'm counting on it." Suddenly, Ginny's door was pulled open. There was a blinding flash as the dancer fell back against Manilla.

"Thanks, girls. One for the family album, ha!" The photographer ripped the door open wider, took a second shot and was across the darkened lawns before their eyes cleared.

"Christ!" Manilla felt her heart begin to slow.

Suddenly, a tall, tuxedoed man reached for Ginny's arm. Gingerly, he said, "May I escort you to your parents, Ms. MacPhearson?"

Ginny recognized him, or, at least she recognized his style. Armed guards — of course. No toy soldiers in her childhood, only these faceless, nameless men filling her home.

He slammed the car door, made a quick motion that Manilla should leave. There was no time to even question. It was Ginny's circus now.

Manilla peeled away, burning rubber in front of a dozen sets of parents headed up the walkway to the formal dinner. Flashbulbs were still spinning in her head as she made an illegal u-turn and hit the gas.

"Where did that idiot buy her license?" Ernest MacPhearson said as he leaned down to peck his daughter's flushed cheek.

In vain, Ginny tried not to flinch at the man's touch.

Her mother caught the struggle and attempted a rescue. "Virginia, you look wonderful! Darling, we're so proud."

Ginny moved past both of her parents. "I think we're holding everyone up. We better go inside."

The handsome dancer moved into the foyer of the mansion. She did not wait for them to follow. Cameras clicked. The crowd parted for her father. Ginny's flesh crawled.

"Just a little while," she thought. "I can get through this evening."

"You'll be seated at my table, of course." Weston's president held out his hand for the MacPhearsons.

He was dwarfed by the tall diplomat.

Ernest MacPhearson answered matter-of-factly, "Of course."

Students were serving the meal. Every time someone passed, the dancer winced. In all her years at Weston she'd never been approached to help serve the President's Senior Dinner. It seemed positively archaic that her friends had been so pressed. Ginny bit the inside of her cheek, kept her mind on Manilla. Manilla, her sanity, her anchor in this sea of sham.

Olivia MacPhearson downed another glass of wine. Her cheeks were the same flushed shade as the liquid. Her gestures were becoming animated, almost wild.

Ginny knew it was only moments before her father would intervene. Pulling Olivia's chair out in such a way that there was no room for protest he would excuse both of them for "some air."

The table would smile, secretly relieved, then nod as the handsome diplomat and his regal lady left. For Ginny, these departures always created a sudden vacuum. She knew, from thousands of dinners before, that no one would speak to her again until her parents returned. They would smile condescendingly, in her direction, even touch her reassuringly, on the back of her hand — but no one would directly speak with her. Ginny knew the script; she'd lived it too often to be unsure.

She checked her watch. Before she could glance up, Olivia had returned. Her mother was more subdued, but much of her earlier grace was gone. A stiffness marked her steps. No one would notice, or, if they did, no one would comment, not even a hushed aside. This was the diplomat's wife.

Ginny closed her eyes at her parents' return. She dug her fingernails into her palms, clenched her fists in her lap. Why were they doing this to her, why here, where she'd come to construct her own peace, her own life?

"This house is so handsomely furnished. Have you been upstairs, dear?" Olivia reached for her wineglass, smiling.

It was more than Ginny could bear. Under her breath, she hissed, "Mother, you didn't have to show up tonight. It would have been enough to come to the graduation. If this is, is difficult, for you . . . and him . . . "

"Why, Virginia, what nonsense! What makes you say such things? We're having a marvelous time. It's such a treat to meet the faculty and administration after all of these years. And the President —"

"Is a crashing bore and a hypocrite!" The stress of the evening was taking its toll on Ginny. She could feel her temples beginning to throb, her muscles shake.

"Virginia! I don't want to ever hear you so much as whisper in such a manner about the host, especially at his own table! You have been raised to know the distinction between propriety and poor taste."

"Mother, you know nothing about this man nor his sexist politics —"

"And you know nothing of gentility!"

Ginny was almost trembling. "At least I'm honest . . . and sober." Ginny's voice was steady, almost calm. There. For years she had wanted to name it. To bring it forward, out of the shadowy hallways and dark libraries where her mother retreated to drink away each day in each embassy. Out of the black holes that made up so much of Ginny's childhood. Now, it had been said. Nothing could take it back,

As if in slow motion, blocking everything and everyone, Olivia turned toward her only daughter. Her eyes were deadly. She gripped the edge of the table with both hands, her knuckles as pale as her face. "At least I am normal." Olivia's voice was a harsh whisper.

"What?" Ginny choked back the sudden burning in her throat.

"I said — " Olivia's voice was tearing with emotion. The strain of keeping Ernest happy, of holding back the brutal disappointment that had come with the letter from Weston's president, their host and friend, delicately informing them of Ginny's liaison with another student, the tyranny of the life she'd led, all ornamental and surface, numbing and caged, all of these things about to be unleashed by this confrontation with her daughter, this public humiliation . . . Olivia's voice rose: "At least I am . . . a woman — a normal woman."

"You have no right!" Ginny was on her feet. Table linen, wineglasses, crashed into the gulf that had risen between her and her mother. Shock. Absolute. A taste like tin in her mouth. When had her parents found out about Manilla? There had been no warning calls, no threatening letters. In the past, when she'd caused some minor infraction at any school, they had immediately descended. No indication of any kind had been forthcoming. Ginny truly believed she'd escaped their clutches. She had truly believed that she was in a new, heady, free life, a life her father and her mother could not touch or control. But now — the reality hit stunningly — now they knew!

"Virginia, when you left us you were whole, healthy, balanced. Now I don't know who or what you are! You're sick, Virginia! Sick! How dare YOU criticize ME? Or my life — your father's life? You are depraved!" Olivia rose to confront her daughter.

The table sat in complete silence. All eyes focused on their plates. Other tables remained oblivious to the unfolding drama.

As her elegant mother stood in front of her, an older, but perfect mirrored image, Ginny felt herself shrivel. Every minute cell in her body screamed for sanctuary, for retreat — to get away!

"That's enough." Two large hands descended upon Olivia's bare shoulders. Ernest stood above his wife, furious.

Olivia began to sob, "It is enough, isn't it?"

Ernest turned to the stunned table. "Excuse us, please. My wife hasn't been well. I believe our schedule has finally caught up with her."

In relief the President and the guests beamed at the handsome man. Of course. It was imminently understandable.

"Stop it! Stop it! You don't have to make any more excuses for me, Ernest!" Olivia staggered, her face contorting with rage.

"I said it is enough." Ernest's expression was tight.

Ginny didn't wait for the rest of the room to realize what was occurring. She backed away from her parents like a terrified animal. And then, she fled.

The hallway outside the dining room seemed altered. Her dress tripped her, trapped her, slowed her escape. She brushed by the last bevy of students and reached the door. She could hear Ernest coming after her.

Outside, the night wrapped a dark comforter around her shoulders. Moist, alive, the lake sang its greeting, a soothing symphony caressing and making her whole. For the first time, Ginny understood Manilla's need to be outdoors — Manilla's constant connection with the wild. There was safety beyond the walls, safety beyond the human cages of rooms and people.

Ginny tore off her heels and pounded across the spongy lawns. Below her, cars filled with underclass women or townies, all sneaking peaks at the illustrious party on the hill cruised Main Street.

Safety.

She tore along the edges of the pine woods, cut to the great ravine that divided the campus in half. Across the wooden footbridge she ran — closer to Manilla. Closer to all she considered home.

Safety.

Her feet were bruised, one toe had bloodied when she slammed into the walk. She hardly felt it, so intense was the horror propelling her. The President's mask-like grin, her father's own well-clothed anger, her mother's betrayal in front of classmates and parents . . .

Safety.

She had to get to Manilla, to the one point of sanity left, away from the monstrous evening, the death-watch of this night.

Then it hit her; Manilla was in danger. Ginny knew the anger and reach of her father. Above all, decorum reigned. No matter his own evil rule, his hateful and unwanted touches, his secret visits to her bedroom — no matter his cruelty and coldness to her mother, the absolute control he demanded at all times from everyone around him — these things were fact, cut into the stone of their lives. She had learned to cope. But the people he felt threatened by — even friends who dared question what went on in his family life — Ginny knew how he dealt with them. Now, Manilla was at risk! Her father would use overkill, of this Ginny was certain. He could destroy Manilla's chances at Weston, disgrace her publicly, set her up and take her down. In places like Weston it was easy to drop a few discrete words and ruin a person's life. Her scholarship, her loans, maybe, even, her chances at grad school . . . who knew what he'd dig up as a means of blackmail? He'd try to buy her and then he'd try to frighten her. Whatever it took to keep appearances up, to keep his family's name pure. Old friend or not, the President of Weston could use a few favors. Ginny was sure he'd manipulate the information. Hadn't he already contacted her mother and set this pendulum swinging? There was no real loyalty in the world her father existed in, in the rooms her family inhabited. There was only survival and evolution — or so her father had made them all believe. Now, she'd stopped believing. She'd become the enemy.

Manilla had taught her to believe — in love that didn't ask for favors, in loyalty based on the heart, in a different world, a different life, a life with freedom at its center. Because of this, Manilla would be destroyed.

There was no safety. There was only the chance of escape — together.

Skirting the shadows and lights that led to Manilla's dorm, Ginny crawled up the mossy bank. There was the possibility of escape. Flight had been the hallmark of her young life. She knew how to pack up and run, to leave behind everything — possessions, friends, pets, even memories. She could teach Manilla. If they hurried, they could beat her father's reach. If they hurried, they could flee before he found them. She had to get to Manilla and explain. There was no more time for secrets.

She knew, as she reached the dorm door, she would now have to trust Manilla with her life.

Ginny heaved the painter's door open.

A half-empty bottle of Coke beside her, Manilla was on the floor, reading. Joni Mitchell wailed "Blue" on the stereo. Ginny fought hysteria at the sight of the warm normalcy of the room.

"Gin, what? What?" Manilla sat up, then went to the bedraggled dancer. Wiping mud and pine-needles from Ginny's face, dabbing at the sweat pouring from her forehead Manilla, expected the worst as she gently pried answers from her lover.

"No rape — not physically — not this time." Ginny moved like a sleep-walker, and sank on to Manilla's bed. The hysteria was passing. In its place, a coldness filled her. This was the feeling that was the herald of her father's presence. Carefully, her voice no more than a whisper, Ginny related the evening's events. She stopped only at the moment when she left the mansion and fled for the dorm. For home.

Manilla did what she knew how to do — she listened. Sitting beside Ginny, covering her with a blanket, offering the warm soda, she paused unsure of what else to do. It wasn't sinking in. Ginny's father, the diplomat, Weston's President, his friend . . . a letter to Ginny's mother . . . danger?

"Who gives a fuck? Ginny, we got 'outed'. That's what happens. I've tried explaining that risk to you for months." Manilla was drowning in unclear details.

"You don't get it, Manilla. Don't you see? This isn't just a college thing — it isn't just a hometown rumor and not being voted Most Likely to Succeed. My father is a very important, highly visible man. He is asked to deal with people, with countries where this sort of thing is cause for death. Worse, this is about my family — blood family. My father, he, he can't — he won't stand for anything that isn't protocol. His friend, the President, all his buddies, his colleagues, they count on it.

"People know. Everyone would love to have my father owe them a favor . . . "

"Ginny, I'm sorry. I really don't get it." Manilla touched her lover's elbow, gently.

"Manilla, I'm sure my mother's known about him, and me, forever. His coming to me — getting me alone — forcing me, alone. He wasn't careful around her. In the privacy of our own spaces he didn't care. He knew he controlled her absolutely, controlled all of us like his private robots. He never even asked me not to tell. Can you believe it? That's why she drinks — and why she's jealous.

"Always, Manilla, I would pray that he'd stop, that she'd find us together and make him stop, or take me away — somewhere safe, that she'd make it safe for both of us. She never did. You're the only person I've ever told. It's so damned ugly. I stopped praying, Manilla. Then, I stopped him. I fought back. Please, believe me. I hated it and I hated him. Hated her, too. Hated her so much," Ginny broke the covering of ice. Hot tears flooded her eyes.

Then Manilla knew it would be all right to take her into her arms, hold her, rock her, to let the dancer cry.

"Manilla, I love you," Ginny whispered, beginning to drift off.

"I love you so much, Gin, so much," Manilla whispered back, whispered into her lover's ear.

⸺

Hours later, they woke, planning the next move. Manilla was sure Ginny was still on the edge of hysteria. Surely, her father couldn't possibly be that powerful — or care that much. Getting "outed" was always traumatic. For Manilla, it had come her first year at Weston. Her art professor. Only a few years older, in her first college position, the woman had reached out to the frosh. She had been attracted by Manilla's talent, by her street-style. Manilla was a dark stone on the white sands of Weston. For the art teacher, Manilla was a kind of prize — the mark of being a professor.

Manilla had grown up around boys and men who expected a woman to be certain things. Lovers, whores, ornaments, mothers, grandmothers. If you didn't fit, you worked at fitting. By the time she'd made it to Weston, Manilla had twisted herself into knots.

Her scholarship got her out of the New England factory town and away from the working-class expectations they'd all tried to pound into her. She'd taken sanctuary in the Art Studio. Weston was bewildering. The money, the attitudes, numbed her personal feelings. She'd focused only on her work. Unable to compete socially, unable to afford the week-end trips or the wardrobe required for the parties the others attended, she'd always found her excuse, her scholarship, her painting. The other Weston students understood ART. Manilla got away with much that would have branded anyone else as outcast — the art had saved her. It had also led her to the Professor. For Manilla, it was an internal explosion. So different from the infuriatingly unfulfilled nights she'd spent wrestling the boys from her hometown — or even the few sweaty interludes with frat boys she'd experimented with. She felt as if some kind of lens had been lifted from her third-eye. This was spiritual — and Manilla had been entirely unprepared.

Always, the encounters were at the Professor's apartment in town. Always they were by invitation only — never for the night. Too much risk. It was clear, from the onset, that Manilla wasn't the only dalliance. Manilla didn't care. She was the only Weston lover. For her, for then, it was enough. The Professor had been a guide over the landscape of Manilla's body and heart. When Manilla tried to reach back, the Professor, like most guides, only laughed. Manilla was a novice in this adventure. As Manilla desperately attempted to equalize the relationship, the Professor drew back. Manilla was shattered. It ended badly. The Prof's appointment ran out and it wasn't renewed. Never assuming she should explain more than perfunctory details to Manilla, she moved to another state, another college. Then, she'd even stopped answering Manilla's calls and letters.

In the ensuing months, Manilla was like a zombie. She'd worked at the college through the summer. She'd been home only once. Her mother and father were horrified at the changes. Hair cut an inch long, denim and army boots, torn tee-shirts and piercings: it was barely under wraps. Then, one morning the summer after her first year, home for a few weeks before the fall term began, Manilla was drinking coffee, with her two sisters. It was warm, bright, the last easy time Manilla could remember in that house.

The morning sunlight streaked it with honey and gold. Em was talking about the date she'd had the night before. Their sister Bryn, was chuckling into her cup. She thought the date was a geek. Manilla only rolled her eyes, happy to be with them, to be accepted and easy and loved. Her siblings had taken the transformation fairly easily. So had her two younger brothers — though nobody wanted the details. But her parents — their quiet rage was barely below the surface. Manilla had ducked every encounter that would leave her alone with either of them. She needed, at this time in her life, the protection of her siblings. Always, she had been the fighter, the protector of the younger ones. Now, they were almost adults. It was their protection she had to rely upon. They hadn't let her down. Unspoken agreement reigned among them. It had been no surprise, this change in their big sister. They'd always sensed a difference. Even as she'd dated, had boyfriends, did the traditional proms, Manilla was at a distance from it all. It went deeper than being an artist.

Manilla seemed like another branch of the family. In their mixed background, a child could be almost any shade — darkest night to the green-eyed sister seated across the breakfast table. It wasn't looks, but a way of being. They'd all known it and accepted it. But, when it burst into bloom, at Weston, it seemed the only people who had been surprised were their parents.

This morning, carrying the paper, their mother had come into the kitchen.

She poured no coffee, put no bread into the toaster. She did not smile.

She sat at her position at the table, the same seat she'd taken for the nineteen years they'd lived there, and lifted the paper to read. The girls quieted, but continued teasing about the previous night's date. Then, the explosion.

Their mother suddenly slammed the paper onto the Formica tabletop. The coffee in all three cups rose in tiny tidal-waves and splashed into the saucers. Manilla saw the liquid movement in slow-motion. Her heart caught in her chest. She knew. She knew what was coming.

"If I ever found out any of my children were . . . were . . . homosexual I'd have them committed. Do you hear me? I think it's disgusting! Unnatural!" Then, as quickly as the storm hit, it blew over. Clutching the newspaper to her breast, as if it were the Holy Grail, Manilla's mother rose from the kitchen chair and left the three daughters to stare silently at her retreat.

Manilla carried no memory of the rest of the breakfast — or much of the vacation. Since then, for the most part, Weston had been where she'd stayed. Her personal life was non-existent. Her political life, low-key — the way the college required it to be. The power of money, was almost absolute. Her focus had been the Art Studio — the classes surrounding it — expanding her into directions associated but not directly related to the art — anthropology, Native American studies, world religions. She'd followed her interests, raised only careful hell, had a few, casual friends, nursed her broken heart in silence and solitude. The painting had sustained her. It had taken all these experiences and synthesized the pain. Then, she'd met Ginny. The sting of being "outed" — by now the rumor of her first affair had traveled throughout the campus — fueled by the fact of the Professor's absence was fading. She wanted to protect Ginny, but she knew that outing was inevitable. Manilla had believed that, so close to graduation, Ginny would escape torment from her peers or any repercussions from old professors who'd known the golden girl in straighter times. But, if they were to be together, it had to happen. They'd never actually discussed the moment, but Ginny had to have known it would come.

Of course, now there was the humongous issue of Ginny's confession — or what felt, to Manilla, like a confession. Ginny had been physically sick after giving the details of her father's atrocities against her.

Manilla wanted to kill him. Never in her life had she wanted to do anything to equal this violent rage. This was Ginny — her light, her heart! And, worse, it had been Ginny as a child — alone, abandoned by an alcoholic mother who probably knew what was transpiring but had done nothing to intervene. Ginny, in boarding school after boarding school, sometimes left for an entire year in a place where she barely knew how to ask for the ketchup — such sad, funny stories Ginny had told over the months. Never, ever letting Manilla suspect the darker side — these cold, strange places the only comfort the small child could depend on. Home was never the nest, the sanctuary to fly for relief to. It was the true prison. No wonder Ginny loved Weston. No wonder she wanted to keep her parents from Manilla — from anything important in her adult life.

When they were children, Manilla's mother had been constantly sick — an invalid. Her cold absence had made it necessary for Manilla to protect, and in some ways, raise the four younger children. Manilla had learned, early on, if one didn't fight one's attackers the attacks would never end. It was a family joke, now that her siblings were all taller than she, but Manilla had been the guardian of them all.

How she longed for a time when she could protect Ginny like that. The street was brutal, but it was clear. There was no clarity here. What could she do to Ginny's father if, indeed, Ginny was right?

"My diaries — I've kept them all, since I was about twelve. They aren't really full, except when . . . I wrote those times down. It was my only sanity, Manilla. They're here, at Weston — about five of them. If he threatens you — or me — I swear, I'll, I'll show them to . . . !" Ginny's voice was hoarse.

"To whomever we have to, Gin. The threat will be enough, I bet. A man like him can hardly — "

"Stand it if he loses — no, we need more. He'll deny the accusations."

Ginny bit her under lip, pulled her torn gown around her, sought some kind of protection.

"I have a few friends in Ithaca. One of them is at the paper. This could be a big story — especially with the readership at Cornell. I mean, the local guys would jump all over this, but you know what it means, if we have to go that far?" Manilla leaned over her lover.

"I have friends, too. The Times, the D.C. papers — yes, I know, Manilla. But, I've already lost both parents. Years ago. Tonight, tonight I know for sure. All I can try to do, now, is to protect you. He'll blame all of this on some target. I know him. You are the closest. If I hold this over his head — and stop him, here, at Weston. Get him here, before his friend, the President, can protect him, he'll try to take your scholarship, Manilla." Ginny began to quietly cry, again.

"Forget it — I'd just like to take the bastard out . . . I swear."
Manilla paced the floor.

"We can't fight him like that, Manilla. Those are terms he's used to. Don't even think like that. One of the reasons I love you is because you are so clean — from any of this. I don't want that spoiled, love. We just need to organize, tonight, these few hours before he finds me. We have time."

———

A knock at the door awoke them. The radiator in the room was cold. Light filtered into the dorm room. Manilla unwrapped the quilt from around them. The door flew open. A man in a navy-blue suit and dark glasses stood there, his face lineless.

Manilla pulled on her glasses, "Who the hell?"

The suit turned toward Ginny. "I'm sorry Ms. MacPhearson. You're father requests that you meet him at the Aura Inn. I'm to accompany you there." The man stepped back into the hallway.

"She doesn't have to go!" Manilla stood in front of the guard.

"Yes I do, darling. It's all right. I know him. I know . . . his men." Ginny's hands pressed wrinkles from her ruined dress. She looked up, speaking to the suit.

"I'll need to change. My room is in another dorm. Meet me in front of the Main Building in twenty minutes."

Manilla was startled. She'd never heard her lover use such a tone. "I'm sorry, Miss, your father says . . . ."

"You have my word. I'll be there. I am not going to run from him again." Ginny swept the golden mass of hair into a bun.

"I'm going with her," Manilla stated.

"Twenty minutes, Ms. MacPhearson. The car will be waiting." The man pulled the door shut.

Ginny touched Manilla's shoulder, "You don't have to do this. You shouldn't come. He'll see it as provocation."

"I've seen the movies, Gin. This is the U.S. of A. So, his kid is queer. He can't kill your lover. You know?" Manilla tried to smile.

"Yeah, well, like they say in the movies, they can make you wish you were dead. I'm terribly serious, Manilla. You don't have to do this with me. I can say you've gone, out of my life, I can lie to him easily." Ginny stood by the door.

"No more lies, Ginny. Not from this point on. You aren't alone anymore. You don't ever have to lie again." Manilla kissed Ginny's hand.

Ginny spoke softly, "He'll call your family — probably already has."

"Yeah, I figured that, after last night. Well, we haven't been exactly close for a couple of years. They were going to find out 'officially', someday, Gin. We are each other's family now, right?"

"We've got fifteen minutes before the second wave hits. Meet me when you're ready." Ginny walked out, holding her head straight as whispers and stares followed her down the hall.

—

"So, you're the one. Interesting." Ernest MacPhearson coddled his snifter, his eyes flat, betraying nothing.

"The one, what?" Her fists hard against her thighs, Manilla stood in front of Ginny. Oh, she would like to strike this man, to make him scream!

"Very witty. I admire humor. Often it's the only way out of a sticky situation — and, my dear, you are in a very sticky situation. Sit down." Ernest sniffed the brandy.

The conference room was one of ten overlooking the lake. Manilla had been there once before, at a reception for a visiting artist.

"Ginny," Ernest said, "you're to come back with us today. We won't go through the sham of graduation. You'll come with us this afternoon. If you want to study dance, we'll arrange something abroad. But, I warn you, you will come with me." Ernest set down his glass.

Ginny glared, "I won't."

"I've called her parents, you know." He jerked his head toward Manilla. "They want nothing to do with her. She will leave Weston. Her scholarship has been revoked. There won't be another school in the country that will take her. I'll see to it." Ernest turned away and peered out toward the water.

Ginny rushed her father, grabbing for his arm, "You can't do this! I won't let you do this!"

Ernest swung around, catching her shoulders and holding her at arm's length. His eyes burned into her as he towered above.

"Let her go." Manilla was quiet, her control absolute, deadly.

"What?" He dropped his hands in amazement.

"Ginny told me all about you — what you've done to her. You filthy, perverted — "

Ernest gestured to the special agent just inside the room, "Johnson, leave!"

As the door clicked shut, Ernest's thin lips became white slits against the scarlet of his chin and cheeks. "No one will believe you. I'll have Ginny committed — all it takes is my word. And you, I'll bury you. There is no way anyone will hear — "

"They've already heard. I have a friend on the Ithaca Tribune who has a copy of the story. Another copy was sent to the Dean. If I don't show up at graduation with Ginny, the Dean will open the letter — and Ginny's diaries. She'll read all about you — dates, places, details only your daughter could know, everything verifiable." Manilla looked at Ginny.

"She's telling the truth." Ginny took Manilla's hand, squeezing so tightly that Manilla felt the blood cut off.

Ernest MacPhearson's voice became dangerous. He began to wheedle, "Virginia, why? I love you. I've always loved you. Why are you making up this nonsense?"

"Stop it! I can't stand it!" Ginny moved back. The smell of her father's breath made her nauseated.

"All right, stay here and rot," Ernest turned from her. "It doesn't matter to me anymore. You went away from me a long time ago."

Manilla kept her voice steady as she could, "It's not enough, Mr. MacPhearson. It would be too easy for you to come after us. We want it in writing — a, a contract. It simply states Ginny gets her trust fund and you continue to support her till it comes to term. No one touches my scholarship. You can't repair what you did to my family, but you can stop here. You can keep from spoiling the rest of your daughter's life." Manilla handed the envelope to the man.

"In return?" Ernest demanded, glancing at the piece of paper.

"You get no trouble from us," Ginny whispered, unable to look her father in the face.

"This is blackmail!" Ernest roared.

"Don't talk to me about blackmail, father, not after all those years you held me prisoner!"

Ernest MacPhearson signed and stood. His eyes were lifeless as he towered over Manilla and his daughter. He held the hand-written contract at arm's length, so that Manilla had to stretch to reach it. Then, he finished his drink.

Ginny's parents left without saying good-bye.

Even as she moved into the Collegetown loft in Ithaca, Ginny refused to speak about it. Cornell's dance program was her focus. That and her relationship with Manilla. Her silence went unbroken. Sometimes at night, believing Manilla asleep, she'd rise. There, by the loft's huge windows overlooking the city, she'd quietly cry.

But, Manilla heard.

Manilla always heard.

PART 2

"More coffee?"

Manilla sat up, expecting to hear Ginny's gentle sobbing in a moon-lit loft. Then, she remembered. Ginny was here, in the hospital. They were both in the hospital . . .

"More coffee, Miss?" The candy-striper stood next to the overloaded beverage cart. She saw the empty cup propped near the lamp. She looked down tentatively, at the smoke-smudged student who had been asleep on the lounge couch.

Word had passed through the ward that this student was the lover of the pretty girl they'd just brought into intensive care. The fire in Collegetown would be all over the morning papers. Word was passed that the burn victim was a diplomat's kid. Queer or not, these two were supposed to be treated with kid gloves — VIPs, no questions asked. Well, the night nurse hadn't been exactly that blunt, but anybody could read between the lines. Heck, even the fire-fighters downstairs were talking about it.

The student on the sofa was filthy. Only mild smoke inhalation, though. A few abrasions. Minor. No admission, even. Still, she'd insisted that she'd wait on the couch if they wouldn't let her into the room with her friend. She'd fallen asleep here.

Nobody was saying what the diplomat's daughter, MacPhearson, was suffering from. She'd been unconscious when the ambulance arrived. Badly bruised, possible severe burns, but something else, something all the night staff was whispering about — an animal bite. Ugly. Somewhere . . . delicate. It made the candy-striper shiver. She looked at the groggy student.

"Coffee?" This time she touched Manilla's arm.

Manilla lurched away. "What? What?"

"Sorry! I didn't mean to startle you. I didn't think you were asleep. I'm really sorry." The candy striper immediately sat down next to Manilla on the waiting-room couch.

Manilla ran sooty fingers through her curly hair. Coughing, tasting smoke, she shook the remnants of the dream from her mind. Gradually, the high-schooler next to her came into focus. After the last few hours, the primly starched red-and-white uniform was such a bizarre apparition, she laughed.

"Uh, you feeling okay? You want me to get one of the nurses?" the candy-striper asked nervously.

Manilla reached for the coffee. "I'm fine. Really. Just dreaming. Thank you. How's my friend, Ginny down the hall? Any word?"

The girl pulled the edge of her jumper closer to her knees. She couldn't look at Manilla, couldn't look directly into those eyes knowing. "Well, you know, they don't allow us in there — intensive care. But she isn't on any of the machines — so that's really good. It means no burns. The police said you guys were really lucky. The building went up like a bomb. Only you two were there, though. Guess your friend was the only one living in the loft, huh? My Dad says it's a sin the city allows those warehouses to be rented to students and artists, just so some people can make a buck. They aren't up to code like regular places. He says a bad fire's only a matter of time."

A large nurse, wearing a pink sweater over her uniform appeared in the hallway.

"Florence? Florence! You leave that young lady alone. For pity's sake, now. Can't you see she's needing some quiet? Get on to the other patients — please. I swear you high school girls just come to gab. Think you'd get enough of that on your own time! Now, get!"

"Okay, Mrs. Mackenzie. I'm out of here. Geez, I was just asking if she wanted coffee." The candy-striper smiled shyly as she rose.

Manilla offered a small wave. "Thanks."

"See ya," the high school girl winked. She pushed the cart in the direction of the floor nurse.

"Girls!" the woman smiled at Manilla.

"Yeah, girls." Manilla settled back onto the plastic cushions of the lounge sofa. Even though her skin was dry, she felt cold, like a sunburn. She pulled her knees up to her chest, then pulled her denim jacket over her. She put her hands beneath her cheek to rest her head. Something scratched! Manilla moved her hands out, into the light.

There was the immediate sparkle of red. A drop of crystallized blood. The stone glinted from its smudged silver setting.

Manilla pulled it off her finger. She breathed on it, then carefully rubbed some of the soot into her coat. Gingerly, she put the ring into the pocket of her denim jacket for safe keeping. Then, once again, she lay back, adjusting the coat, best she could, like a blanket. Slater's ring. All that was left. Manilla fell back to dreaming.

———

The night was cold. Winter would be early. Sinking into the damp moss at the edge of the golf course Manilla stopped her run. Inhaling deeply she pressed her sweaty forehead into the luxurious green. Incense. The forest edge was like the entrance to a great cathedral. For her, it had always been. She breathed deeply, letting her heart slow, letting so much of the past months slip away.

The forest saved her. The haunted ground of Weston College held her close. It was so strange to know that. But, even when she was little, running to the woods had kept her safe. Hadn't her family always chided her about it? Called her "changeling" — the elf child left in place of a stolen human infant. They were only half-kidding. Hadn't they always known she was different?

Now, their worries had been validated. Ginny's father had seen to it — put an official, black seal upon it. Upon Ginny, too. Both of them, cut off, cut away, like any imperfection, you wiped them out. Now, Ginny was her family, her life. And she would have to be Ginny's. It was so much pressure — to live up to that. But worth it. Manilla looked up into the crystalline sky and thanked whatever spirits could hear her. Of course, even separated by thirty miles of lake front, with Ginny firmly ensconced at Cornell, it was still worth it.

Only a year left at Weston — then grad school, art school, maybe even time off just to find work in a gallery? Like Ginny said, they had a life of options — a life. It had struck Manilla like an arrow, piercing her through. A life. Combined existences creating a new whole. Yes, whatever it took to get them through this last year of separation, Manilla would do it.

Ginny needed her in a way which didn't suffocate, a way that gave without demanding twice as much, in return, just to prove the love. Ginny burned for her. She devoured Manilla when they made love, pushing past skin, past muscle, past bone. Ginny entered her heart, pumping through her like blood.

Somewhere an owl called. A breeze made its way past Manilla's neck. Needing the hard press, the solidity, to ground her, she slumped against a sugar maple. If Ginny had been there, Ginny's presence would have had the same effect. But, Ginny wasn't. Now, it was up to this hallowed ground. She closed her eyes, waited for her pulse to slow. Sometimes, sometimes even the glare from the stars hurt.

So much was hard, harder than they'd anticipated. Where were the role models? Shit — who could tell them how to finish school, do their art, keep their lives clear and connected while fighting out of the closet — especially now that they were separated by the lake? There were no lesson plans, no blueprints. Increasingly, just talking on the phone was a pain that only re-enforced the separation. The forest, the sky and water, only these offered sanctuary. Even knowing it was stolen ground didn't totally tarnish the feeling. Hell, the whole planet was ripped-off merchandise — right? Weston and Cornell had been built on Indian land that was finagled in shady and violent deals. A few, token scholarships to Indian kids, a couple loads of vegetables and farm equipment and a cow or two, the archaic payments made, still. Hardly a fair exchange. So much blood in the ground, so much sorrow. Even the place where the Boathouse had been built — once a peach orchard, had been burned to the ground as the first act of the European explorers who reached the shore. Hell, someone had erected a bronze plaque to commemorate the atrocity. Maybe that was why the forest felt safe, especially at night. The trees knew; they witnessed and remembered. Like them, in the deep nights, Manilla blended. They recognized her skin. They held her in leafy embrace, allowed her tears to salt their own.

The stillness began to filter in. The sudden silence — no more owls, no more night animals rustling in the brush. Even the breeze had quieted. Manilla opened her eyes. Then, she saw it.

Carefully, Manilla crouched, trying to hide behind the trunk of the maple. A scream formed in her throat; like sickness, it rose. She dug her nails into the rough bark, tried to muffle the sound. The figure beyond her in a clearing in the trees, didn't turn. Manilla was forced to watch.

The sickening sounds were worse than the vision in the moon's half-cast glow. Wet flesh. Wet flesh to wet flesh. A kind of tearing. The dying animal heaved a final sigh; then, it was still. The smaller figure, moving over it, creating the sucking sounds, continued. Braced above the bovine, ribs filling both fists, the figure seemed to bury its head in the dead animal's neck. Blood flowed blackly in the clearing.

Manilla's heart was roaring in her chest. Yet, whatever had killed the calf was too small to have transported it there — surely. This was no mountain lion preying on baby animals — it was human. And, there was no glint of metal, no smell of gunpowder on the still, night air. How had the act been committed? What was going on? The closest farm was on the other side of the golf course. The calf would have staggered a man. This was no man feeding on the flowing blood. Long hair had come loose from a tucked bandanna, a dark flag at the figure's back.

The adrenaline in Manilla's system went into overdrive. She inched her way, almost belly-to-the-ground, backwards. Then, sure, even if she were spotted she could get away. She stood, broke into a full run. The lights of the Student Union, lower on the hill, crashed through the matte of trees. Manilla almost wept in relief as the feel of solid concrete came into contact with her sneakers. She had to get to Ithaca. She had to tell Ginny what she'd seen.

Shocked and yawning, Ginny answered the door in her bathrobe.

"I didn't call cause I had a chance at a ride," Manilla told the story.

"We've got to call the cops — the sheriff — somebody." Ginny picked up her phone.

"Gin, they won't believe me. They aren't going up there, in the dark, after some cow. God, I was afraid you wouldn't be here," Manilla looked up at the sleep-softened woman.

"Hey, you, where'd you think I'd be? Manilla — " Ginny grabbed the bedraggled painter, shaking her like a kitten, then pulling her close.

"You know, fool, it's dangerous to hitch," Ginny purred into Manilla's ear.

Fingers found buttons, grasped and pulled off clothes. Everything tangled in a heap at their feet. The scents of damp flannel, blue jeans and soft powder filled the studio. For Manilla, though, the image of the dead calf kept breaking in.

———

Manilla pushed the soggy eggs around her plate. The dining hall was almost clear. She was procrastinating. She had to make the appointment to meet the new advisor. Fourth advisor appointed to her in four years — a Weston first. Nobody knew what to do with her. She wasn't just an art major — she'd blasted past that her sophomore year. Weston prided itself on individualized programs. A few religion Profs had approached her about doing a double focus, even one of the Soc guys. But, always, Manilla proved to be too much to handle. They were used to sophisticated students who didn't take them on, toe-to-toe. Manilla's rough edges scratched. Now, the new anthro department head, a woman, a newcomer, was going to be her advisor. Manilla wondered what lottery the woman had lost.

She played with the cold mess of breakfast, killed time.

"Hey, you, girl! You hear what went down in the lab last night?" Jamie Jones pulled a chair across from Manilla. Hanging a limp wrist out at Manilla, the handsome junior rolled her eyes meaningfully.

"No. What?" Manilla put down her fork.

"Somebody took the monkeys out of their cages — or left the locks unlocked! Girl, those apes were all over the place when the cleaning ladies went in! I think some of the maids are still running! C'mon, you can catch the show!" Reaching for Manilla's shirt sleeve, Jamie stood up.

"Can't James, gotta see my advisor. Take notes, okay?" Manilla smiled, fighting a sudden chill.

"Whatever. Catch you later." Jamie started out.

"Hey," Manilla called, "did they say anything about the animals being . . . uh . . . hurt . . . cut or anything?"

"Girlfriend, you're mixing biology with psychology — these were the psych lab's monkeys! You artists are so weird! See ya." The junior swung her mini-skirt perfectly as she made her way to the big, oak doors.

Manilla pushed away from the table.

———

Manilla knocked gingerly.

Had to make the knock perfect — too loud and it would be chalked up as typical, but too soft and she could make a wussy first appearance.

"Come in."

Manilla eased the door open. Her new sneakers squeaked as she came inside. She winced.

"Manilla, isn't it?" Professor Katherine Slater stood from behind the rosewood expanse of desk. She almost smiled. Pointing to an overstuffed chair, directly across, she motioned for Manilla to be seated.

Manilla sat.

The woman was lovely. Manilla felt an unusual pull in the vicinity of her heart.

This was not only unexpected; it was different. Slater's eyes caught Manilla's wary stare. Like a forest — Slater's eyes were that green. Something else — as if the older woman could see inside her head. Manilla almost felt her there. Weird. Shivery weird. Then the feeling passed. Manilla eased into the chair, relaxing. It was clear, somehow, this woman was not the enemy.

"So, your paper is completed?" Slater leaned over the desk, palm upraised, expectant. Again, the forest gaze went into Manilla.

Manilla struggled out of the depths of the upholstery to hand over the report.

Her first impression in print, for the new advisor. Mixing art with anthropology — not a huge stretch. Manilla was actually excited. Maybe, maybe this time she'd click.

Her friends raved about their relationships with advisors — hell, Weston was known for it.

She'd never made that connection. Like so many other misses, Manilla merely let it go. She was not one of them and she knew it.

For long seconds, the professor hung onto the folder, her eyes searing Manilla's. Something strange and more than a little sad rippled through the student. Then, shaking her shoulder-length hair from her face, the woman moved back, gently tugging the report out of Manilla's grasp. There was the tiniest of electrical shocks at the separation.

Manilla moved to her chair. She noticed the long, slender fingers of the woman as she held the file.

Slater tucked Manilla's paper into the file envelope and put it into her top drawer. "Manilla, I have a proposition for you. I'd like to get to know all of my students, especially the seniors, closely. I know Weston has a tradition of encouraging that and I think it's a good idea. Your interest in combining your art major with anthropology is of particular interest. I'd like to talk with you, at length, about graduate school."

There! Manilla felt it again! She opened her eyes wider, finding the professor almost staring her down! Another minute electrical shock, running up and down her arms . . . not sex. Not danger. Something, something she'd never felt before! Exciting. Maybe a little alarming. She couldn't stop the color that was rising in her face. Something more. When was the last time a professor had taken her seriously? Forget about anyone caring to ask about her post-graduation game-plan. The blush deepened. Her pulse quickened. She knew the woman could see it, but somehow, with this woman, it would be understood not misread.

Slater stood up and came round the front of the desk. She held out the slender, strong hand. She smiled gently.

Manilla was hesitant. Her palm was so hot she was almost embarrassed. Then, swallowing as unobtrusively as she could, Manilla allowed the grasp.

This time it was as if their arms were high-tension wires — the current a river of fire and light moving through Manilla's whole body. She was riveted, her eyes locked as deeply with Slater's as their hands. What was the Prof doing to her? Why was this happening? Was she such a weakling that the fall's challenges had reduced her to needing a, a what? Surely not a mother-figure — no, not the other, either. No! For a full second Manilla fought the overwhelming sexual surge — then, just as quickly, it was gone — vaporized! In its place, this warmth, this delicious, safe, almost melancholy feeling. All Manilla knew was that, for the first time in her entire life, she absolutely trusted a stranger — this magnificent stranger holding her hand.

"Tomorrow evening, my house, by the lake, around nine?"

Slater's hand loosened.

Manilla nodded still transfixed. Her hand dropped away from Slater's. Slater moved back to her desk.

"Good-bye, Professor," Manilla said, softly, somehow making it to the door. Then she was in the hallway, feeling like a sleepwalker, drifting away.

———

Manilla flipped on the dorm-room light. "Ginny!"

"Where have you been, Manilla? I've been waiting for hours!" The dancer rushed across the room.

Manilla, trying to read her lover, pushed away. "What are you doing here?"

"I tried to call, but you know this damned place. I took a chance and drove out. Oh — just hold me, please!"

Manilla moved Ginny to the bed, cradling her, waiting for Ginny to talk. She stroked the blonde head lovingly, pressing her lips to Ginny's hair.

"Steady, Gin, I don't follow," Manilla propped up on one elbow, tried to read the dancer. Ginny gave clues through her body when she couldn't find the words.

"I wanted to call you right after it happened but she talked me out of it. She said there wasn't anything you could do; why get you upset? Last night, after class, a man, a man tried to . . . tried to . . . Manilla, I was so scared! I just froze!"

Manilla sat up, searched Ginny's face, "Did anything happen? I mean . . . ."

"If Darsen hadn't been there, oh, Manilla, that's why, when she asked me to come across the street to her studio, for dinner, I couldn't refuse. She's that woman from the cafe, at breakfast that day, remember?"

Manilla flashed on that morning, waiting for Ginny, outside the restaurant in Collegetown. She'd been glancing at the newspapers on a rack when a sudden shadow made her look up: a woman, tall, tall as Ginny, dressed entirely in black, wearing some kind of poncho, her hair long and straight, the color of a raven's back. The woman had been in front of her, then, somehow, Manilla was up against the brick wall of the building.

Then, the heat. A wave of fire as the woman fell against her in a full-body press. Fearing she'd faint Manilla had braced her hands against the wall, for balance. Her brain was aghast at the forced dance. People moved past, seemingly oblivious.

The woman had moved her leg, forcing Manilla's knees apart. Her thigh had pressed hard into Manilla's crotch, causing the heat to focus, building there. The blood rose, pounding. Manilla was swollen, wet, so open to the dark stranger!

Only Ginny's appearance caused it to stop. Ginny was there, as suddenly as the stranger had been there, just as suddenly they weren't against the bricks, but at the news rack, part of the street crowd. The woman was touching Manilla's face, again, explaining to Ginny that she feared she'd whirled around and caught the edge of her poncho's trim on Manilla's cheek. She apologized profusely, even charmingly. She introduced herself: Darsen. Darsen.

She didn't meet Manilla's eyes. She simply slipped off into the moving river of college kids.

Manilla had never mentioned the interlude. Chalking it up to just another oddity in a very odd autumn, she'd withheld it, maybe not quite believing it had happened . . . not wanting to dwell on what she couldn't explain.

Now, the clammy feeling Darsen had left had returned.

"Darsen happened to be at the cafe that morning because she lives in the loft across the street from me." Ginny was calming as she told the story to Manilla. "The other night, there was this man, he must have followed me from the Dance Studio. I was just about to put my keys in the lock. Darsen heard him, saw him grab me — "

"Gin . . . "

"She used some kind of self-defense — really creamed the guy. She took me to the police, stayed with me — Manilla, it happened so fast — I wanted to call you, but it was late. When she asked me to come to dinner, tonight, well, I couldn't refuse, after her help. I tried to reach you! I kept trying to call!"

"You're all right?" The queasy feeling in Manilla's stomach remained. She hadn't been there, hadn't even known about it, till now. But Darsen had.

"Tonight, I was just going over for dinner, to talk with her. She's fascinating, Manilla. Her life, well, it's been so much like mine, like mine used to be. She seemed so kind, like she understood me, my past. She's a wonderful painter — these amazing jungle scenes — huge canvases. But, after a while, I started to feel strange, almost like we were in the jungle and I was, well, being hunted. I mean, first that bastard on the street and then Darsen — Manilla, it hurt! Betrayed — she betrayed me after reminding me so much of, of my mother, of home." Ginny's voice cracked.

The pain was choking. Ginny sobbed against Manilla. "Forgive me, I should have sensed it, seen it coming. I've never been unfaithful, Manilla, never to you. Please, love, say you don't hate me, say it's still all right between us."

Manilla fought her own tears. No anger. No rage — just the absolute white light of terror. Its frigid hand pressed against her heart. No one had ever come between them — not even the huge vortex of their families had pulled them apart. What was she to make of this? The first issue, the attack, seemed almost extraneous, a bad dream explained away. Ginny had been saved. But the admission that something had gone on between this stranger and Ginny — something Ginny felt guilt over . . . Manilla's universe reeled.

She wrapped her arms around Ginny, a human quilt, trying to ward off the icy feelings, to fight the dread. "Shhh, nothing to forgive, nothing happened, not really.

"I'm just glad you're all right. I hate that I wasn't there — when that man — I would have castrated the son of a bitch! I'm glad she was there — thank God! Gin, tonight, it was just some cosmic reaction, you know? This whole year has been like that. It's not really us. Look, that woman, well, I didn't tell you everything that morning at the cafe. It was like a fever dream. I wasn't sure it happened. She had me pressed against the building, tight. Before I could stop her, you were there and we were like, uh, four feet away. There's something dangerous about her, Ginny. Something psychotic. It's in her eyes. Don't talk to her, don't go near her anymore. Tell her you've got this stone butch lover who'll take her apart if she tries anything. We can call the cops on HER, no lie. Or, move you out of the neighborhood. I could quit Weston, transfer, maybe move in with you, full-time — "

"Manilla, stop it! Your scholarship, my father! It will be okay. Any loft I can afford will only be in a worse section of town. I won't be pushed. Not by anyone, not ever again. She didn't force me, Manilla. It was unexpected, that's all. Maybe I miss you, maybe too much. More than you know. More than I say. Sometimes I just shove my feelings down until they implode. Look, just promise me you'll come to town for the whole week-end. Just spend it with me?" Ginny brushed Manilla's cheek with her lips.

The ice softened in the pit of Manilla's stomach. Her muscles unclenched. "It's going to be fine, it's got to be, Gin. We'll make it okay. I promise." Manilla wrapped her fingers in her lover's hair and pulled Ginny into a kiss.

━━━━

Slater's front door opened at Manilla's first tentative knock.

"Hope you like fish — a friend came by with some red snapper. Thought it would be fun to share. Come in." Slater smiled.

"Thank you." Manilla entered shyly. The house was one of the oldest in the village. Built on the lake as a summer home, it was charming, airy, what Manilla would have chosen for herself — for herself and Ginny, someday.

The hardwood floors and matching bookcases gave a feeling of warmth, of solidity. Manilla was surprised at the sheer number of volumes lining her walls.

"Yes, well, I know it can be intimidating, but I've been collecting for a long time." Slater came up behind Manilla, silent as a cat.

The tears sprang up, coursed down Manilla's cheeks. She felt Slater behind her. Even as the Prof stood, separated by mere inches, the heat from her body flowed over Manilla. It made her ache. From the first introduction, there had been this exchange, this energy. Not like Ginny, not like anyone Manilla had ever met before. This was purely from the Professor. Here, in her private quarters, surrounded by so many words, so much polished copper and brass and golden lamplight, the patina of a life spread before her — why was it so familiar? Why did it make Manilla so sad?

She'd always prided herself on running from hearth-scenes; prided herself on being the wild-child-rebel. Weren't she and Ginny glorious because they hated conventions like these? They were artists — not home-owners, not bookish teachers caught in tenured amber. She and Ginny despised the act of acquisition merely to define oneself — and wasn't this home exactly like every other professor's home?

Slater hadn't moved. Manilla could feel her warm, gentle breathing, could feel every inch of the tall woman behind her.

A flood of images roared through Manilla's mind. Partly childhood, partly things read, all combining into a kind of truth. She longed for a home, for knowledge at one's fingertips — more than a printed screen, actual books, their weight attesting to what they contained. She longed for a well-lit sanctuary exactly like this. She recognized this place because it had been at the core of her dreams forever. She recognized Slater.

Ashamed at her tears, the ridiculous emotion, unsure how to explain, she wiped at her face brusquely.

"Manilla, what's wrong?" Slater's voice was so soft, Manilla barely heard it.

But, even though the older woman had not moved, Manilla felt her voice like a touch. So familiar, so understood.

"I don't . . . I'm sorry. I never cry, I can't." The onslaught of images roared again, an immense wave washing over her mind. Images of New England blizzards, absent adults, frightened and freezing children, the constant yearning for someone, someone stronger, bigger, able to protect, someone to help because she couldn't, she couldn't . . . .

Slater moved even closer. Her voice was almost hushed, as if muffled in velvet, "It will be all right. I promise. You are safe here. Maybe I understand more than you know. You have to sense this — deeply. You have to trust me, Manilla. Come. We'll both feel better after we eat." Slater pulled a linen handkerchief out of her pocket and dabbed at Manilla's face.

Manilla allowed the unusual tenderness. No fight left. No fight at all. No defenses with this woman. Why? She simply followed Slater to the table.

"I want to thank you. I don't get many home-cooked meals around here — and Ginny's loft doesn't exactly have a four-star kitchen — " Manilla caught herself. Slater couldn't know about Ginny. Not that it really mattered — or would it change Slater's view of her?

Slater's hand reached across the table and touched the back of Manilla's. "I know all about Virginia MacPhearson, Manilla."

The lids suddenly weighted, Manilla's eyes began to flutter. Something, something in Slater's touch, the focus was growing fuzzy, her mind widening, as if it were opening, like a book, another volume for the professor to read. No question of holding back, something between them, the past welling up, just like the first time, in her office, their handshake — and earlier, when Slater had been behind her — that strange current, moving through and over — now it was pulling all the contents of her past into view. Slater knew everything.

"Manilla, your life is here, for me to read. I won't play games with you. Or, I'll attempt to keep the games from becoming a barrier. Don't be frightened. I, I know you. Somehow. I'm not positive, but I am sure. You and your friend, Ginny, there is a connection. There are some things you must know, now, if you are to help me — I need your help, I need your strength. But you have to trust. In your heart, Manilla, so much is clear. If you can't trust me, this power, trust what you know to be true in your own heart."

It was as if Manilla were both present, in her body, yet distant, watching the woman hold her wrist and speak to the comatose student. What Slater presented, Manilla could feel, could experience, but she was also under the watchful gaze of the older woman as they sat at the table. It was intoxicating — and terrible. It was also total. Ridiculous, whatever, whoever this woman was, ridiculous to even think she could resist.

Slater continued, "My power would allow me to wrest what I need from you, to take away your will and make it my own. But, I do not want to do that. I'm making a request. I am taking the risk of asking permission. If you agree, you won't remember this encounter, not until I feel it is safe for you to do so. But, you will remember our pact and this bond. This is a friendship that goes deeper than any you have ever encountered, even with Ginny. I am going to ask permission to communicate with your soul, Manilla. It will be frightening, maybe it will even border on madness, but you must trust me. I will not let you be harmed. I swear, if you allow this, I will never betray you. Somehow, you've been sent to me, at this time, to aid me and I both recognize and honor the Power that sent you. I also honor your free will. This is beyond understanding, for now. But, if you will think of it as, perhaps, the missing links of your life, an answer to questions that have always arisen, your acceptance of what I am about to share may mean that something absolutely evil which has manifested in this world will come to an end. It is something so hideous there are no words for it. You can become instrumental in stopping this monstrous force, if you agree to come with me. For a long while, you will not consciously know what you are being led to do. Only in the right moment will it be revealed. That is part of the pact, the permission. Don't question why — it's for your own safety — trust. Feel in your heart and test what I say."

Slater gripped her wrist more tightly. Manilla both watched and felt the action. This probing of her mind, of her spirit, was like a needle. But, even in the panic and pain, Manilla knew the truth. Manilla answered: "Yes."

A silent, long, wrenching scream: the panoply of the most gruesome history of this planet played out, unreeled in front of her: before recorded time, through the rising and falling back of countless species, innumerable civilizations; then, closer to her own history books: the Dark Ages, the Holocaust, continental famines and the ravages of global disease: every horror poured on mankind, created and kindled and manipulated against and by mankind. She was drowning in the excruciating and irrevocable certainty that she'd been part of it all. Victor as well as victim. So many times she had acquiesced to the evil, so many times she'd said "yes."

The images were torn back from her mind. A sense of floating, of drifting. She was removed totally from her body, from its past and present. Warmth. Blue and white light. A cessation of horror. Only Slater's voice to crack the stillness:

"In each of us, is this bud of evil. A seed, long planted, needing only the right gardener to bring forth fruit. Needing only some monster to water and nurture to maturity the destructive potential that is sleeping in us all. We are not apart from it, Manilla. We are part of it — or, more precisely, it is part of us. The depth of the sleep is determined by choice. We choose our circumstances, all of our circumstances. Oh, the consequences of poor choice! I have met the gardener, Manilla. I know that every atrocity that has been committed on this planet can be traced to single decisions made by individuals — decisions prompted and nourished by this virago."

There, in the middle of the floating space, in the middle of the cocoon of Slater's voice, had risen the beautiful, horrifying face of the Dark One. Manilla recognized it!

It was Darsen!

Manilla panicked, trying to pull away, feeling Darsen's presence as real as the presence of Slater. She moaned with the effort, even as she heard Slater's call.

"From the first meeting in my office, that afternoon, I knew you, Manilla. I also knew, somehow, Darsen had entered your life. I believe, from what you've shown me, in your mind's recollection, in your heart, she's also entered the life of Ginny MacPhearson. I believe she may be stalking Ginny, even as we speak. Will you help me, Manilla? There is so much more for you to learn, but I can't go any farther until I have your answer."

Manilla suddenly understood. Everything she'd witnessed, the amazing epic of the ages, the bi-location, even the brief image of the calf on the hill, all of it came down to a single, laser point. Everything else was overwhelming, but she could hang on to this last fact — Ginny was in deadly danger. Whatever their connections to the past — or their obligations to the future, however much Slater could be trusted or not, Manilla's heart knew one certainty: Ginny had met Darsen and Ginny was in danger.

Of course, there was only one answer.

So, it was sealed.

Wherever it would lead, it was sealed, between them.

Slater increased the probe's power one more time.

In that second, Manilla learned the truth about her advisor.

In that second she knew how close to death Ginny really was.

———

The door to the loft smashed. All Manilla could see over Slater's shoulder was Darsen, Darsen atop Ginny!

Before she could push past the Professor, Slater screamed: "Darsen!"

The scream brought the monster up snarling.

Darsen whirled around, off the still dancer. Manilla cringed at the mask of raw hatred covering Darsen's face when the vampire saw Slater.

Again, Slater screamed: "Darsen, no!"

Darsen moved toward them in a single leap. Her arms knocked over several candles eerily placed around the bed. They fell to the floor, instant fire.

"I thought you were dead!" The voice was Darsen's but unlike Darsen — almost bestial.

Slater stood between Manilla and the approaching animal. "You knew I was alive. No more lies! You felt me tracking you. You plotted to kill me, tonight, here! Don't try to cloud your mind — your arrogance will be your last mistake!"

Slater bounded across the distance between them. Manilla was frozen, in absolute disbelief as she watched the transformation in each of the women. Through the rising smoke, the snarl of animals locked in deadly combat filled the room.

Some sound from Ginny broke Manilla's shock.

"Ginny!" Manilla was held back by a rising wall of fire. She couldn't get to the semi-conscious dancer.

Through the flames, Manilla could see the continuing transformation of Darsen.

It roared, its unearthly screams were matched only by the leathery sound of its huge wings as they beat against the smoke.

Smoke obscured everything. Its boiling, dense waves curdled Manilla's vision. For a moment she believed there was a second monster, rising , flying above the fire, matching Darsen's screams.

Then, Ginny called her name.

Beating through the heat Manilla managed to reach the engulfed bed. Ginny crawled on to the floor. Manilla tried to pull her up, to force her out of the inferno but the dancer was conscious only for moments. Then, Slater was behind them hoisting Ginny over Manilla's shoulders, draping the dancer so Manilla could get them out. Slater helped them to the loft's exit, pushed them through — before Darsen could witness the flight.

Down, down, through the crackling tile and warping wood, over the cement stairs, down. Ash coated everything. Manilla could feel Ginny's ankles as they scraped against the stairs —

she couldn't help it. Ginny's height made it impossible to do more.

Finally, the sudden miracle of cold. The night air surrounded them. The milling crowd enclosed them — so many people in the street — sirens, students, everyone screaming, pointing up.

Ginny was coughing, gulping for air. Manilla couldn't understand what she was saying. Didn't matter. All that mattered was getting her to the ambulance, letting the fire-fighters know there was still someone up there — Slater had to be rescued.

Manilla dropped Ginny in the first arms offered. She screamed for help but was restrained. Breaking free, Manilla pushed past the crowd, clawed through the billowing smoke. Sparks danced over her hair, the heat drove her backwards, but she fought it, moving forward by inches, knowing Slater was alone with the monster.

Fire licked into the stairwell. It scorched Manilla even though she held her jacket over her face.

The denim was singeing. She could smell the cotton and her own hair as bits of debris floated down on her. She beat out the flames now moving upward. She tore open the door, then almost retreated from what she met.

The horror of the noise was almost worse then the fear of flames. Metallic clicking, like nails or worse, fangs missing their mark, as two huge predators slashed, bore down on each other in a fight to the death.

"Slater!" Manilla had to reach her. They couldn't make it down the front stairs anymore, but there was a chance — the bathroom — a window outside, there. The fire couldn't burn the tiled room, surely.

The thundering battle roared around Manilla's head. She ducked, she coughed; the air was becoming so dense that she was losing consciousness. Then, in the middle of the hell, Darsen. Darsen beyond Manilla's worst dreams: a monster unleashed, with clacking fangs and enormous, blackened wings beating at the scalding air!

Where was Slater? Manilla tried to retreat, to call out, anything to get to her professor. A blast sent her spinning like a child's toy into a melting corner of the studio. She held her fists to her ears in an attempt to keep out the bone-chilling cacophony.

A deafening explosion sprayed shards of glass like shrapnel through the ruptured loft. As she tried to stand, to run, a fireball hurtled over: enormous, alive, shrieking, even as it burst into the writhing night, high above the heads of the throng in the street.

An arm, human, solid, strong, grasped Manilla's. It pulled her toward what remained of the bathroom. The door closed behind them. Against the flames and fury. The window to the fire escape outside, was broken. Manilla gulped at the clean air. Turning, she tried to wipe the blood from her eyes. Through this distortion, she saw Slater.

Slumping to the floor, the older woman reached out. Manilla tried to hold her. Slater fell, dragging Manilla down.

Manilla pressed the dying woman to her own heart, sobbing, wanting, somehow, some way, to pump the energy that beat inside her back.

Slater raised a blackened hand to touch Manilla's cheek. Only a hoarse whisper, all she could finally manage — for Manilla — for herself:

"It's done . . . be glad . . . if only . . . we . . . a long time ago . . . it might have been different, Manilla . . . maybe . . . ."

Then, Slater's weight was gone.

In Manilla's arms, only ashes. Slowly, they began to rise, mingled with the drifting smoke, floated out into the uneasy night. Manilla watched, transfixed, till they vanished.

Tears wrenched her throat, burning as the fire could not.

She felt something in her hand. Opening her sooty palm, she found the silver and ruby ring that had been Slater's! Manilla pushed it roughly on to her finger.

Hacking and wheezing, fighting for air, she made her way to the window.

A fire-fighter met her on the escape, hauled her down even as the building began to crumble. The ambulance below waited. Ginny was on a stretcher, inside. An oxygen mask was clamped to her ashy face.

Manilla held Ginny's cold hand all the way to the hospital.

Quietly, the floor nurse came toward the lounge to check on the student. The woman held a blanket. Carefully, so as not to disturb Manilla, she tucked it all around. The smell of smoke was acrid on the girl.

"Lucky kid," the nurse thought, moving silently away, up the deserted corridor.

Beneath the blanket, Manilla shivered, un-hearing, knowing only the numbing fear and questions of her dream.

PART 3

"Not a bad room, eh? I'm sure you've seen worse." The businessman stuck his graying head out of the shower.

The sixteen-year-old sat on the bed closest to the outside door. He eyed the twenty the man had left for him. It lay like a dry leaf on the other bed. The boy was desperate; the bill might blow away, might evaporate or burst into flame, might become lost, like so many before it. He weighed the realities: the possibility of escape, clothes in one hand, the twenty between his teeth . . . .

Too late.

The guy was back, streaming water, a towel tucked around his paunch, the expensive wallet tucked into the towel.

The man watched the boy's eyes, baby-blue glancing furtively from the abandoned bill on the bed back to the wallet. The man chuckled. The voice was high, higher than the boy expected. The sound made the boy shiver.

"Look son, I'm no rube. Maybe you're new in town. Haven't heard about me, yet. The others will vouch, I pay when I play. But I don't take shit and I don't take shinola. You got that, son? Save the sob stories. Don't fuck with the wallet. We'll get along just fine."

The skinny blonde kid with the big blue eyes tucked his own towel tighter. He was hungry. No lunch. No breakfast. His stomach growled. He'd lost weight, though. At least that was something good, right? In the last two months maybe it was the only good thing.

He could get through this date. Hadn't been able to get high, earlier, but he could get through this. Focus. Something else in the room. Go farther away — the bus station. The bus ticket. This was the bus ticket home — last time he had to do it with a creep.

Going to go home, getting out of the life. Whatever it took, however hard it would be back there.

Okay, maybe, at first, he'd liked it — the attention, the sex, in the beginning. All right. In the beginning, when semi-decent guys picked him up, picked him out. But pretty soon he wasn't such fresh meat. Pretty soon he had to get into stuff he didn't like, didn't want to do. Stuff he hated. Pretty soon he looked way older than sixteen. He knew it, could see it for himself.

Even the good sex wasn't. Syracuse sucked. He didn't care what they did to him when he got back home. Anything was better than the streets of this town. These jerks, their middle-aged dicks . . . when did they ever spring for a decent room? Always, like this, cheap; cheap and cold.

The boy looked away. The businessman picked up the kid's discarded Mega-Death tee-shirt. The man fingered the gamy cloth, bringing it up to his nostrils, sniffing at the armholes. He inhaled deeply.

The boy kept his eyes on the silent TV. The tacky curtains. Even the mildewy steam still rising from the shower. Anything but the man and his actions. They repulsed him, but they didn't surprise. Nothing the johns did surprised him. They were a lot of sad sickos these days. Just like his bastard cousin. Wasn't that the real reason for taking off? Shit, that and school . . . when they caught him with the football player.

The football player's family had publicly denied the rumor, then privately come looking for him with a baseball bat. He'd tried to make it to NYC. Never got far enough. Always something to snag you, to hold you back. Syracuse would have to do. Big enough to get lost in, big enough to have its own hustling scene. Found that easy. Trucker who gave him his last hitch dropped him off in the middle of it.

The trucker had liked the way he smelled, too.

"Come here, Joey." The businessman sidled up to the boy. The boy tried to smile. Tried to keep his mind riveted to the bus depot. The easy thrum of tires on wet macadam, the night as it would look when he sped from this place. He tried to smile. He almost made it.

The businessman shoved his cock into the boy's soft face.

It was almost blue with the blood the boy caused to rise. The man rubbed it across the boy's tight lips. The man moaned. Oh, yeah, this was a choice one. Not more than peach-fuzz on that face, oh yeah.

The boy snapped back from his bus depot dreaming.

"Wait, mister, wait! You said a hand-job, a hand-job for ten and the other ten if I let you jack me off!"

"Listen punk," the man grabbed the boy by the hair, jerking the kid's unbelieving face upward, the hard cock bobbing just below the boy's chin, "that was then, this is now. I want a blow-job. You got that? Christ, you cock-suckers are all the same. Freaking whining fairies. Trying to wheedle out of a deal every fucking time. You ain't gonna get more money, punk. You got that? You suck or I fuck, pretty boy. That's all the choices you got left."

The boy felt the anger rising from the older man, hardening his cock fully. The boy could feel it without having to look. He knew this kind of fury. His own cousin, when he was little. He had to get out of this room, fast. Fuck the bus ride. It wasn't coming from this john!

The man felt the boy's panic as it telegraphed across the pale body.

"Sit down, queer!" The businessman shoved the boy hard, sending him to the floor. The boy's towel came undone, slid beneath the bed. Seeing the kid, suddenly naked, made the man shiver with pleasure. Oh, yeah! He knew he could take this chicken anywhere he wanted — easy. The kid had to be, what? Fifteen, sixteen tops? Very nellie. So what? He'd paid — up front. Didn't he always pay? They played their faggoty games thinking they could weasel out some more cash — well, think again, baby. He'd paid and if he wanted something extra, well, he'd pay a little more. But damn if he was going to give this fag piss ant the satisfaction of knowing that before they were through! A hand job? What a cunt! No better than the wife . . . come here, go away . . . fuck them all!

He slapped the boy. Hard. His hand left a clear, red imprint on the kid's cheek. The boy tried to stone-face it, but tears danced around the edges of his eyes. A thin line of blood escaped from one nostril.

"On the bed, faggot!" The man's voice was much higher. A small vein stood out on his neck, throbbed.

The boy didn't argue. Cupping his genitals pathetically, he crawled backwards, onto the bed. The man wasn't much taller than he was, but the guy out-weighed him by fifty pounds.

The businessman clenched the boy's shoulder with beefy hands. He let his nails dig into the freckled flesh.

The boy choked on his tears. "Okay, mister, whatever you say. Please, just let me get a rubber. Protection, you know?

Please!" The boy was frantic. He never did anything without protection. Some of the others didn't care but they were so high they didn't care about much. He was terrified. Didn't care who laughed. Had even passed up "dates" if they wouldn't let him use a rubber. He always carried skins. Anyway, he wasn't really a hustler. He was only doing this till he got a better plan. Maybe fell in love with Mr. Right, got his head together, made enough to get home again, start school over.

"You fucking crazy, kid? A raincoat? No way! If I wanted to wear a rubber I'd stick it in some cunt. Who the hell you think you're dealing with, homo? I'm clean. I'm no queer-boy. You're the one gonna die from the plague, pal. You and your buddies. Now, open that pretty mouth wide — I've got a real treat for you, Joey. You really don't mind, do you, Joey? I can tell you want to." The man straddled the teen. He forced the boy's mouth wider. This time when he struck the kid, he used a closed fist.

Blood spurted from the boy's split lip.

"Christ! Now look what you made me do! I don't want your homo blood on my cock! You just remember, Joey, from here on in, you made the choice. You live with it, queer."

The man raised his thick torso and grabbed for the boy's legs. The boy was openly crying. He pleaded for the man to stop. Again, the heavy fist squashed into the smooth face.

The boy stopped struggling. He merely whimpered as the man raised his legs higher.

The businessman grunted in pleasure as he fell against the hustler. In one swift, terrible motion — the man's stiff cock ripped into the teen.

The boy screamed.

The scream caught in the back of his throat. The pain checked everything. Never had there been such pain nor such terrible weight. The fire in his bowels was the only feeling he knew. The skin ripped around his anus, pulling and tearing in the tempo of the man's thrusts.

"OOOOOOOIEIEEEIEIEE JOOOOEEEE, yessss!" The businessman spurted deep inside the boy.

The boy felt the scald in the pit of his stomach, envisioned the spore infecting his soul. His breath was ragged and rushing and this time he could make sound.

Again, the man grunted. He pulled out, rolled over, nursed the final spasm from his shrinking cock.

The boy squeezed his legs together as tightly as the pain would allow. He felt split in half, as if the rip would widen, move upward, tear his belly and chest and skull apart like a doll pulled by two feuding children. His mind moved from his throbbing body. Flashback . . . to where there had been other children, one older, much larger cousin. A cousin big enough to want to try his advantage out . . . an earlier nightmare come to life.

"Dammit, son, that was good! Never thought I'd get a cherry ass . . . well, I didn't think you were telling me the truth. You know, like you wanted to play rough — heehee. Hell, I'm a fair man. I'll throw in another bill, just to make it square. All you nellie-boys squeal. How's a guy to know you're serious, huh? Maybe you should just be glad it's me and not some maniac. Yeah. You just think on that one, son. You can add this number to your little bag of tricks, right? Shit, I got to get on the road. The wife'll have a cow. You keep the room. For the whole night, all right?" The businessman slapped the boy on the flank, then moved back toward the still-steamy shower.

Light spilled out from the bathroom, across the beds.

Shuddering the boy crossed his skinny arms over his chest. The pain was terrible. He reached around, gingerly, bringing his fingers back with blood. There was blood.

He listened to the crazy whistling and the running water and the buzzing of the cheap electric clock beside the bed.

He moved his fingers.

They were glued by the blood.

———

Ginny MacPhearson woke up in the hospital bed holding back a scream. A fluorescent buzz crackled above her — sounding dangerous — like something somewhere else . . . Darsen's loft . . . Ginny blinked, choking, attempting to keep the noise from filling her, sending her, yet again, to the monster's house.

Her lips were cracked. The taste of smoke was deep in her throat. Her lungs ached. It ached lower. But, she didn't want to touch, to confirm the wound. Not yet. God, please, if she could find a way to make the past months another memory — evil, horrific, a nightmare come to its own frightening life. No. They would remain. Inside her head she knew that they could not be erased. Unlike the memories of her father's atrocious acts, she knew, just knew, these could never be frozen. Never be blunted.

She reached for the water by her bed. As her hand encircled the plastic cup, a wave of nausea engulfed her. The curdling image of Darsen moving on top of her, pressing her to the bed, making her weak, open . . . her legs, her sex, open to that blood-thirsty mouth . . . .

Bile rose in her gullet. Before Ginny could scramble from the high hospital bed, she vomited violently. The cup was sent spinning out and over the linoleum floor: the water arching, then spreading, mixing with the ruby spew.

Ginny sank back, shaken. She wiped sour lips against the back of her hand. Pink. Pink stained the ashy skin! God — she was so cold. Ginny closed her eyes. She did not call for help.

———

"Nothing? You didn't hear a thing?" waiting for an answer the cop scribbled on the dog-eared pad.

The motel clerk looked like a ferret. He constantly tugged at his thin mustache while glancing over the cop's shoulder.

He shook his head nervously. The clerk hated cops; he hated trouble.

The cop rolled his eyes at his partner. Disgusted. Same old same old when it came to these losers on night shifts. His partner kicked at a stone in the poorly tarred lot.

"Hey, boys," a voice behind them called, "it's a fuck-by-the-hour palace. That dude means he didn't hear anything except what passes for white noise around here. Ha!" The detective moved closer to the three men. With long strides he avoided major puddles. His worn bomber jacket covered a white shirt and half-knotted tweedy tie.

"Gunner!" The first cop grimaced. "Who put you on this?" The cop's partner moved the clerk back towards the empty office.

"Morning, Sam. Who do you think? Got the call an hour ago. I've worked this kind of thing in L.A. Don't take it personal, Sam. No hard clues, right? Plenty of mess. Nobody, heard anything till the maid screamed. Same MO every time. Like they took a course in it. Hell, maybe they did — the street's a night school, right?" Gunner scratched his wrist. He glanced at the watch he hated wearing. Seven-fucking-thirty. Too early to be giving philosophy lessons to the uniforms. He wanted coffee with lots of cream and sugar. He wanted eggs. Maybe bacon. Definitely toast.

"Yeah, Mr. West Coast Refugee, this ain't L.A., maybe, but we ain't farmers. Some of us been around. We read the material, too, Gunner. Ya know? So, Mr. Bigshot, it's sado-masochistic, body tied on the bed with pieces of tee-shirt. Mega-Death shirt. My kid has the same fucking one — gives me the willies. Over-kill scene, big time. John whacked from behind, while he was tied up. Maybe. Hustler used one of the lamps. Watch where you walk in there. It's slippery — brains, blood, what's left of the lamp. Wallet's still inside. All plastic intact, far as we can guess. We'll have to confirm. No cash. Kid probably took that. But that's it. Guy's watch, tie-tack, even the fucking wedding ring — all gold — all left. My take on the scene: well, the john went too far. Kid goes ballistic. I haven't been on this kind of case before, Gunner, not till today, but I do read the frigging literature, man. Hey, don't take my word for it. Check it out. Nobody's been in there since the murder, except for us — and the maid. She didn't stay too long. All we did was establish a crime scene, buddy. Period. The clerk never even saw the kid. Says he recognizes the stiff, though. Been in here more than a couple of times. Different boys every time, mostly. Nice, eh? Listen, it gets better. Now we gotta call the wife. Sweet thing to drop on her for the holidays, eh?" The cop shook his head in disgust.

"Yeah," Gunner scratched his wrist again, "Happy Thanksgiving. Well, okay. We'll do what we do. Let's go. It's getting cold out here."

"Way cold. Maybe snow. Maybe tonight. Man, it's gonna be a long winter," the partner came back from the office.

"Maybe." Detective Gunner moved heavily toward the open motel room door.

It was seven-forty a.m.

━━━

"I could move in. I should have moved in with you, last summer, in the old place. Maybe if I had — " Manilla shivered lightly.

"If you had Weston would have taken away your financial aid — you know their archaic policies. Besides, we've only got my VW between us. How could we both go to school full-time, and get you up and down the lake, thirty-miles, every day? You have to finish your senior show up there and I have to do the dance program here, Manilla." Ginny turned, abruptly, dropping the box she'd hauled inside. She grabbed Manilla's arms, forcing the young painter to meet her gaze. "Manilla, you couldn't have prevented what happened. I couldn't, either. It's a bad horror film, honey. I don't even believe it, not all of it, anymore. The only people who could have helped were killed. You, we, we have to forget and forgive ourselves. We have to forgive each other and just move on, Manilla. Just try to focus — your work at Weston, helping me set up this new house — us! I'm going to need you more than ever. Please, please — for me?" Ginny kissed the top of Manilla's head.

"It's just still so new, Gin. I mean, one minute you're safe, in Collegetown, in your own loft and the next minute we're fighting a monster — " Manilla's voice cracked, even as she held on to the dancer.

"Manilla, I was never safe — it's all relative!" Ginny looked over the curly head, past her lover, out the windows which faced the lake.

"What?" Manilla squirmed, but Ginny held her fast.

"We'll never be totally free from my father, for one. Two, even in Collegetown, in that fire-trap of a loft, remember the guy who grabbed me? Manilla, it was Darsen who got him off me!" Ginny's voice was husky as the scene played over in her mind. The feeling of the stranger's iron-fingers as he grabbed her throat, his sudden weight, the cold, oily smell of the rain in the night street — then, exhilarating freedom as the weight was removed from her. Darsen had done that — thrown the man against the brick building, smashing his head like a pumpkin, saving her.

Whatever else Darsen had done, she had, one time, saved her. It gnawed at Ginny's mind and memory, like a rat. She owed Darsen for that.

"I can't believe you're saying this!" Manilla wiggled free from Ginny's embrace, "She only saved you for herself — because she wanted you, for herself!"

Ginny turned, fully facing the windows, watching the sun move toward the cold horizon, as she answered, "I know, Manilla. I know."

"She killed Katherine Slater, Gin! If I had been living with you, I wouldn't have known Slater — I would have been kicked out of Weston, working, full-time, living with you in Collegetown. Maybe, maybe Darsen never would have found you — or Slater would never have been drawn to Darsen — maybe Slater would have lost the trail and Darsen would have hunted elsewhere! If I had been with you things would have been very, very different, Ginny." Manilla's hands pounded the back of the new couch.

"Maybe, maybe." Ginny touched the cold windowpane, watching her finger block out the setting sun.

Beyond the glass she could hear the warning cries of Canadian geese as they came across the freezing water.

Manilla didn't notice.

——————

The moonlight was waning. It peeled through the makeshift curtains Manilla (in her New England insistence) had made her hang. Not enough moon to see the edges of Manilla's lips, yet Ginny COULD easily define those tiny curves. Not enough moon to count the lashes on the delicate eyelids, yet Ginny had, indeed, done just that. She couldn't fall asleep. Even now.

Not enough light to watch the throb and thrum of the almost-hidden vein behind Manilla's left ear, yet, Ginny SAW everything.

She sat, now, inches away from the slumbering Manilla. She sat, absolutely awake, absolutely famished.

Twice she'd risen, just to scrounge a snack in the ramshackle mess of kitchen. Things weren't entirely unpacked, but there was food.

Twice she'd put it all back, nausea, distress at the textures and smells. But, she knew the food was fine. Fresh. She'd bought it herself.

On the second excursion, she'd realized Manilla had not so much as shifted in her sleep. Wiped out. Maybe still shell-shocked from all the previous week's events. So should she be. But she wasn't even tired.

So, Ginny sat — sat in the illuminated dark, listening.

The new cottage by the lake was alive with night sounds: the tremble of the storm windows on the lake side, the creak of the hardwood floors in the early winter cold, the rattle of the refrigerator and the hiss of the radiators — so, it wasn't the best digs and it wasn't very new — a refurbished summer rental got for an excellent price because no one in their right mind would rent such a house during the winter. But, it was new, to her — to them. Fresh start. Away from Collegetown. Five miles closer to Weston. A new, better beginning.

Then, Ginny heard the scurry of a mouse behind the wall, near the front door. She shook her head to clear it. She pulled the down comforter closer, wrapping it all around her, as she sat listening. Then, again: unmistakable.

Four tiny, racing feet. The sudden rodent stop, the pounding of a miniature pulse, the infinitesimal squeak of whiskers as the mouse groomed itself nervously. Ginny was unsure where the predator was, but positive one lurked nearby; the animal was jumpy.

Ginny heard all of it: everything. More disturbing, she suddenly understood what she heard.

Outside, the moon dipped behind a cloud.

Darker, inside.

Ultramarine to cobalt blue, Manilla would have described the change in light, too dark to see. Manilla snored softly in the bedroom. Manilla saw nothing.

For Ginny, everything had simply become more acutely defined.

She looked out the windows. No moon. No moon left, at all.

Again, her vision shifted. Unfamiliar sounds began to rise. Much closer — as if a leather bag filled with water were being dragged across a gym mat. Manilla?

Ginny heard the noise even before the movement occurred. Manilla turned over in their bed. Head and shoulders preceding rib cage, stomach, the sex, thighs, knees to calves and feet, all slipping across the expanse of new sheets. So much blood, organ and bone. Ginny knew it, heard it, felt it. It thrilled her most minute cells and synapses.

This time, the artery in Manilla's neck, completely exposed, throbbed in that surreal light. In Ginny's vision, it hummed, giving off a pinkish glow, like neon or a hot, machine coil, the energy packed and rising in constant flow. Ginny's eyes watered, strained to clarify the vision. No illusion, this; no mirage.

For the rest of the night, Ginny sat up, knees tucked against her pounding chest, arms wrapped under the comforter.

Terrified.

She was terrified.

The wounds on her labia, unexplainably healed even before Manilla had seen them, took on new importance.

The bad dream was alive and pulling her along with it.

Only when Manilla reached out for her, half-awake, did Ginny allow contact.

Even then, Ginny MacPhearson did not reach back.

━━━━

The car drove by slowly. Big car, little man. It turned the corner, disappeared behind the street lights and trees.

Hands crammed into the cheap, flannel-lined windbreaker, the boy walked a few feet. Head down, low. Eyes unfocused. He could feel the return of the car as it came up behind him. This time it stopped.

The boy moved to the parked vehicle. He stuck his head into the open passenger's window. "Want a date?" He glanced down, checking out the driver's shoes. Too expensive to be a cop.

The interior smelled civilian, too. Dirty enough to have been used but so clean that his mother would have driven in it. His mother.

Stop that.

Couldn't go there.

He had to wipe out the image.

His mother wasn't going to get him a place to sleep tonight, and damn straight she wasn't cooking his dinner. Had to wipe it clean. Think of something else. Far away. The new Mel Gibson flick. The sexy Calvin Klein billboard.

The driver leaned forward, unlocked the car doors. "Yes, uh, please, get in."

The boy slid inside. He was grateful for the warm air. "So, what'll it be?" he asked, pulling a cigarette from his pocket as he reached for the car lighter.

"Uh, would you mind not smoking? See, my wife, I mean, I . . . just quit," the balding man blushed.

"Whatever." The boy stubbed out the cigarette in the ashtray, then retrieved the butt and put it carefully back into his pack.

The man glanced nervously into the rear-view mirror. It was as if he expected to see cops or worse, his wife.

"Uh, there's this little motel out by the thru-way. Do you mind if we drive there?"

The boy swiveled around, stared directly at the man, "It makes no difference. It's your date, man." The boy's voice came from faraway.

The driver loosened his tie. Maybe the kid was on drugs? He didn't approve of drugs, per se. Didn't really even drink. Not really. Maybe he should just let the kid off. But how would he get rid of the hustler? He was already in the car.

"Son, uh, look, I'm not into anything weird, or, uh, heavy — no kinky, druggy scenes. You understand?" The man kept his eyes on the road. Traffic was heavier than he'd ever noticed it. He didn't like it. Not a bit.

The boy chuckled. His fingers drummed against the clean dash.

The driver cleared his throat loudly, but he kept his eyes on the road, "Son, I'm serious, now. If you want to do that sort of thing, maybe I should take you back to your, uh, your corner."

The boy slammed his open palm against the imitation leather car seat. "Man, you are pathetic! You're the one who wanted this date! You picked ME up. You should have thought about that crap back there, before you lured me into this heap!"

"Wait, wait just a minute, now, no need, uh, to get hostile, is there? I'm glad you got in, really. It is just that I don't do well around illegal substances. I just wanted to be on the safe side. Maybe I'm, uh, a square, huh?" the driver sneaked a sideways glance at the teenager.

What could he do? He didn't want the kid screaming at him. Caught — and nobody to blame but himself — he'd just have to go through with it. Hadn't he dreamed about picking up one of these boys a million nights? All right. Decision time. Finally: action. The boy was no innocent. He knew what he was doing. Probably a good kid, underneath. Eager, even. Just edgy. Probably hadn't had a good meal in days. Typical teenager. Well, first they'd take care of that. Get some hot food, good coffee, maybe even chat a bit. Yes. That was what they both needed. Make it a bit more personal. Heck, the kid had called it a "date," hadn't he? They could always head out for the motel later. He was the adult here. He could afford a little extra tact. Just had to relax. Be like his wife said, a bit less uptight.

Smiling crookedly he turned toward the boy.

The boy didn't return the grin.

"What's your name, son?"

The teenager turned to gaze out the side window, "Joey."

"Hey, then, Joey, how about some fried chicken, maybe a big, old cheeseburger, cup of Java? That sound good to you, son?"

"Sounds fine," the boy pulled the stubbed-out cigarette from the crushed pack in his pocket. He stuck the butt between chapped lips. Then, he reached for the car lighter. "Sounds great, man."

———

The phone machine wasn't on.

Gunner reached for the receiver, blindly, knocked the alarm clock from the night stand into his cowboy boot.

The buzzing was muffled, but still obnoxious as hell.

"Hullo? Jeezus, just a minute — I said, wait a minute! Christ!" Gunner felt around with one hand till he hit the heel of the boot. He shook out the buzzing alarm. It bounced off his woolly chest, causing him to wince. Smacking the little demon silent, he went back to the phone.

"Okay, I'm awake. What's up?"

The voice on the line crackled and faded. Damned cellular phones; talking on them was like listening to ghosts. Gunner pressed the receiver tighter to his ear.

"What? You sure? Same MO . . . ? Sweet Christ, I don't know! Could be, or could be a copycat. Not as rare as you guys keep thinking. Times are hard. All right. Give me twenty minutes. Fuck, no! I mean it, Halloran. I gotta get a shower and some coffee or I'll take somebody's head off for sure. Right, twenty minutes. And you tell them not to touch a fucking thing! You got that?"

Gunner lurched into sitting position, the clock ticking ominously, lost in the sheets. Four-forty-seven, in the god damned a.m.

That's what it had said, before he smacked the fucker.

Four-forty-seven.

The motel maid had come in early.

———

"You have to be careful what you feed them, Ginny. They're very temperamental. I've lost a few just from drafts." Kelly James tapped the bronze cage carefully and set the finches to chirping.

"Kelly, it's so sweet of you! Thanks." Ginny accepted the caged birds, moving them to the coffee-table in her living room.

"The entire dance department feels so bad about your fire, Ginny. Especially the first year grads. I mean, nobody really knows anyone else, yet, we're all a little shy. This seemed like a good idea — just an excuse, really, to see your new place, see how you're doing." Kelly stood in the doorway. Her coat was still buttoned to her chin.

Ginny walked back toward the dancer.

The scent off the woman was sweet: roses, maybe mixed with citrus? The dancer's hair was freshly washed, but she used a cheap creme rinse. Her hand lotion was from the health food store just off the Commons — beeswax and lavender — unmistakable.

Invisible condensation on the wool of her jacket reminded Ginny of winters at Weston; hallways filled with ancient steam radiators — mittens and socks were piled high, drying, after the snow.

The woman's lip gloss was flavored; there was a chemical base — a sun block? The flavor was cherry. Definitely cherry. She used "Secret," but not the antiperspirant, roll-on, regular scent. She was sweating now, but not from the cottage's heat; the woman was nervous. Her scent was acidic, a little acrid. It rose from her clothing, cut through the other odors she'd brought in.

Ginny tried to ignore them. Tried to clear her mind. She didn't want to know these things about the graduate student. Didn't want to have to deal with such personal details. Ginny passed a hot palm over her own forehead.

Kelly James moved closer, "Are you all right?"

"Fine. I'm really fine. It's just the stress of getting the house together so quickly after the fire. Honest. I don't mean to seem rude, but I have to get back to it, Kelly. It takes forever, you know?" Ginny back-pedaled as far as possible. The heavy perfume, the heat off the student hit her like a wave, sending her under, desperate for air.

Kelly froze, mid-step.

She saw something in Ginny's face, her eyes. It was almost as if Ginny had seen an enemy.

Ginny felt the girl's rising concern; she tried to relax.

Immediately, Kelly's good humor returned, her unease abated.

"So, when are you coming into the Studio? This week?" Kelly forced a smile, but she also reached for the doorknob.

"Um, not sure. I'm behind — even if the fire hadn't interrupted. Minx will kill me if I don't get some work done by the end of the month. I better not push my luck with him, or so I've been told." Ginny could breathe as the space between them widened.

Kelly opened the door all the way. She knew she must leave. Had to get out. Get away. Now!

Not a conscious thought, not even a feeling. It was as if she'd been programmed or commanded. She was simply supposed to go. Now. She would do it. No upset. No anger. Nor even confusion. She didn't even question how odd it must look to Ginny. In fact, it was as if Ginny were, in a strange way, part of it.

Kelly began, "Just remember Minx is a pig. Everyone knows it — but he's also the best choreographer on staff. He likes your work, Ginny. Don't worry — and don't let him push you around." Kelly couldn't stop talking. She was wound tightly, now sprung loose. Finally, she just turned and began the icy ascent up the walk, back to her car.

Her face was burning. She opened the car door and crawled inside. Maybe it was just meeting Ginny, at her house — the reputation of Ginny's family and all. Or maybe it was because on the night of the fire, in Collegetown, Kelly had been in that crowd on the street watching the inferno. She'd seen Ginny's loft explode, watched as that fireball hurtled overhead.

Ginny MacPhearson shouldn't be out of intensive care, let alone moving into a new place. Kelly turned on the engine. She hit the gas, hard. She prayed she wouldn't spin out and she prayed Ginny wasn't watching. She'd figure it out later — over drinks.

Inside, Ginny was watching the birds.

They were mesmerized by their new mistress.

Ginny heard their tiny, drumming hearts. She closed her eyes. The drumming slowed. Eyes open, the miniature organs sped up. Fascinating. Ginny experimented for several minutes.

"Oh, God, I'm sorry!" She suddenly realized this wasn't good for the birds. So, to calm them, she began to whistle. A lame apology, but the only one she could muster.

To her amazement, the finches moved in, closer.

She whistled again.

Cautiously, their tiny heads pressing against the bars of the cage, their bright, beady eyes inches from Ginny, they hopped across the perch.

Awkwardly, Ginny attempted a few lines from a Bach piece she remembered.

The finches chirped back, note for note.

Ginny giggled.

It couldn't be real! She felt light-headed.

Another song whistled, another perfectly returned. The birds hadn't missed a beat.

Ginny drew as close as she could to the shining eyes and brilliant feathers.

She felt something warm and wet against the back of her hand.

Glancing down, she saw it was saliva . . . a thin string linked it up to the edge of her mouth.

———

"Bus 28, departing for NYC and all points . . . ." The voice on the loudspeaker crackled and popped.

"Classy, huh?" Reggie spit out the toothpick. He missed the sand-filled ashcan by several inches.

"It's just a bus station." The girl answering him was maybe fourteen. Her straight, red hair was tightly pulled into a pony-tail. She clutched a beat-up "Simpsons" duffel bag in one hand and a pair of purple suede gloves in the other. Her parka was open; the depot was steamy. She'd been waiting for four hours. Her boyfriend was not going to show. She finally believed Reggie.

"Honey, eighteen ain't the age for settling down, take it from me. Personally, I think the dude must be blind to keep beautiful women like yourself waiting." Reggie smiled through capped teeth.

She was tired.

She was burned out, distracted.

At least Reggie had made her less uncomfortable, less self-conscious about being at the station for so long.

Dick was supposed to meet her in Syracuse. He was supposed to get the bus after his history class. They weren't leaving together because it would be suspicious. He would meet her half-way, half-way to The City. He was now four hours late.

For the first time in her life, she'd actually acted on a plan. They could get fake id. Once they got to The City they could start taking acting classes. They had real talent. Back home nobody appreciated real talent. It would be different in New York. Hadn't Dick scored all the leads in school productions? Since his frosh year! And every-body was always telling her what a killer bod she had. What model ever came out of their hometown?

They had to split. Quick. While they could. They had to get out together, pool their money and believe in each other. Dick was carrying most of the cash. He was older and, well, he WAS the man. She had a twenty left. After lunch. Now, Dick was four hours late. All the buses had been on time. She'd risked calling him at home, but his father had answered. She'd hung up.

Cassie sat on her duffel bag.

"Look, babe, it ain't worth it. Hey, girl! You got a million dollar face! Now, you know I'm no creep, here. I've been talking with you and hanging out with you all day. If I was a creep I'd a snatched your bag and be gone by now, right? Have I done all that? But this IS gonna sound like a creepy line, I admit. He ain't gonna show, honey. I seen it a thousand times — every night when I walk by here to pick up a paper. Just like today. Now, you can cash in the rest of your ticket and head home to Mom and Pop — but what they going to say? You want to face that every day, for the rest of your life? Your friends, too, they all know about it, right? Or, you can make him sweat. Make them all sweat and respect your pride — you tried. More than they could. You could come home with me for a few days.

"I got a nice job at the University, working in the garage. The University's always hiring, honey. For part-time, you hardly need any id. I could fix it so you work in the cafeteria or even housecleaning. You could stay with me for a while, till you raise some dough, get your head clear. Hey, I know what it's like being dumped, being alone in a city where you don't know anyone, don't have enough for a hotel room or nothing." Reggie watched the girl's face as he played her out.

Cassie paused. Maybe she could pass for eighteen. With make-up. And heels. People were always saying how built she was.

"Don't get me wrong, honey. If you decide you do like it around here, then, you gotta get your own place. I'm not offering a crash pad. I don't do this for most people but there's something different about you, something special. I can see it. I know students, right? I work at the University. A few nights, max, help you get connected, get situated, make some pocket change. Then, you decide. Back home or here. But leastways you still got your pride. Here, you can take some classes, meet some real people, people who recognize what you got, not like the weasel of a boyfriend that yellow, fake-boy playing at being grown-up. You hear what I'm saying, honey?"

Her face flushed, blushing mildly, Cassie squinted at Reggie. His speech was half-street jive, half-sincere. But, he had watched her bag while she went to the bathroom. He'd even offered to buy their lunch before she pulled out her money. And, he hadn't touched her. Not once. She couldn't go home. Couldn't face the parental units. Couldn't even face Dick — never mind her friends. What an ass she'd been — she'd told everybody.

Decided, Cassie stood.

She was about to hand over her duffel bag to Reg when she felt an intense wave of cold come over her, run almost electrically through each vein.

Cassie couldn't move. Couldn't speak.

"So, baby, you coming or what?" Reg reached for the girl's hand.

Before their fingers touched, two men were on either side of him, flashing badges.

"Okay, Reggie, it's over, man. We got you on tape this time. How sweet it is!" One of the cops drawled.

The second plainclothesman snapped cuffs on Reggie's thin wrists.

Cassie didn't react. She remained frozen, the acid-cold shunting through her. Her breath was quick and shallow. Nothing seemed real. The bus station, the cops, Reggie. Nothing to do with this freezing coursing through her body. Inside her, like something inside her, alive, separate, squeezing her heart.

"Hey, kid, what's your name? You aren't in trouble. You can go, get out of here — unless you want to file a complaint against old Reg? We just need your name and — hey!" The cop called to his partner as the girl melted into a heap on the floor.

The crowd gathered around them, blocking out the lithe figure of a woman, a woman in black, standing back from the confusion. She was there, staring. She was gone.

She had been only mildly amused as she watched them take Reggie away.

———

The bar was smoky. Only the regulars knew it stayed open till four. Reggie was a regular. He brought the third shot of cheap whiskey to his lips.

"Seems to me, Reg, if they really had a case, they would have kept you," the bartender said as he swabbed a spot directly in front of Reg.

"What you mean? I'm innocent, man! They got nothing! Well, entrapment, maybe. Fuckers!" Reggie tossed back the drink.

"You need another line of work, man." The bartender kept swabbing.

"Easy for you to say, white boy. I been running pick-ups since I was old enough to take them home. Man, I don't need anything more strenuous. I got a bad heart, man. What you suggest? Running rock? Or maybe selling doobies out of a plastic briefcase at the lunch rush, huh? Give me a fucking break."

"Admit it, Reggie. You got a soft spot for the little girlies."

"I got a HARD spot, man," Reg chuckled. He wiped a line of spit from his lip with a wrinkled handkerchief. A tap on the shoulder sent him spinning from the barstool.

"I like a man who carries a handkerchief." The voice moving between the empty seats at the bar was cold, but melodic.

"Say what?" Reggie looked up at the tall woman in front of him.

Her hair was tied into a French twist at the back of the handsome skull. Dark. Dark in that blue-black way a raven's wing is dark. Smooth. Fine as excellent silk. Equally black, the leather jacket, cinched at the waist. Narrowest waist he'd ever seen! She wasn't like a lot of these body-builder women. No, her figure was lean, feminine. Old-fashioned, almost. His type. A thoroughbred. Those nails — that wicked, wicked mouth! Forget the little girls. Her eyes shone like sapphires, they made him weak-kneed. She was looking right through him. Something cold, cruel made him hate her for the desire she made rise. The hate made him desperate.

"I'd like to buy you a drink, Reg. It is Reg, isn't it?" The woman reached inside her jacket.

So smooth, she was so smooth. Reg could only shake his head drunkenly as he watched, mesmerized.

No one saw them leave.

The bartender cursed when he found Reg's seat vacant and no tip in sight.

——

The town house was dark.

A single, silver slice of moon filtered inside. Reg swore as he caught his boot heel on one of the rugs.

The woman merely laughed. Low. Dangerous.

A quick flash of a match in the dark; scents of beeswax and spent carbon. Reggie screamed as he saw a lion's jaw by his foot.

Again, the woman laughed disdainfully. "Really, Reg, I shot it myself, years ago. Can't hurt you tonight. Nothing can hurt you here." She smirked.

"Except you?" Reg shuddered. He realigned his belt and sucked in his gut all in one obscene motion.

"You are such a bright man." She moved before he could take another breath.

Reg felt his body go stiff with the immediate cold. He couldn't breathe, couldn't feel his heart anymore. His eyes were horribly open, staring at her approach, lips back, her mouth revealed not the bud of tongue he'd hungered after but something monstrous. Something forked, almost reptilian, something deadly.

Then, he saw her fangs.

"Reg, you interrupted me at the bus depot. You stole my dinner right from out of my arms. It's only fair you pay me back. Now, don't look like that! You are actually one lucky man, Reg. Your last day has been pleasant and full. It could have been much worse. I was almost angry enough to follow you to the city jail. I could have ended it in the middle of a stinking cell, Reggie. Behind bars. Like an aging zoo specimen. Nobody to hear you screaming. I'd say tonight was a gift. The best drunken luck of your life, Reg."

The monster hissed as she held him by the throat, cutting off all air. His eyes rolled back, mercifully, into his head.

"Good night, sweet Reggie. Good night." As Darsen bit into the quivering flesh, she could feel her own climax rise. So odd. Perhaps the oddest of all, that even this creature could give her so much pleasure, give her such release. If she'd been the Creator she would have used far more subtlety, built in some finesse . . . Darsen finished the voluptuous suck with a last sigh.

And then, she slept.

———

The dried bouquet was beautiful. Still, Manilla preferred roses. But roses in winter were far beyond her means. Anyway, the dried blossoms would last longer.

"I like them, too," a familiar voice interrupted her thoughts. Manilla turned in the small shop and bumped directly into a young girl in a bright down vest. The young woman was pretty. Manilla couldn't help smiling. Something so familiar . . . .

"You don't remember me, do you? From the hospital, the night of the fire?"

Of course, the candy-striper pushing the coffee-cart! Her gentleness amidst the chaos of that devastating evening. "I do remember," Manilla answered.

"I'm Florence. Florence Kray, candy-striper!" The teenager laughed shyly, her eyes sparkling.

"Thank-you, Florence Kray, candy-striper. You were the one bright note in a lousy evening. I wish I could have told you then," Manilla leaned against a stack of harvest pumpkins.

The girl checked out Manilla. Straight girl cruise, nothing romantic, just . . . interested. A mild flirt. She liked something about Manilla, about the way Manilla had waited for Ginny MacPhearson, about the way she didn't care who knew they were lovers. Something almost, almost like a movie, in that. Besides, Manilla was cute — tomboyish, but, cute.

"You look way better than the last time I saw you, that's for sure. You live here?" Florence dropped her backpack near the dried flowers.

"Actually, no. I go to Weston up the lake. I'm an art student. I paint. But my friend, Ginny — " Manilla felt the color deepen in her face. It never was easy. Not with strangers, not with teenagers. You'd think, after so many years of being out, it would get simple. Like breathing. Maybe, for some people, maybe it was. But she always expected judgment, evaluations to fly in her face. Would it ever get easy? Weston didn't help. At Weston she faced the bowed heads and only partially shielded gossip or the averted eyes when she passed someone she didn't personally know in the hall. Giggles, even from the frosh, when they thought she'd passed by — as if she were the only lesbian. It was partly her, of course. So many people still blamed her for "turning" Ginny. As if anyone could turn Ginny into anything.

Florence brought her out of the awkward silence.

"Yeah, your bud, Ginny MacPhearson. We were so worried about her."

"Not to worry anymore. She's doing great. Really. Losing her loft was the worst blow, but we found her a new place and — "

"A new place? " Florence Kray looked confused.

"Yeah, her loft was a dancer's studio, she's a grad student at Cornell. The new place is only a cottage, but . . . ." Manilla watched Florence carefully.

"Wow, I didn't realize she was a dancer! God, it must be horrible for her, I mean trying to get along with that terrible bite and all — the nurses said they'd never seen anything like it."

Manilla felt the cold begin in the pit of her stomach. She grabbed the candy-striper by the arm. "Bite? I don't understand what you mean."

"She didn't tell you? Nobody at the hospital told you?" Florence Kray winced.

Manilla's grip tightened, "Tell me what?"

"Oh, shit. I'm going to be killed if anyone finds out. Maybe you're friend is just self-conscious. It's really none of my business." She'd blown it. She'd blown it big time. No going back now. The depth of hurt on Manilla's face precluded that. But if they were lovers, how could Manilla not know? It was so obvious, and so gross.

Florence felt Manilla trembling. "Okay, but look, you didn't hear it from me, all right? Isn't Ginny still on her meds? Painkillers and antibiotics?"

Manilla's eyes began to tear over. Around them, the scents of lilies and roses seemed to be suffocating.

"Florence, please, tell me!"

The teenager glanced around nervously. All she needed was for some friends to see her with a hysterical dyke attached to her elbow. She wanted out of the shop, away from the mess she'd made.

"You both were filthy from the fire when they brought you in, right? Maybe it was just soot or, or some debris? The nurses on duty that night could have been wrong. That happens way more than they want the public to know. She's fine, your girlfriend, right? You said she's moving into a new place? Well, I do know everyone was surprised how soon she was discharged, so it couldn't be that bad, right? Maybe just a big, ugly scratch or even dried blood. I mean, when I first saw her on the stretcher she looked like a piece of fried bacon! Could have just been gossip." Florence pulled gently away from Manilla's grasp and reached down for her backpack.

Lop-sided grin in place, Manilla jammed her hands into her pockets. Of course — a scratch — healed over now. Or it could have been all that soot — lots of scrapes that night. A miracle they'd both come out without any burns — a miracle. Florence was exactly right. Hell, if anyone knew the sadistic power of gossip, Manilla did. Besides, if there had been anything, wouldn't she have seen it? Wouldn't Ginny have told her?

"Hey, please don't hold this against the hospital, please. Basically, they, we do a good job. We really try. Honest. Tell your friend, tell Ginny, I'm glad she's better." Florence Kray backed away, hurrying out of the store.

Outside, the afternoon was graying, turning to rain. Cold enough to become sleet by sundown. Florence stopped at the curb, buttoned the down vest all the way to her chin. A tap on the shoulder made her spin around. It was Manilla.

"Florence, I'd like you to have these. Just, well, as a thank-you. For the other night." Manilla held out the dried bouquet.

The potpourri scent wafted warmly on the chilly breeze. It reminded Florence of her grandmother's attic in autumn. She didn't know how to respond. Not many people had given her flowers. Especially not other women.

"Uh, you don't have to give me these," the teenager blushed wildly.

"Yes. I do."

Waving once Manilla disappeared around the corner of the Commons. Her dark curls were plastered to her head from the rain. Her denim jacket looked far too light for the weather.

"Take care," Florence Kray whispered, watching till Manilla was gone.

———

On the second re-dial, Ginny threw the phone across the room. Still no answer at Manilla's dorm. Dinner. All the perfect Westonites filing into the stone dining-hall. Dressed, pressed and ready to chow down — just as she had once been. More than likely Manilla was holed up in the Art Studio or grabbing something quick at the Student Union.

Out of the corner of her eye Ginny noticed the finches. They were nervous, chirping madly. Ginny came across the room toward them. Something about their activity was exciting.

She whispered as she approached, "Shhh, all right. Everything's going to be all right. Just fine."

Eyeing her curiously, the male fluttered to the highest perch. His brilliant cap and cape made him seem like an animated jewel. His heart was beating wildly. Its tempo increased as Ginny neared. He would not back down. His eyes were bright beads. Their fierce protectiveness toward his mate not lost on Ginny. The hot fear so evident in the finch's stare caused needles of absolute delight to course up her spine. She was angered by the small defiance. She was fevered, growing unaccountably furious.

"You aren't afraid, huh?" Before she had formulated the action, before it even clarified in her mind, Ginny had the male out of the cage and in the middle of her left hand.

She trembled. The bird was still. In a state of shock, its body had gone limp. Its eyes were dull, glazed, its beak slightly open, its breath infinitesimal. Instead of horror at her deed, she felt excited by the sight of the bird's comatose body. She reached for the cowering female, scooping it from the cage with her empty hand.

A snarl more animal than human emanated from Ginny's throat. She ripped the heads off both birds, sucking the spurting bodies until they lay shriveled balls of fluff with unmoving claws.

Ginny dropped the bundles and sleep-walked toward the bathroom. Night covered the house. It had been dark outside even before her first call to Weston. Yet Ginny could see everything in her path. Each object seemed illuminated from within its own core. Each shadow receded beneath her new night vision.

Something was happening.

Something was happening to her, there, in the cottage.

She needed an aspirin.

She needed a Prozac.

In the bathroom, out of habit Ginny reached for the light switch. Pain sparkled deep in her joints. In the muscles of her arms and legs and back, tiny points of fire began to glow. Penetrating, as if after she'd danced very hard. Sweat beaded her forehead, ran down her cheeks, to her lips. She felt raw. She was exhilarated. She closed her eyes halfway as the first tingle and smell of her open sex rose. Surprised. Surprised and delighted. Her earlier fury had vanished. In its place came a sense of building excitement. She needed what? What? She fiddled with the handle of the medicine cabinet.

She needed to get out.

She needed to search. Whatever it was, she would find it away from the house. She would find what was necessary. Ginny turned off the light. In the mirror, it caught her gaze.

Almost too bright, the overhead lights reflected in the silvery wall of glass and masked the image. Now it stared back at her unmercifully. Ginny fought the rising scream. Her hands rose, touched the slimy cheeks, cradled the blood-soaked demon who glared back from the mirror.

——

The park was not empty, even though dark had settled in. Floodlights illuminated the abandoned tennis courts, spilled on to the swings and monkey bars. A light rain soaked everything. It was just above freezing. Still, a number of kids from the nearby junior high hung out, talking. They barely glanced up from their intense circle as Ginny passed. But she noticed them.

Every sweaty boy, every waft of cheap, teen-aged cologne, every Bonnie Belle faced girl, every flavored lip gloss and sweet shampoo that floated to her, Ginny noticed. Deeper, still, in rising alarm, Ginny could discern cooking odors from their homes, chalk dust from the classrooms, disinfectant one of the boys must have brushed against in the locker room. Deeper still, the musky, mushroomy scent of the boys, in their more private zones — some wearing talc, others clearly unwashed that day. And the girls, the girls! Their intimate aromas almost made Ginny salivate. Shocking, even to herself.

The childhood visits, the unwanted attention from her father, they came streaking into her consciousness like errant stars. Had his hunger been this insatiable? Had her scent aroused such fury in him? No! It was intolerable. How often had she become physically ill after hearing about adults who preyed on children? Now, in this very playground, she, she had come here, specifically. She knew the older children would still be out, after dark, knew exactly which area they'd gather in. She had come here, stalking them, even as her father had stalked her!

Rising from the bench at the sandbox edge, Ginny began to run. Faster, faster, not stopping for so much as a backward glance, needing to get away, she ran on, away from the children, out of the park!

All the junior high students noticed was a flash of tan trench coat, the streak of muted gold which was the dancer's hair as it came undone from its braid, the rapid exit of another nameless adult from their intense, young lives.

Immersed, once again, in each other, they were unaware of how close, how close they'd really come . . .

———

Walking to the Student Union, Manilla realized it was only an hour till closing. She'd arrived later than she'd expected. Upset over meeting Florence Kray and the fact that Ginny had had an injury she didn't share — healed over or not — had all but destroyed Manilla's balance, her timing.

That first night together, after the fire — Manilla was positive —there had been no mark, no scab, no scar — definitely nothing that could warrant being called a wound. Florence had to be mistaken. Besides, the nurses didn't share that kind of information — especially around a motor-mouth like that kid! The high schooler, however well-intentioned, was just dead wrong. And Manilla was not going to cause Ginny any more angst by making her think there was yet another wild rumor floating out there.

Darsen was out of their lives. Whatever had happened in that inferno, nothing was left of Darsen. If she were going to show, she would have showed. No, the vampire was banished. Maybe, even, please God, dead.

So was Slater.

Manilla felt the familiar lump in her pocket. Slater's ring. Hadn't taken it out since the hospital. Ginny wasn't around when she thought of it, too much else to think about when Ginny wasn't there. A tightness in her throat, the scald of tears held in abeyance — all of these sensations had grown as familiar as the ring, itself. She didn't want to re-live the past months' panic in her waking hours. Weren't dreams enough karmic payment? Manilla shook herself, as if she could literally shake the images pouring through her mind. Then, she pushed open the doors to the steamy Student Union.

Almost empty inside.

Even the jukebox was quiet.

High, oak booths lined both sides of the large room. All were vacant, as was the pool table, lit eerily as a night-time lawn, in the corner.

Manilla was relieved. She didn't need to bump into anyone else.

Behind the counter, a student sat on a stool. She was absorbed in her paperback volume of Yeats.

The cooking smells of fried onions and burnt meat were sharp. Manilla hadn't eaten since morning. Maybe that was why she was so damned emotional. She swiped at her eyes, pretending it was merely the stinging, outside cold which had left her bleary.

Coming up to the far counter, she pushed three bills across the greasy surface.

"Burger, coffee, please." Manilla tried a smile.

"No buns. White or rye?" The student-cook barely glanced up from her book.

"Rye's fine. I'll be in the back booth," Manilla answered, dropping all pretense of pleasantry.

"Whatever." The student slipped the Yeats into her smudgy apron pocket and sluggishly moved from the stool.

Manilla had no more than removed her jacket when the front door of the Union blew open admitting a roar of frigid lake air. The immediate scents of wet rocks, wet leaves and pine trees swept over her.

"Ginny?" Manilla rushed from the booth toward the tall woman in the trench coat, admitter of the wind. Ginny looked as if she owned the place.

Ginny crossed the room and squeezed them both back into the booth.

"Manilla, I knew you had to be up here. I called the dorm and even the Studio. I'm so glad I caught you!" Ginny touched the painter's hand with her own, colder one.

Immediate connection, the familiar press of thigh, of arm, the liquid gold light of the hair as it tumbled across Ginny's shoulders and brushed Manilla's warming cheek. Any thoughts of misplaced phenomena, misread symptoms, misunderstood affairs, vanished. Ginny WAS veracity.

Manilla moved her thigh as tightly as possible against the dancer's leg. The tense muscles made Manilla pause — she took a closer look into Ginny's face.

"What's wrong?"

Before Ginny could answer, two students, their gray and scarlet school scarves knotted high beneath wind-burned faces, entered the Union. The self-absorbed giggles stopped the moment they caught sight of Ginny MacPhearson in the booth next to Manilla.

Hurriedly they crossed the room and whispered loudly to the cook when they reached the back counter.

Manilla's voice rose, " Fuck you!"

Ginny turned, staring at the group intently. "Manilla, don't get mad. It's what they want. Keep cool. A few more months, that's all. Don't give anyone the satisfaction of blowing it now." Ginny's voice was surprisingly gentle. The student's entrance had given her a few moments to settle her still-racing mind, to find a way to explain the early day's events. Now she found the urge to confess diminishing.

The dancer wanted to take Manilla from the Union and back to her bedroom. This other hunger was beginning to burn again. She needed Manilla like oxygen. Manilla fed her, grounded her, kept her sane. She reached for her lover under the table. She let long fingers brush delicately but insistently, at the inseam in Manilla's crotch. She felt the almost immediate warmth and hot, wet spot her touch caused. She, alone, heard the quick intake of Manilla's breath. Ginny wanted Manilla, wanted out of there, now.

"Burger's done." The waitress dumped the greasy sandwich in front of the two with a thunk. As if disgusted she even had to wait the table, she set down the coffee so hard half of it spilled and sank into the bread of the burger.

"Hey!" Manilla came out of her torpor, as if awakened from a dream.

The waitress didn't stop for a second look. She moved back to her post before anything more could be said.

The connection momentarily broken, Ginny's mood turned darker.

Manilla saw the strange light flash across Ginny's face. "Have you eaten anything today?" Manilla asked.

"Sweetie, I'm a grown-up. Don't worry, okay? Eat and let's get out of here." Ginny tried to make her face twist back to nonchalance, but the sounds and scents coming from the group by the counter kept distracting her.

"I'm not really that hungry, Gin. Honest. Let's go." Manilla pushed the plate away.

Ginny had caught the attention of one of the girls. Something about the shortest one — something was infuriating — irritating. Ginny's eyes locked with the student's. The young woman grew pale. She couldn't take her glance off Ginny MacPhearson.

Noting Ginny was staring at them, the other girls began giggling maliciously. All but the shortest one bowed their heads conspiratorially.

Only the sudden, shocking gasps for air made them look up, look over at their friend. The girl was clutching her throat. Eyes rolling back, she was gagging.

The student-cook vaulted over the counter, attempted to beat the girl on the back, to beat air into the lungs. Hands clasped to her own open mouth, unable to do more than stutter, the second friend stood first on one foot, then the other. It was a macabre dance.

Ginny enjoyed it immensely.

Chuckling, she turned back to Manilla.

"Hey, she choking? Maybe I should — " Manilla began to slide out of the booth.

Ginny's hand stopped her.

"She has all the help she needs. We should go." Grasping Manilla's wrist, Ginny led the painter to the front door. Then, before opening it, Ginny kissed Manilla, full, open and very, very hard.

Outside, the dark was a welcomed friend. The wind had calmed, leaving the air crystalline — freezing, but pure. Still feeling confused by Ginny's presence on a week-night, the choking scene in the Union, and Ginny's heavy kiss, Manilla was silent.

Ginny knew Manilla's questions.

For the first time since the transformation had begun, she could see and hear Manilla's mind. With the other girls the images were less direct, more out of focus. But, Manilla was open to her and so, invited, she had this access. It was both terrifying and wonderful. What else? What else?

Head against the soft breasts, arms wrapped loosely around the slender waist, Manilla stopped. She pushed into Ginny. Inhaling, as if it were incense, she took in the essence of the dancer. Yes, yes, it was still Ginny — but, something else. Something not felt nor smelled nor even seen — something was different.

"Why did you come, tonight?" Manilla couldn't look at Ginny's face. Something in her own head made her gaze, instead, at the tortoise shell buttons on the trench coat. One of them was almost off, the thread worn, fraying. The button was close to Ginny's heart.

"You asked me, up there, now I'm asking you, Manilla — what's wrong?" Ginny put one hand under the painter's chin, tilting it upwards. Unless Manilla wanted to close her eyes, she couldn't avoid Ginny's probing stare.

Manilla did look up, then, but past the dancer. Around the black outline of Ginny's head, stars arched and burned. The entire sky seemed to be there only to offer back light for the dancer. Manilla's heart began to pound. The stars seemed to swoop closer, dancing almost in a halo over Ginny.

The touch — Ginny's touch on her, against her held more than the usual electric charge — Manilla's gaze went directly to Ginny's eyes.

In the black hoodish outline that was Ginny's head, two pure points of red glittered. Manilla froze, bird before snake, caught. Her heart roared for release, pounded in her head, pounded for her to go — escape — run.

This was Ginny, yes, but something more. Manilla recognized the fast-forward motion, the immobility now flooding her muscles. "Oh, Gin," Manilla moaned. Then, she went down into the floating, flooding blackness, alone.

The probe.

The same flood of darkness . . . the same falling . . . both inside and outside of your own body, both watcher and actor . . . but not Slater. Not Slater probing, this time . . . Manilla tried to calm her racing consciousness . . . she knew, from the last encounter, if she didn't fight it, if she let herself float almost, like learning to swim, don't thrash, relax, the drowning sensation would stop . . . her head would stop its stroke-like pounding . . . her heart would calm . . . Manilla tried to breathe again.

"It's only me. Manilla. It's just me." Coat still on, her hand touching Manilla's temples, stroking them so lightly, Ginny sat on the floor by the dorm room bed. The down sleeping bag just covering the top of Manilla was unzipped.

Manilla's feet thrashed twice, the heels connecting with the lumpy mattress, then stopping. Everything just stopped. She was in her dorm room. One light on the desk burned. Ginny sat beside her. They both had their clothes on. And she felt as if she'd been hit by a truck. Her entire body was sore. "What?"

"You . . . passed out . . . I carried you back. No one, no one saw us. Probably from not eating all day — " Ginny kissed Manilla's forehead.

"Stop it!" Manilla dragged herself up on one elbow.

"Stop what? What's gotten into you? Do you want me to call the infirmary — or drive you over? Maybe it's the flu." Looking huge in the shadowy room Ginny stood up.

"That! Exactly that!" Manilla kicked free of the sleeping bag. Against the protest of her body, she sat up. The room lurched and then refocused. She wasn't going to heave. She was going to do this — now!

"Manilla, I . . . I don't know what you want." Ginny, surprised, stepped back into a darker corner.

Manilla moved more swiftly than she would have believed she could. Grasping Ginny's arm, she tried to pull Ginny into the lamplight by the desk.

"Ginny, I know what you did — to me — just now, outside. I don't know how and I don't know why, but I recognize it. Now, you can tell me or you can kill me, but MacPhearson, you ain't leaving this room till I know what the hell is going on. All of it!" Unsure whether she could really back up the threat, Manilla felt her voice quaver. But she didn't move from her position blocking the door.

Ginny simply dropped like a rag tossed into a laundry basket. No fight. No tension. A weird smile played across her lips.

"YOU know what I did? How? How? I don't even know what I just did!" Ginny's long legs spread out before her. She held her hands to the sides of her head in some vaudevillian pantomime of upset.

Manilla moved the desk chair between them. Every cell screamed "Leave! Get away from this predator, while you have the upper hand." Instead, over-riding the instinct, Manilla turned the chair around. She sat like a cowboy. The back of the chair propped her arms and chin, making her gaze eye level with Ginny's.

"I know because somebody did it to me, before — " Manilla's voice grew hushed.

"Katherine Slater?" Ginny's eyes sparkled, but this time, the bloody-red hue was diminished. Only small points of fire seemed to dance in the darkened pools.

"We haven't had much time to really talk — about what happened, with me, with Slater — before the fire, Gin. That's been . . . my fault." Manilla swallowed hard. She had meant to tell Ginny — everything. All of it. But it had begun to fade — and with the strong images, so, too, the belief that anyone —even Ginny — would understand. Ginny, of course, believed her, would believe her, still, but understand? Besides — what Slater caused in Manilla's heart — lay a secret she never wanted to have Ginny unfold. It would damage them both. She'd hidden the ring, still, from Ginny.

"Gin, I had dinner with Slater. At her home. I thought it was just going to be one of those senior things Weston encourages, you know, Slater being the new advisor and all. But it wasn't, Gin. I didn't tell you because, until the night of the fire, I didn't have the memory available — it was buried."

"C'mon, Manilla, who 'buried' it?" Ginny's voice was edged in sarcasm, even though she knew Manilla was telling the truth. Something about Slater — even now that Slater was dead — stood between Manilla and Katherine Slater. Ginny had sensed it from the start. Ginny had never let on that she felt more than passing concern. She kidded Manilla about teacher crushes and all. But the feeling was strong, seemingly stronger now that Slater was dead. Ginny couldn't hide the jealousy that rose even as Manilla began to speak.

"She did, Slater. It was too much. In the beginning — before — before I really understood who Darsen was — or who Slater was."

"My God — it wasn't the smoke — what I saw Darsen become, what I saw Darsen fighting — it was Katherine Slater?" Ginny lunged forward. In an instant, faster than Manilla could speak, Ginny held Manilla's hands in a crushing grip.

Again, the connection. Head lolling back, a flood of images crashing through her brain, Manilla swooned. The pain of centuries was written in Darsen's hand, written with human blood. Manilla's muscles began to spasm. A seizure began to take her. Ginny dropped the hands. Connection broken, Manilla fell from the chair unconscious.

This time, when Manilla woke Ginny was gone.

━━━━

The motel was the best he'd ever been in. Had its own fridge and bar, lots of thick, wide towels and a water bed with a heater that didn't take change.

"What'd ya say your name was?" the lawyer asked, putting down the phone.

The hustler answered without looking at the man. "Joey."

"Really? I used to play basketball with a Joey. Joey Martin. Kid down the street. Wonder what the hell he's doing now? Probably a proctologist in Beverly Hills, huh? Well, Joey, you aren't Mr. Martin and I'm glad. Here. Try some. It's good blow." The lawyer held out a mirror striped with neat, white lines.

Silently, the boy accepted. The buzz slammed into the middle of his head, then whipped through his spinal cord, coming out of his cock, or so he visualized. He was huge, hard, hungry.

"Well, kid, I don't have a lot of time to play, so let's get to it. Thought I had the night off, but word's out. I have to get back to the office. Special papers due tomorrow. Ah, the legal life. Anyway, you can stay the night in the room, whatever, but, let's do this good. Okay? You ready for that?" Stepping from the paisley delicately, the lawyer dropped his silk boxers.

He worked out twice a week, kept the fat mostly under control. He wasn't really large. He was a foot shorter than the hustler. The kid wasn't that butch, which was okay, too. He didn't like guys that were intimidating. Soft tops, his particular fantasy. He didn't like being responsible for the evening's performance, wanted to just lie back and let it happen.

He handed four scarves to the boy.

"I presume, since you are professional, you know what to do with these?"

"You got that right, pal," Joey pushed the man onto the bed. "Roll over."

The lawyer obeyed. A shiver held him in its shimmery embrace. Just what was necessary. Just what he needed to get through the night. Good dope, good sex and later, a great meal. A nice red to bring him down, even him out from the coke. There was much to be said for pampering oneself.

"Spread them," the boy's order was a short bark.

"Gladly," the lawyer quipped, belly flat, face to the side.

The boy tied the scarves tight enough to cut the pale flesh of the man's wrists.

"Hey, that hurts!" the lawyer squealed.

"Isn't that what your paying me for?" Joey moved to the man's feet.

"You don't get it! I'm not into pain — none of that kinky stuff! I like bondage, Joey and well, maybe a little dominance — maybe. Just, well, a real man, on top. Can you be a real man? A nice man for me, Joey?" the lawyer wheedled.

Joey was disgusted; pallid buttocks, the thick, stiff red hairs across the ass, the spattering of freckles on the shoulders reminded him of nothing so much as splashes of dried blood.

Joey reached across the bound man for the cocaine vial. Neatly separating the powder into two, long lines, Joey inhaled.

"Hey, leave some for me!" the lawyer yelled.

Joey stopped, mid-sniff. "What?"

"I said, uh — " the lawyer's anger dribbled away. He wasn't sure if this was part of the scene.

"You suggesting, maybe, like, I'm being a pig?" Leaning down and close to the rosy face, Joey straddled the naked man.

The lawyer answered, "No, not exactly. I mean, I was simply worried there wouldn't be any, you know, for later . . . for both of us."

"Look at me when I'm talking to you!" Joey yanked the man's hair.

The attorney began to breathe very fast. Maybe it was a mistake, this kid, trying to get a quickie in. No good, mixing business with pleasure. The coke was pretty pure. Better than that kid usually got, for sure. It had probably zoned the hustler. Maybe he should just offer to pay and get out.

"You think I'm just some street scum you can order around, toss away like Kleenex when you're through? You get me all riled up, you and your grade-A blow and your silk undies and fancy suit — listen, Bigshot — this is corruption of a minor, you know that? You listening to me? I know your type — all my life. If you go, now, you run to the cops, tell them I threatened you or I'm dealing or some kinda shit. Blame the kid — your kind of rehab? Huh? Who do you think you are, fucker? Who do you think you're dealing with?" Joey reached into his work boot.

The man was absolutely still. Suddenly, he felt something hard, something smooth and metallic-smelling, under his nose. The steel was cold. Then, a simple, caressing tug, right below the nostrils. There was the taste of iron, of salt, followed by almost sweetness as the blood ran over his lips, into his mouth. Several seconds passed before he felt the stinging. The blade was that sharp.

"Jesus Christ!" the attorney felt his bladder release. The stench of hot urine rose from beneath them.

"What a kick, Lawyer Man! Mr. Hotshot wets the bed! What a crack up! Do they know this in court? Wonder what's worse, having to admit your a fag or that you wet the bed? Sorry, buddy, Jesus Christ is dead. I'm the only one who's listening."

Joey began to slice.

———

The TV glowed blue, but the sound was off.

Didn't matter.

Joey had learned to tune out almost everything. When he was little, when his cousin would take him down into the cellar, Joey could hear the adults laughing and talking, upstairs. They were oblivious that the sixteen-year-old cousin was sneaking the five-year-old boy into the womb of the house. Joey could hear them upstairs, happy, drinking and eating, laughing, unworried about anything. They could not hear him. The sounds never worked in his favor. His cousin knew it and he knew it and so, he'd learned to tune it all out. His cousin threatened to kill Joey if he even whimpered. Then, to insure there would be no screaming, the sixteen-year-old thrust his thick cock into the child's mouth. They never heard him retch, never heard him choke. And Joey had learned to tune out the sounds of his cousin's pleasure, to tune it all out, to go far away where there was only silence and blue-white light.

Not even the low gurgling from the dying attorney on the bed disturbed his peace.

Joey sat in front of the TV, a can of honey-roasted almonds in one hand, a bottle of bitter, imported beer in the other. The razor was neatly folded, cleaned and shining and tucked back into his work boot.

He did not so much as glance back at his carving job.

He did not listen.

After it was done, he never looked or listened. Not since that first john. Something in him had changed. Joey had turned a corner and there was no going back. Whatever innocence had been in the runaway trying to get off the street was dead now. He'd gone to the end of that lane. Another route, another twist in the road. The runaway was dead. Something was beginning to grow from the compost of the corpse. Something that was seated in the middle of the paid-in-full luxury room.

The heavy curtains moved slowly from the wall.

Joey didn't react.

But, he did see her — tall, dark, coming between the TV's blue glow and the bed.

She was solid.

She was not part of his memories nor his dreams.

"Ahhhh, Joey, I don't think you're piggy at all. In fact, you've left all the best parts for me — haven't you? Just like the last time. Hmmmm . . . " Purring, she moved past him, toward the bubbling man on the bed.

Darsen fed while Joey drifted, lost, beyond her, in his own head.

Darsen fed until the attorney was a corpse.

She left a little blood, just enough to confuse those who would find him, enough to make them believe he'd died from the wounds which marked him open and shut, like an accordion.

A delicious game — using the boy like this! Why hadn't she thought of such a diversion long before? It grew so tedious, especially in these smaller cities, no play, no stretch. The hunting was almost a bore. In fact, if not for the burning cold which could incapacitate if not heeded, she wouldn't feed every night. Using Joey was the perfect answer — dinner and entertainment! She'd seen him and the others a hundred nights before, but they seemed such an unwashed bunch. Her sensibilities were of a different order. But one night, again, out of sheer ennui, she'd followed Joey, let him play out his game. He'd delighted her with his hidden talents. She'd stepped in only after the brutal act was done — no need to mess herself when the boy clearly liked his work. No, she'd slipped between the acts, as it were, finishing off the still breathing victims while the boy merely watched. He was mesmerized by her. She knew it. She had read his mind from the first. He thought she was an angel, then a goddess, then . . . now, now his mind was fragmenting, breaking up. She knew they would have to part company in the near future — but not yet. It was still too diverting, too delicious. Syracuse was such an ugly city, so pedestrian, so gray, this game was her only recreation. It was so good, once again, to be held in awe and reverence. Joey was her hand-maiden. Ha!

Darsen licked the last of the blood from her perfect lips. Then, coming behind the boy, she rose. She stroked his temples, promised him protection, promised him life. She would never let the police capture him. She would never leave him alone. Wasn't this everything he longed for? Such a sweet covenant . . . .

Darsen's voice was like silk. He could feel what she said, see what she said. The images flowed, under his skin, flooded his mind, made his own. Anything. Yes. He would do anything for her, because, because she knew him. She would protect him. She would never abandon him.

He felt all the hairs along his scalp line rise. Her breath was lilac and lily. So cold, so cold, but still, he didn't want her to stop. He could come just with the sound of her voice — the only sound he couldn't shut out. Wouldn't shut out. He wanted her close, beside him. Always. Beside him. He would never be alone again.

And when The Nightmare came, when the bodies rose, up from the sidewalks, clinging and clutching and pulling him down, she would be there. Beside him. She would speak softly to him, rock him out of the hellish place and bring him back. She would watch him as he slept, watch over him. She'd promised that.

Joey smiled. He was disentangled from the blue-white place and the silence. He listened to Darsen's voice and then he was back, in the room, in front of the TV. He was free.

"Yes, Joey. Forever. Just like I promised." Darsen moved the corpse to the far side of the soiled bed. She stretched out, smiling, smiling at Joey. Her Joey. Her Joey in that cold, blue light.

———

Ginny turned her key in the lock.

She knew what was waiting inside.

More than the empty balls of fluff, it was the monster caught in the mirror, reflected but living inside of her.

It was still dark.

She had to leave Manilla.

Manilla would come out of the swoon. Temporary. How did she know? Unsure — unsure even, quite, how she'd done it to Manilla — but when she'd touched a pulse point, the power blooming inside her opened Manilla up — as if Ginny could step inside Manilla, inside all of Manilla's memories, dreams, feelings.

She'd only stopped when she'd come across Darsen!

So horrific — to find Darsen inside of her lover — like a tumor — hideous, alive — the memory so guarded yet so powerful. Ginny had to believe Manilla when Manilla tried to explain — Katherine Slater had been one of them — like Darsen — but no one was like Darsen! Katherine had fallen through Darsen — it was Katherine Slater that had led Manilla to Darsen — and of course, ultimately, to Ginny's own liaison with the vampire.

Katherine Slater was a vampire — but why hadn't she taken Manilla? Surely their connection was that strong — Ginny felt the memory of Slater, still living, in Manilla. She hadn't realized so much of what Manilla was going through — so wrapped up had she been in her own life in Ithaca and with dealing with Darsen — but Manilla had had a drama of her own — and Slater was at its core! Manilla had hidden it from Ginny for months — why? Surely, she would have known if Manilla were in love with the professor? Even as Darsen began her seduction, Manilla had felt it destroying Ginny — wouldn't the same hold true in Manilla's case? Wouldn't Ginny feel it, know it? But, Katherine Slater wasn't Darsen — she wasn't evil. Yes, she'd been responsible for putting Manilla in danger — but Manilla was already enmeshed. Katherine Slater had saved them all. At her own expense — the key to what was happening lay with Katherine Slater. What did Manilla know? What was still in her subconscious?

Ginny hadn't been able to continue with the probe. Its power was too unpredictable. Her knowledge too incomplete to use without damaging Manilla's mind — or her heart. The sudden apparition of Darsen, in Manilla's memories, made Ginny unwittingly increase the probe. The surge sent Manilla into a tailspin edging on heart-attack or stroke. Ginny had pulled back when she'd realized it. Manilla was asleep, exhausted, but not comatose. Not hurt. Ginny had to leave her — staying was dangerous. The hunger was beginning to over-ride caution. Manilla's sweet body, the absolute helplessness, was almost too much to endure. Ginny knew if she didn't leave, she'd hurt her lover. Even Manilla could be fair prey.

Ginny stepped into the quiet house.

Another place of blood. She pushed the front door closed. Immediately, the stench of the dead birds filled her. It clung like smoke clings, long after the fire is out.

Slowly, Ginny moved toward the carcasses. Tears, slightly stained with pink, fell, as she gingerly carried the small bodies in the palms of her hands. She went to the back door. She pushed hard, breaking an icy film that stuck the bottom of the weather-stripping to the porch. Freezing rain began in earnest.

Night stained the lake still. Ginny moved through the dark, down toward the edge of the water.

On the rocky shore, she stamped a hole through the crusty ice and slipped the silent puff-balls under along the lake's lip. She was thankful for the cover of the storm.

Ginny could see beneath the ice. She watched as the current caught the bodies. She watched until they were carried away.

Another vision crowded in. When she'd been in England, the year before arriving at Weston, she'd spend a summer studying literature, made a field trip to Virginia Woolf's country house. Virginia Woolf — her favorite writer. Manilla called Ginny snooty for her preference, but she didn't care. Something in Woolf's brilliance and lonely madness spoke to Ginny. So, too, the death of the writer. Plagued by an oncoming bout of mania, the author had quietly stolen down to the river behind her home. Sure the terrific current would move her body far from where anyone who loved her could find it, here, she'd stuffed rocks into her pockets, and then walked out into the water. She had not been able to face the madness one more time. She had not wanted to cause suffering to those who would have to bear the changes with her. Woolf had seen visions, heard voices, been visited by demons.

Ginny looked out over the black ice and frozen waves. Suddenly, she understood Woolf far better than she had ever understood anyone.

When the sun rose, it rose pale and cold.

Facing the rising light, Ginny huddled beneath the down comforter. She had not slept. The cold was growing, even as the sun burned through the lake side windows.

From her toes, the soles of her feet, the palms of her hands, the cold was moving toward her heart. The comforter was of little help. Not along her skin, no, it was deeper — inside the flesh, moving past muscle and ligament. The cold had penetrated bone.

Ginny attempted a drink of water.

Immediately, the liquid came back up.

No use. She knew what was necessary. She knew and she loathed the need. She'd fight it as long as she could. Conquering the body was something every dancer dealt with. When all was pain — and even pain wrung out — still, you moved, you went on. One more leap, another arabesque. You pushed and flew and slid long past the point of bloodied feet. Ginny understood pain.

She also understood the cold.

In Spain, in convent school, the girls' cells were unheated. Ginny had managed by wearing all the clothes she owned to bed. For two years she'd lived like that. So much darkness, so much ice. Constantly alone. She learned the native language out of desperation. She had been unable to ask for a drink of mere water without it. How much worse not to be able to ask for kindness? A child's comfort? A simple confidante? Yes, it was in Spain that Ginny came to understand cold.

The lessons continued in her family — her father, tutor of all frigid acts — taught her how ice can form around a beating heart. His own heat only caused her ice to thicken. The absent mother, lost in her bottled dreams and drowning in 'Jack Daniels': she, too, had reinforced the winters between them.

Ginny had survived by learning to become part of the tundra. Caring less and less for people, she found solace in art. In dance. Art became her suckling mother, her protecting father. Music was her religion, her dance, her prayer. Through them what little melting had been possible occurred.

Then, the hejira: Weston College.

Manilla.

The fire between them, the burning connection, had broken and re-made her. But now, a killing frost had returned.

Ginny needed a new arsenal.

Even Manilla couldn't aid in this siege.

Once again, Ginny MacPhearson was completely alone.

———

It was dusk, again.

Manilla knocked before she tried her key.

No answer.

She opened the door for the first time since she'd helped Ginny move in. Ready for anything, she tentatively called, "Ginny?"

The harsh, industrial overhead lights nearly blinded Manilla. They hadn't had a chance to shop for lamps. The furniture had come with the cottage — a rag-tag assortment of summer people's leftovers. Evidently, people did not leave lamps. Noticing how cold the house was, Manilla went into the kitchen.

"Gin?" she called, again, half-expecting the dancer to jump out of the shadows. It had been more than disturbing when Manilla woke from the probe, alone, near noon. She felt as if she'd had a case of beer the night before. After the hang-over, she'd tried to sort things out. There was no disputing the facts — the probe was unmistakable. But Ginny hadn't used it the way Slater had. Slater had taken her backward and forward, had allowed Manilla to react, to question, to even move within the confines of the dream-state. With Ginny there had been no warning, no preparation — a slamming into Manilla's mind. It was as if some dream surgeon had carved slices from her gray matter. Such was the invasion. Then, the horrible falling and the darkness, awakening, finally, with sounds coming from the corridor, people on the phone, people in the hallway, the noon-time bells from the tower. But no Ginny. No note. No answer when she'd tried to call the cottage.

Manilla's mind was working its way around the inevitable. What if what the candy striper had seen was true? What if she had heard those nurses correctly, had witnessed more than ashes and soot on Ginny as they had pushed her through the hospital emergency room? How would such a wound heal so quickly? Why hadn't Ginny mentioned it? Why had Ginny avoided almost all discussion of the night of the fire?

Manilla wanted to believe, was desperate to believe the experience had been too painful for the dancer. Too horrific. Maybe they were even experiencing some sort of stress syndrome like survivors of disasters or wars experienced. There would come a time to reveal all — both sides, a time when Manilla would have to tell Ginny everything about Katherine Slater — including her confusing feelings, a time when Manilla wanted to know everything about Darsen — especially the hours before the fire. Slater had warned her how much at risk Ginny had been, how no one could resist the vampire. Manilla had believed her love for Ginny would protect them both.

The image of Ginny's ruby-eyes glowing in the dark the night before, the image of Ginny's sudden crossing of the dorm room, the image of grasping Manilla's wrist, pushing Manilla into the dark place. Ginny's retreat left Manilla with no explanations, left Manilla sick and questioning.

All her life she'd been around people who avoided answering questions. When her mother had been ill and so often taken to the hospital, no explanations were ever given to the children. When her family's drinking relatives caused huge scenes, when objects were broken, doors smashed, windows cracked, furniture flew and all the little ones scattering for cover, trembling, hiding, with only Manilla to round them up, joke them out of their fear, wrap them in blankets and hide them in bedrooms. Only Manilla was left to protect them with her own wakefulness and all-night watch. There had never been explanations offered. No apologies, no answers. Growing up, demanding that the blanks be filled in, that she at least know what was coming so she could protect them, Manilla had tried. She had been told children should be seen, not heard, that children shouldn't speak unless spoken to. Anyway, she didn't protect anyone. Her father protected them, her aunts and uncles and grandparents — where did this savior behavior evolve into a nine-year-old kid?

In catholic school, Manilla again demanded answers about God — a God who allowed such things to happen to children she'd seen in that factory town; slaps, detentions, notes home . . . but no answers. So, she'd learned to gather the information she could herself, then sift it through, discard what was unreliable, unsure. In matters of regular life, it had made her a fighter and a survivor. In matters of heart and spirit, it had left her vulnerable, street-wise but vulnerable. In matters of heart, she let the questions hang on in the open air. In matters of spirit, she sent up prayers like sparklers into the dark, but she felt, so often, removed. There, too, she found no obvious answers.

So, in this dark place, with Ginny, Manilla waited, refusing to scream out. Perhaps, perhaps Ginny's contact with Darsen had imparted some kind of energy exchange — like, like an apprentice to a healer or psychic. Perhaps Ginny had somehow picked up the residual charge. That would explain why the probe had been similar to, yet not as damaging, so different from the probe Slater had employed. They had to talk, now. They couldn't wait for time to pass, to heal them over. There was no one who could act as translator or therapist. If they were going to survive together, the time to be honest was now. But where in hell was Ginny?

Manilla began hunting for the thermostat. One thing she could fix was the temperature. She could also softened the light in the little house. Make it warmer, make it safer. When Ginny came home it would be to a kind of sanctuary, not to face an adversary or argument. They would get through this, together.

The thermostat was nowhere to be found.

Manilla decided she'd make a fire. There was wood on the back porch. There were matches on the mantle. Clearly, the fireplace worked.

It took the artist only minutes to coax a roaring flame from the logs. The fire did much to dispel the drafty feeling in the house. Sweet wood smoke perfumed the living room. Just fragrant enough not to bring up bad memories. Besides, the fire in the loft had reeked of burning chemicals, of sulphur.

Manilla decided to check out the kitchen. She'd missed lunch because she was fighting the hangover. Then she'd spent the early afternoon in a meeting with the committee that had been hastily put together to replace Slater. Slater's disappearance had been covered by Slater herself. When she'd realized how close they were to finding Darsen, and what that would mean, she'd sent letters of resignation to the President and Dean of Weston. She'd cited "personal, family matters." They were still scrambling, trying to locate her so that she could deal with her household responsibilities and various forms of paperwork, but, the explanation and resignation were accepted. What else could they do? Slater had let Manilla know she'd taken care of it all — the "signal" would be a note, left behind, for Manilla, the kind of note any advisor would leave behind in similar situations. Family problems, health matters, legal complications — in polite College society a student wasn't expected to question these mysterious comings and goings of the faculty. And, of course, only cursory explanations would be offered.

Slater had banked on this protocol. She had covered well. Her "note" to Manilla had been delivered during that long week while Ginny was in the hospital. Manilla recognized the pre-arranged signal. She knew that Slater had, once again, saved her. Manilla was publicly noted as the last person Katherine Slater had been seen with prior to her departure. Manilla, like the rest of Weston, was off the hook. Slater had protected them all.

So, a committee had been formed — a committee of three — one from the anthropology department, one from the sociology department and, of course, the head of the art department. Nice enough men, who vaguely understood what Manilla's senior project and exhibition would be, but who did not really know what to do with the senior. Clearly, they were also uneasy in matters touching upon Katherine Slater's absence.

They'd spent the afternoon parrying with Manilla — trying to get a quick fix on the senior's plans, to develop a strategy for her senior show.

Manilla knew the recent work had been impacted by the fall's drama. She couldn't very well explain that to them. Slater's death had pushed her work into a tailspin. Her painting was a way to deal with all she couldn't speak — it had always been. The violence of the last year, her knowledge of the virago in their midst, her almost losing Ginny — these things could not be painted. What emerged was an amalgam of half-hearted attempts at what a committee from a cultured college would deem appropriate. As unsure as they were of the student, herself, they had seen earlier work and they felt that the recent painting was a deep disappointment. It almost seemed as if it hadn't come from the same painter.

The meeting had ended badly. Manilla was in trouble. Everyone that afternoon knew it. They'd granted some small leeway in that Katherine Slater's surprising exit could account for Manilla's difficulties — but it was November. Manilla had only one choice left. She must scrap the year's work and begin again.

Begin again — God knew she'd give anything to do precisely that!

The kitchen was still partially in boxes. The fridge contained only two apples, half a carton of turned skim milk and an unopened jar of instant coffee. Typical dancer's fare. What was unusual, however, was that there were usually a half-dozen bottles of water in the refrigerator and a half-dozen empties, stuck in the beverage holder on the door — one of Ginny's idiosyncrasies. No water . . . no empties.

Manilla took one of the apples and shut the door.

The living room was beginning to get toasty. Manilla pulled two cushions from the couch and propped herself by the fire. She took off her jacket and noticed a little "thinggk" as something fell from the pocket onto the hearthstone.

Slater's ring.

Manilla pushed it onto her finger.

Hidden in the jacket, all this time, hidden, still, from Ginny — this was the night to wear it, to use as a prop in dealing with the whole story of Katherine Slater. The stone seemed to gather the firelight and keep it at its own center. Deeper than ruby, it was almost violet. Heart-blood. Or so it seemed, from the most hidden places.

Manilla lay down, her head cradled in her arms and watched the firelight dance in the core of the jewel.

"Darsen is the promise, the artifice of human love." Katherine Slater was standing in front of Manilla.

Manilla shook herself like some cartoon character trying to wake from a dream.

"Katherine — you're dead — how?" Manilla stared at the anthropologist.

Slater was beautiful — her skin creamy, her hair full and dark, brushing the strong shoulders, caressing the firm neck. She stood, tall, erect, but easy. Her denim shirt and Levis made her look as if she had just come from a dig or was about to go into the forest.

The professor didn't come any closer, but she continued, "Ginny doesn't see Darsen, even now, as Darsen truly is.

Ginny's experience only encompassed what Darsen allowed. Manilla, no matter what happens, you cannot hold Ginny fully accountable. You have no idea how powerful Darsen's pull can be! If you have ever truly loved Ginny, you must focus only on that, put all of your energy into a single, brilliant point and using that power, fight for her. This will be the greatest battle of your lives."

"Katherine! I'm so glad to see you — but how? How?" Manilla stepped closer.

The older woman reached out and lightly grasped the painter's wrist. Immediately Manilla felt the probing begin . . . the sudden weakness, the falling, the black, and then, that melding. Manilla began to go where Slater's mind, Slater's words led. Slater was in Manilla's dreams even as Manilla was in Slater's. There were no boundaries, no laws of time or physics here. It was all a great river, a constant flow.

Slater pressed only slightly harder, "You can never understand Darsen the way Ginny does. When Darsen found me in the Amazon Basin, I was lost. I was delirious. She saved my life — and then, she took my life in payment. She walked with me in my dreams, Manilla. When I'd wake, she'd talk to me about those dreams, as it we'd simply strolled in the jungle or had tea together. All edges were blurred until there were no edges."

"Like now, like this," Manilla whispered.

Slater went on, "There are no limits to that kind of seduction, Manilla. Never forget this. As women, so often we've been taught that we are nothing alone. Merely incomplete creatures, biding our time until someone finds us worthy enough or desirable enough to rescue. To fulfill our empty lives. We are drilled to desire, always, another half. Darsen's hunger is total. When you are the subject of that kind of desire, especially if you are a woman who has been taught to seek out and to measure yourself by that kind of desire, it becomes absolute. More than sex, more than gender, Darsen deals with soul-hunger. She will be satisfied only with total possession.

Some deep part of Ginny had to be open to that kind of need. Goddess knows, we all are . . . Darsen discovered the exact loci of Ginny's wounds. For Darsen it is always so easy, so clear. Once her kind has revealed itself, there is no turning from them. The person Darsen chooses is in constant turmoil and danger.

Manilla, the power Darsen offers is her final seduction. She offers what she appears to be — forever youthful, powerful, wise. But there is a universe we pass through daily and never heed. Most cannot enter — even in their dreams. Darsen and her breed pull back that curtain. Then, everything can be revealed. Everything! Manilla, Darsen has the power to bring you face to face with your God!"

Manilla tried to pull back, to erase the mounting fear in her gut, to ease her pounding heart. If it were Slater, here, with her, where was she? How had this happened? Where was Ginny? And most important — where was Darsen?

Slater did not ease her grip. "I was a pawn and a witness. Some things cannot be shown to you. There are no words and your mind would tear at the visions. Know only these facts: Darsen and her kind were the first; they are evil incarnate. And those of us they do seduce, are half-demon ourselves. Only by drinking human blood would we join, fully, into their ranks. Ironic, isn't it? The potential remains, a constant temptation and torment, each night of our lives. Until something destroys our bodies, fully, until we are reduced to ashes, only then, some relief. But still, till the end of time, when all things will be judged finally, until then, all that is given to us is this limbo."

"Katherine, I don't understand, I don't know where this place is — where you went after the fire. Is this death?" Manilla touched the solid body of the woman.

"Oh, my friend, for me there is no death. No re-birth, either, not till the end of time. Such is the price of the seduction. But all energy goes on — human or otherwise. Nothing is ever fully destroyed. At least, here, I can do no harm, am removed from the hunger. Here, I might repay my mistakes, here, I may yet learn how to do great good."

Tears began to form in Manilla's eyes. Hot, real, they coursed down her face.

Pulling closer to Manilla, Katherine Slater touched them, "Manilla, you saw my body freed from Darsen's hold — now I must work out the price of falling to her seduction. For my kind, the kind she makes of her human hosts, for us, this is our realm. She cannot follow me here — she cannot come to this place of light. She does not, as I once feared, still own my soul. Don't weep for me, Manilla. There is much to do. Do not be afraid. I will be with you — till the end. Our connection goes forever."

Manilla felt Slater's touch lessen. The image of the professor began to shimmer, to break up, to fall into a million points of light.

Manilla sat up.

The room had cooled.

The fire was out.

Her hip and shoulder were sore because of the odd angle of her sleeping.

Some gentle movement, directly across from her, in the darkness, caught her eye.

"Who?" she tried to cry, but her throat was constricted.

Two burning coals of eyes approached, hypnotized her into paralysis.

Just as they came down, upon her, she managed to raise a hand.

A single laser-like beam of violet-red light shot from the center of Slater's ring. It struck directly between the two eyes.

There was a gut-wrenching scream and then, silence.

━━━━━

"Bag him." Gunner scratched at the loose watch. Someday he was going to get the one his grandfather had left him fixed. A pocket watch. Civilized. Not some god-damned gee-gaw hunk of Jap metal that made him itch.

"Real butcher job, this time." The sergeant coughed back the bile rising in his throat. It had been an effort not to lose it in front of Gunner. This time the victim had been hacked to inch-wide ribbons, clear down to the bone.

"Yeah, the kid's getting good. Least we know for certain that the weapon's a straight-edge razor. Probably snatched it from the dude the night of the first murder, right out of the guy's shaving kit. The kid's got style." Gunner reached into his bomber jacket. Pulling out a fresh pack of menthols, he stopped. Thought better of it. The Sarge already looked a might green. Cigarette wasn't going to help.

Gunner shoved the pack back into his pocket. "One thing's bothering me, though."

"What?" The sergeant focused on the cold ground.

"Not enough blood. Not for a butcher job like this. We're down a few pints." Gunner scanned the cop's face. If the guy was going to hurl, it would be now.

Holding his beefy fist to his chin, the cop gagged but he was all right.

"How do you know? Blood's soaked clear through the mattress." The sergeant was about fifteen years younger than Gunner. He knew what Gunner thought of the local PD. He swallowed, hard. His spit was dry and sour.

"NAM. Clean-up detail, after we'd 'officially left country,' I saw what we'd left — took apart booby traps and mines. Put together people who found them before we did. I know how much blood a human body holds. The kid did it on the bed. Isn't likely he stopped to get a bucket. Hell, don't take my word, Sarge. Wait for the coroner — and the splatter expert. It's gonna be a while." Gunner decided it was safe to smoke that cigarette.

The wind was stiff. It whipped color back into the younger man's cheeks.

"Gunner, this is creepy, man. I mean, between you and me, this is fucking weird! You still sure it's a kid?"

"Absolutely. Gotta be a hustler. No doubt in my mind at all." Gunner watched the ambulance pull into the lot. He inhaled deeply.

"Gunner, if we don't get him soon — "

"Listen, Sergeant, all my time in L.A., the thing I learned fastest was that when we get one of these kids going ballistic, he ain't gonna stop till we stop him — or the street does. But something WILL stop him, sooner or later. These kids are walking dead. Stats say three months out there and you ain't never coming back in. Old is twenty-one, on the meat-rack. Street snatches you, Sarge, it snatches for good. We'll get this one, one way or another." Gunner pushed past the younger man.

"Hey, Gunner! This Zen street-crap is a lot of — hey! You listening to me, man? Come back here, we aren't through — " Sarge held his ground but his voice grew shrill.

Gunner didn't turn around.

"Yeah man, I hear you."

———

Darsen opened her eyes.

Night.

The town house was dim, but not dark.

Night.

Usually, it opened her wide, ripping and cold as a claw. But not this night. She'd fed well that morning at the hotel.

Now she could rise, open crates of canvas and linseed oil and turpentine and paint. Or, if she chose, listen to music or watch old films in relative peace.

She rose from her black satin sheets. Pulling on a silk kimono, she moved toward the immense windows. Below her, the city was all light, all movement. She could sense the approach of a storm. It was going to be a harsh winter. Still, she couldn't leave. Could not go south to the cities she most enjoyed. Two matters required attention. They were the only reasons she was chained to this post-industrial University hell-hole.

Syracuse was not her idea of charming. Only its proximity to the schools and its closeness to Ithaca allowed her continued patience. Syracuse was large enough to disappear in when it was necessary, but easy to move in. Easy to stalk.

Who would have believed that she, Darsen, would wind up in such a spot? Feeling frustrated, she ground her scarlet nails into the pale palms. Her hunger was beginning to rise.

Long enough.

This wait.

Almost over. The power was beginning to take root.

Even at this distance, she could feel it. Weeks now. Only through proper gestation would Ginny MacPhearson's transformation gain a suitable hold. Debacles, like that of Katherine Slater, had taught her this much.

Slater had made her stupid, sloppy in her passion. Never again! Only through sheer luck had she discovered Slater's presence and approach! It was that small, dark one, that Manilla, Ginny's lover. Her heart had sounded the warning beating like a band at their approach, tipping the scales. It would never happen again. She'd taken care of Slater and she WOULD take care of Manilla.

Their untimely rescue had bought only a brief respite for Ginny. The hunger and its resulting agony began to overwhelm the dancer. Darsen would wait, would hide until the transformation had fully begun. So much easier to allow the suffering to peak! Then, Ginny would embrace her gift as it should be embraced. Then, they would go away, together — their destiny, as cohorts, complete.

Perhaps the south of France, or maybe Switzerland? Someplace clean, private, where she could work the dangerous magic necessary, teach Ginny how to survive in her new body, in her new life. Only in this way would Ginny be able to live out the life span a human vampire might expect. Darsen would teach her about their Power. Ginny was lovely, a fragile flower in need of such tutelage. Darsen had been craving such a one for centuries. Cultured. Almost European in her tastes, a member of an aristocracy that bled back in time to the days when Darsen had first walked the earth. Only such a one would satisfy Darsen now. Forget the more independent, modern women — hadn't her lust for Katherine Slater almost destroyed her? No, she needed to satiate her thirst for reverence with another type — someone like Ginny

The hunger of sex was another matter.

Like blood craving, this appetite did not change with the eons. It was the reason she constantly sought out human companions. Creating a vampire through human seed, she could keep her lover for centuries. Without the transformation, connection on any real level aside from death was not possible. It always ended in failure. Aside from simple longevity, it was the temptation of human blood that she could not put in abeyance. The scent of human flesh, the flavor and its heat, the hearts and pulses, much too close to the surface — especially in the midst of passion.

Too infuriating to withstand for long: she would be forced to take that final drink, the last, deep suck. Perhaps this was her worst punishment for being who she was . . . this loneliness.

Her breed could scarce stand each other's company, so jealous were they. Given half a chance, they preyed upon each other. Always, always, Darsen was on watch for other members of her own race: vultures, carrion pickers, devious since time immemorial. Even the lesser, human vampires were a minor threat. She must constantly be on alert, constantly protect herself and any companion she chose. It was part of that Divine Order — one of the only parts she was forced into accepting. A way to keep her breed in check. Unfair, really. Unfair and uncomfortable, but as much part of her existence as the blood.

Darsen smiled at her own melodrama.

She moved away from the windows, into the luxury of the larger rooms. Under her bare feet, the thick rugs were like meadow grass. Their softness only interrupted by the softness of the animal hides: furs littered the plush carpet, much as islands litter the great seas.

Throughout the rooms, she wandered, switching on the soft lights, peeling away the darkness, readying the space for her art.

Whatever else she was, Darsen was an artist. A painter, first. It had been decades since she'd exhibited. Superstitious citizens in past centuries had cost her valuable work. Her art was too refined, too fantastic for their feeble minds. Burned by clergy, vandalized by the ignorant, she'd been forced to hide, to watch in silent fury as they destroyed work she could never replicate. True, she'd had her revenge, but even those lives could not replace the original vision. Great fiend? Hadn't they made her cruel? Hadn't she merely sought, always, that which was most beautiful? Most pure? Always, always, and first, an artist. If only these humans had respected that . . . .

In these times, there was a chance. Camouflaged by daily discoveries in technology, cocky in their new-found toys, she could play priestess to their new religion. Science. Hah! Mere play. Nothing was impossible, they believed. In this belief they were oh so much more gullible! Vulnerable! In these times she could, once again, come from her hiding places, show her masterworks with impunity. This time she might actually receive the accolades she deserved. Might actually be crowned as the genius she was. On her own terms. With her own visions worshiped. She did not need the power of blood for these ends.

She did, however, need Ginny MacPhearson. A glorious consort — the perfect mate. The dancer, alone, could understand the artist, would share in the accolades. Ginny, in her time, would also become legendary. Left to her own human talents, she had some promise, but the gifts had been neglected. Now, with this newly given vitality and the years of work it would insure, she could rise!

She and Ginny, together. What a time this would be! Such beauty, such grace. When, before, had there ever been such a coupling? They could bring truth to this savage planet of fools. With Ginny beside her, she could rise as the new savior, the greatest master, the most powerful creator the world had ever known! Hers would be the New Light, a light born from the seed of darkness.

How perfect for this dark globe!

Darsen moved toward the vast room that served as her newest studio.

She needed to unpack the supplies, to begin the fresh work. Only through activity could she bear the wait. A few more days of hunger and Ginny would begin to burn. The fever was insidious. Then, Darsen, brilliant archangel, would descend. This time, there would be no Katherine Slater to interfere. This time there would only be success!

Darsen knew Ginny MacPhearson's soul. It was not strong enough to withstand the onslaught.

As for the little, dark one, well, Manilla was so much bone and dust. Yes, Darsen would take her — in front of Ginny — perhaps — delightful! The raggedy upstart who dared fly at the vampire would become grist for the bloody sacrament itself. Perfect. In a few, short days it would be Manilla's still-pumping heart that Darsen would feed to Ginny.

Her laughter echoed through the room, careened from the high-beamed ceiling and ricocheted across the white walls. If anyone had been present, had been witness, they would have seen the razor fangs and slit tongue of the virago.

———

Joey was sweating again.

He sat up, drenched, the good sheets soaked. Clenching the terry cloth robe Darsen had brought him, he moved from the sodden bed and into the kitchen.

Opening the refrigerator, he found beer, cold cuts and a bowl of soup from the deli downstairs.

He retrieved one of the beers.

Draining it, he felt chilled.

"Shit!"

Joey ran for the bathroom. Turning on the shower full force, he watched as steam scudded around the tiled walls and floor.

He stepped under the hot water. It burned, it burned badly, but not as bad as the cold. He forced himself to stay under it until he felt warmer.

He needed to get warmer.

He needed to get clean.

Nothing he did seemed to keep the chill away.

Then, night sweats had come.

They were the precursors of horrible dreams — especially if she wasn't there to wake him.

He stood under the shower, sobbing.

Oh God, would he ever get clean?

———

"Put it away!" Ginny's voice screamed from behind the couch where she'd fallen. Manilla, not pausing to think, tore the ring from her finger and pocketed it immediately.

Then Manilla tried to reach the wounded dancer.

"Stop! Don't, not yet . . . I'll be fine . . . it will heal in a few minutes . . . but don't come closer yet!" Ginny stood, shakily retreated into the deeper shadows of the room.

"It's Slater's ring — Ginny, I don't know how — " Manilla stood still, searching for an explanation.

"As long as it's put away right now. There's something more important I need your help with — we'll figure out the rest, later." Ginny didn't come into the arc of light where Manilla was standing.

"What can be more important than this? Fuck, Gin, Katherine Slater's ring just shot a laser beam at your head — " Manilla approached carefully.

"I said don't touch me! You don't understand — you can't touch me. Not now . . . not for a while . . . but I need your help!" Ginny kept her face covered.

"Gin, let me see! Are you sick? Should I get you back to the hospital? Maybe you've got some weird infection, something they didn't notice when you were there before, something they all missed." Manilla's mind overflowed with the images: flower store, Florence Kray, Ginny's probe, dream of Slater.

"My God, Manilla? An infection?" The dancer dropped her hands and began laughing. The sound was cruel and hollow.

In the half-light, Manilla could only make out portions of Ginny's features. Her skin seemed streaked with dirt. Her hair had bits of leaves and twigs tangled in it. Her coat had a button missing. Then, Ginny looked at her, fully. The ruby glow of each eye was back.

Manilla stepped backwards, stammering, "It's true. I didn't want to believe it, but it's true!"

Ginny moved like lightning, over the couch and suddenly, directly in front of her lover. But she did not physically connect. "Don't, Manilla, please, not now. I know how frightening all of this is — I'm scared, too, but if you leave me, now, if you leave, Manilla, I'm going to die!" Then, she reached out tentatively, unsure herself of the result.

Manilla didn't bridge the gap between them. Something primal kept her from allowing the touch. There was the rising panic she had to push down. There was that urge to flee — evil was there, maybe right in front of her! But, it was also Ginny — Ginny was caught by it, too.

She fought to stay put, to slow her heart, to breathe once, twice, release the terror. It was still Ginny, whatever had happened. It was still Ginny pleading for her help.

"Gin, what can I do?"

The woods were empty.

In the day, the park was patrolled by rangers, but at night, the designated wilderness at the edge of the city was abandoned by humans. A final nod to what had once been virgin forest. Unspoiled falls, streams fed from far-off mountains, all fenced-off into an area whose boundaries lay flank-to-flank with the town's.

Yet, there was wildlife.

As they have always done, the animals who could tolerate the development survived. Some, in fact, thrived. Most of the natural predators had long since been trapped or forced out. Humans came, leaving garbage, easy pickings, wherever they walked. The forest was full of animals who knew almost nothing of being stalked.

Manilla waited in the car. She knew what she'd witness if she followed Ginny. It had been Katherine Slater's nocturnal feeding that Manilla had come upon that night, so long ago, on the golf course — the mysterious stranger killing the calf. Now Ginny was doing a similar sacrifice. Manilla didn't need another view.

Along with so many other truths, Slater had confessed to the killing of the calf. Desperate, unable to sustain herself simply on lab animal specimens, she'd been forced to kill farm animals up and down the lake. It was that or . . . but Slater had never given in to the other. She had died, still half-human, never having tasted human blood. Manilla reflected on the dream. If she could only believe what she'd seen — if Slater were safe, somewhere — not lost, not destroyed like a comic book character. And the ring? Why had it reacted to Ginny? Slater herself had worn it — had even told Manilla how Darsen had given it to her when Darsen had transformed her in the Amazon. It had always been a vampire's ring — why had it hurt Ginny? What had changed?

Before Manilla could take the ring out to examine it closely, Ginny tumbled from the woods.

Most of the blood had been wiped away. She was naked. Ferns and wet leaves clung to her skin. She could barely stand. The long drink from the coyote had been like a drug — hot and sweet and incapacitating her. She had not been sickened by her own acts — it was strong medicine. It was natural as any predator — going far past reason or morality. The human part of her recoiled only a little, but, when faced with its own death, the body will allow much. The birds had only whetted the insatiable appetite, awakened the natural killer inside. After that one act, she'd been revolted, hated herself, hid the tiny bodies out of a murderer's guilt. This time, it was different. The universe had suddenly shifted, taking her with it. She was changed in ways she had no words for. She had preyed upon the coyote and its death had stopped her own. Nothing evil, nothing sinister, nothing out of hate or greed — it was a pure act.

And now, she was tired.

She had to sleep.

Find a safe place and simply sleep.

There was no more to it than that.

Numbed, Manilla watched Ginny's approach. She did not help the dancer into the car. She merely held the blanket out for her as Ginny crawled inside.

Then, they drove.

"What did you do with your clothes?"

"I buried them, deep." Ginny's answer was sleep-filled, fuzzy.

"And the animal?" Manilla felt, no matter how ridiculous, she could gauge how far Ginny was lost, by this answer.

"It was a coyote, Manilla. I put the body on top of my torn clothes." Ginny was overcome with the effort of explaining. Her eyes were closed, heavy; her breathing, deep and regular. Even as she was covered with the gruesome clues of the kill, like some angel of death, she remained beautiful.

———

Manilla turned the shower on full. It was awkward, helping Ginny under the water. The dancer was almost a foot taller and slumping, literally asleep on her feet. Propping her up, Manilla sopped off leaves and residual gore from the creamy skin. It took two soapings. It was as if Ginny were a little girl who had come in from making mud pies; it took two soapings to get her clean.

Unmindful of the trail of water she left in their wake, Manilla stepped from the shower.

Swaddling Ginny in a beach towel, Manilla half-carried the woman into the bedroom. There, she unbundled the dancer and slipped her beneath the covers. Flooded with sudden tenderness at the helplessness she saw, Manilla pulled the comforter under Ginny's chin. Ginny was like a co-ed who had been the unwitting victim of a spiked drink. She was now in deep need of Manilla's care.

"Oh, Gin," Manilla whispered, leaning over to tuck in the sheets.

From her virgin slumber, the new Ginny reached for Manilla. Pulling the younger painter close, Ginny smiled sleepily.

Against all reason and judgment, against considerable residual fear, Manilla moved under the covers, moved next to her lover.

"Manilla." Ginny sighed, as if from very far away, as if she had no real hope that her lover would actually hear and yet, she could not stop herself from whispering.

"I'm here, Gin. I'm right here."

Morning sun drenched the room. Ginny rolled over, her skin suddenly feeling electric as she came into contact with Manilla.

As if every cell along her surface began to burn, each brushing against Manilla inflamed her. Ginny watched the small mouth, the gentle exhalation of the breath, the tangled curls like dark ferns in the night forest, now splayed upon the pillow, the long eyelashes, equally dark, each so perfect. The perfection caused its own ache in Ginny.

As she lifted the edge of the comforter, the sudden rush of warm air greeted Ginny like fresh bread coming out of the oven. So much warmth, so much scent! Clean, open, Manilla carried her own perfume and it maddened Ginny with its power.

Ginny's hand began a long glide over the rounded hips and strong thighs of the sleeping painter. Barely brushing the flesh, Ginny could feel the skin react, feel it as if she were touching herself, feel each goose bump, each erotic swell, feel it along Manilla and along herself. No separation, no edges. This power, whatever it had done to her, it had given her this. Ginny was heavy with the rush and wetness of her hunger.

Her hand brushed the tight curls of Manilla's mons, then, still so gently as not to waken the girl from sleep, Ginny dipped her fingers in. Wet. Yes, even in sleep, Manilla sensed her there. Ginny slipped beneath the comforter, inhaling deeply, like a swimmer gulping air before a very deep dive. Manilla's sex scent rose, heady, intoxicating, almost maddening, filling Ginny's nose and lungs. She could smell her own scent, mingling.

The rising thrum between her own legs was growing. Her own clit was engorged. She felt as she'd often imagined a man must feel before he comes. She didn't want to come. She wanted to prolong the ecstatic agony, to make Manilla come to her, first, to feel that power as her own.

Lower, lower, the dancer swam down. Carefully, slowly, gently, she wanted Manilla asleep until she exploded. Ginny tickled and tangled the dark hair between her fingers. A soft moan escaped the still quiet painter. She was dreaming and Ginny grinned, feeling the dream.

Her fingers dipped in deeper, swirling and probing the sweet, hot moistness beginning to saturate Manilla's lips. Ginny brought her head down to those depths, her mouth opening only a bit, her tongue beginning a quick flick and lick, tasting the salt and the honey there, drinking in what she had caused to erupt and overflow.

Ginny's head began to spin. Like champagne, this elixir was making her drunk, making her giddy. Again and again she sipped, her tongue beginning a deeper probe. Her own lower lips were full, throbbing. She ground her pelvis into the bed, thrusting there, in time to the soft licks and nips she was bestowing upon Manilla.

Then, she heard Manilla.

The painter was awake, dazed, gasping.

Manilla spread her legs wide, beginning to open deeper, to push closer to the hungry mouth devouring her.

"Ginny, Ginny — " Manilla cried, clutching the pillow, feeling the climax building, ready to explode.

Then, as if running out of oxygen, as if suddenly realizing what was happening Ginny burst from under the covers, crying, pushing Manilla away from her, almost sending the painter off the bed.

"NOOOO!" Ginny sprang from the room, rushed into the bath, locked the door behind her. Sobs came from behind the door toward Manilla.

Gathering the wrinkled bedclothes around her, Manilla sat up. Her body was still screaming for release. Bathed in sexual sweat, heart pounding, head reeling, she ground her teeth together, got her bearings, tried to come down from the height Ginny had taken her. Then, slowly, it dawned on her — where they had almost gone.

Manilla began to shake uncontrollably.

It was over an hour before Ginny unlocked the bathroom door and came back. Manilla, as promised, was waiting, but dressed. Manilla sat on the edge of the now-made bed. She'd left clothes on the end, near the footboard. She watched as Ginny silently slipped into the faded Levis and white turtleneck.

Ginny pulled on socks and boots, then sat on the edge of the bed two feet away from Manilla.

"What do we do, Gin?" Manilla's voice was calm and quiet. Inside, she was screaming, wanting only to rush to Ginny, to hold her, rock her, tell her it didn't matter. But she held on to the evenness out of fear.

Ginny was not human, or, not only human.

There was a large part of Ginny, now, that was closer to a wild thing.

Instinctively, Manilla understood. Any sudden motions, however well-intended, would make the dancer bolt. Manilla needed Ginny to stay. They both needed Ginny to stay.

"I'm so frightened, Manilla. I'm so . . . ashamed." Ginny began to cry.

Again, resisting the urge to go to her lover, Manilla sat stiffly. Her voice would have to be the comfort now.

"Gin, listen to me. Listen. I've had a long time to think this over. I haven't clarified all the details, but I 've got some clues, some ideas. Listen to me!"

Ginny gulped, then turned, looking at Manilla for the first time since they'd awakened.

"Ginny, I had a dream, before you came back here the other night. A dream about Katherine Slater. It was as if I went to her — where she is now — "

"She's dead, Manilla — " Ginny sniffed, reaching out a tender hand toward the painter, then, thinking better of it, retracting the touch.

"But, what's 'dead'? I mean, everything we thought about death and God and good and angels, all of it, it's all dashed to shreds, now, isn't it? Look what we've seen, Ginny!" Manilla's voice rose.

"Yes, I guess."

"All my life, Gin, I prayed to saints and believed in angels and devils and Jesus and the Virgin — fuck, even the little drummer boy! Then, learning about other religions, other spiritual ways, I began to doubt the whole scene. It's so fucking confusing! Everyone tries to explain the whole enchilada from their perspective — but, what if, what if it takes all perspectives? What if built into every single human being and every single living thing — hell, every single THING — what if all of those perspectives are necessary? Only when you crash through time and space and gather and put together every single thing in every dimension backwards and forwards and sideways do you get the truth. What if every piece is necessary and important because without it, you can't get the whole? See, then — "

"Then everyone is right — as far as each piece — but nobody has the whole picture." Ginny's voice grew low.

"Manilla, that isn't exactly a comfort right now. It would mean anything is possible — anything at all! It would mean there is as much evil as good — or possibly morel It would mean we are in way deeper than the Dark Ages — that we can't possibly know what to do — there's no hope with that perspective because there's no end!"

"Yes, it could mean that, but there's some Indian philosophies that help straighten some of this out. I don't know what tribe, exactly, but I know that the Europeans got it all wrong when they translated the Indians idea of 'a great spirit.' The truth was, the Indians were just being polite — trying to accommodate their guests' ideas, trying not to laugh at the whites. Truth is, there is no persona of a Great Spirit — the Great Spirit is all things, maker and inhabiter and arbitrator and host to all things. Unnameable, unknowable — and, get this — supposed to remain that way — unknowable, in our lives. The Mystery is supposed to remain a mystery. We aren't supposed to use up our lives attempting to figure it out. Ginny do you see?" Manilla was getting excited. This was beginning to come together for her, a way to handle what was occurring, a way to deal.

"Manilla, there are other religions who share some of those ideas." Ginny shifted uneasily. Prickles of excitement began to sparkle in her mind. This made some weird kind of sense. Manilla was going somewhere with this and Ginny could follow the path.

"Right! Because it is true! Somewhere, in each of us, we are wired for this truth. Maybe it takes a kind of horrendous event or loss of all faith or a miracle — whatever — but when the right combination of things happens, the wiring gets the juice and this idea comes up! It feels true. And if it is true, Ginny, then, we aren't crazy. If it's true then what we thought we believed about death, about devils and monsters, what we were taught — it isn't true! We have to start rethinking this, paying attention to things we used to just throw away."

"Like dreams?" Ginny moved closer to Manilla.

"Yes. Yes. Because Slater told me when she was alive that Darsen changed the boundaries of life for her. Darsen could walk in her dreams, could interact, could play out things in

HER dreams. Then, when she was awake, Darsen spoke of the dreams as if they were everyday occurrences. When Slater used her probe on me, to tell me about Darsen, to warn me and show me who Darsen was, I was in that place, as if I were walking around in Slater's dream. Only, I couldn't talk to anyone else there, not even Slater — I felt things, saw things, smelled things . . . but she controlled it all. I remembered only what she wanted me to remember, Gin. That's why I haven't told you everything. But what I do remember was real — as real as my dream the other night. Slater was in the dream, Gin. She said her body had been destroyed in the fire but her soul was still in this place. She'd always feared that Darsen owned her soul — that once she'd become what she became she gave her soul over to Darsen. But now she knew it wasn't true — and she wanted me to know, because of you." Manilla's voice broke.

"Slater knew what I was becoming? You knew, all this time, too?" Ginny's eyes began to tear.

"Oh, Gin — I didn't. I didn't because I didn't want to know. I ignored all the clues. There was even a candy-striper at the hospital that saw some kind of bite."

"Jesus, Manilla. I couldn't tell you. I was so terrified. I didn't want to believe it — " Ginny couldn't look at Manilla any longer. She stood, ready to run.

"Ginny! Don't go!" Making a grab for her lover's sleeve, Manilla reached across the bed.

"If I stay around you, Manilla, I'm going to hurt you — look what almost happened this morning!" Ginny pulled away.

"But it didn't! And it didn't happen last night, either! Ginny, you're like Slater was — you aren't like Darsen! Slater told me, unless you drink human blood you remain only half-monster. That's why she didn't lose her soul, why she's in that place, that dimension. She says she can't be reborn, that's kind of the karma she's got, now, but she isn't damned — and she's finding out more as she goes on. There are chances she can still do good — still help. She wanted me to know, to tell you. So she's got to know about you! If Slater thought you'd kill me, she would have told me to run — right? Or told me how to destroy you — right? But she didn't, Gin! She didn't!" Manilla grabbed Ginny's arm tightly.

"But what if the dream was only a dream, Manilla? I know how you felt about Katherine Slater. I know how you still feel." Ginny turned to face Manilla.

"I've wanted to tell you, to be honest with you about that, Ginny. Like you about this other stuff. I didn't know how, didn't want to hurt you." Manilla dropped her grip.

"It's okay. Even before Darsen, when you first began talking about your 'new advisor,' I could hear it in your voice." Ginny managed a small smile, remembering that still innocent part of autumn.

"Why didn't you ever say anything about it?" Manilla asked quietly.

"I kidded you, a couple of times — but Manilla, I trust you, fool. I might be a little jealous, but I know you and I trust you. After Darsen, well, then everything changed."

"Ginny, I trust you. Even now. Even after Darsen." Manilla reached up, touching the dancer's lips with her fingertips.

A single, pink-tinged tear rolled down Ginny's cheek.

"As far as Slater's warning me about you — I think she did — when you showed up here, in the dark, before you told me you needed help. It's connected to her ring — I don't understand the logistics and I don't want to fool around with it if it can hurt you, but it kept you off me, kept you away from me. I didn't think the light from the ring, like a weapon or anything. It just happened. It was her gift to me before she died. It's connected to Darsen, too. Darsen gave it to her! We've got to find a way to get more information about the ring, Gin. And about what's happening to you."

"I think I should go away, Manilla. I know I can live off animal blood — but how can I do that, regularly, and keep a normal life, here? Not much call for zoo-keeper dancers, is there? And I'm not a scientist, like Slater. I can't get a handy supply of lab animals to bleed. What about you? What kind of life can you expect? We can't sleep together without endangering you — and I'm like some dangerous exotic pet you have to keep worrying about. We don't have any idea where this will lead. I won't do that to you. I'll just . . . go away." Ginny's tears flowed freely. But she didn't push Manilla aside.

"First, Ginny MacPhearson, if you had some terminal disease, would it be acceptable for me to bail? I don't think so — at least not acceptable to me. And if I had a terminal disease, would you bail? Would you even want me to slink off, play the noble one? No way. You'd be pissed off big time! You'd hunt me down and carry me back, bound and gagged, if you had to."

"Well, yeah, I guess." Ginny smiled.

"You aren't an animal — and you aren't a monster. Far as we know, unless we get stupid or careless, this isn't communicable. There are too many pieces we can still gather, Ginny. And let's just play with this a little. What have we got to lose? If there is a slim chance that my dreams are more than dreams, I can communicate with Slater and find out what she knows! Besides, vampire lore goes back centuries. A lot of it is crap — but some of it probably has pieces of truth. It's the pieces we can gather up, Gin. That's what will save us. Maybe never the whole mystery, but enough. Enough for us to have our lives." Manilla hugged Ginny tenderly.

"Are you positive you want to do this? Are you absolutely sure?" Ginny hugged the painter back.

"Gin, I once asked you the same question."

———

It was mid-afternoon.

Ginny would need to go out again, soon. They both knew they would have to wait for cover of darkness.

"Hey, maybe this is where all that mythology about vampires being allergic to sunlight comes from — what do you think?" Manilla, washing glasses, called from the kitchen.

"Manilla, not funny. Listen, though, the more I run through all of this, the more I come back to your ideas about the dream time. And the probing — Manilla, if I tried to do it consciously, lightly, not like the night at Weston where I didn't know my ass from my elbow or what was going on, but softly — you kind of leading me, telling me, as we go along — would you be willing to try it?" Ginny walked into the kitchen. She could feel the cold beginning to tingle along her ribs. She didn't want to think of that. If Manilla was willing, an experiment would keep her mind from feeling the hunger build.

Manilla put down the glass she was wiping. "For what reason? I mean, you already know everything about me. I don't have anymore secrets, Gin."

"Not conscious secrets — but what if I could access what Slater planted in your head? Maybe you could show me what she showed you? At least that much — so I can know her, at least a little bit. What do you think?"

Manilla spun around. Her eyes were wide. "Ginny, that's brilliant! I bet it will work! I didn't think of it, but why not? Computers are designed like brains, right? So, you should theoretically be able to pull what Slater put in, out! It should still be there — like a program, still be accessible. I mean, even in hypnotherapy people can retrieve images — that probing power you have is way more intense! Besides, you could experience it for yourself and pick up details that for me, at that time, weren't so important. If it works the way Slater made it work, you will have an actual experience, not just my memory of her story. We've got nothing to lose — just go easy, okay? I hate the hangover you left me with the other night." Manilla grinned.

"I am so sorry. I swear to you, Manilla, I will never hurt you again — not if my life depends on it."

"Gin, I was kidding. Look, you have to lighten up a little, here. We're both going to need Prozac if you don't, okay?" Manilla mimed a punch at Ginny's jaw.

"Okay"

More from a sense of security than a need for light or warmth, they built the fire up. Then, moving all the sofa cushions on to the floor, Ginny positioned herself so she could keep a constant, light pressure on Manilla's wrist. Manilla was lying down, her arm outstretched on Ginny's lap.

"Ready?" Ginny whispered.

"I should be asking you that!" Manilla smiled.

Then, she felt the cushions melt from under her.

There was the spinning cold, the blackness and suddenly, the thrum of plane engines as she awoke in the small cabin, Ginny beside her.

Ginny looked startled. She touched the ripped upholstery of the plane, then reached over and touched Manilla.

"It worked, we're here — I remember!" Manilla yelled over the mechanical roar.

Ginny glanced nervously at the pilot, the man sitting in front of her, and a much younger Katherine Slater.

"They can't hear or see you, Gin — at least they couldn't when Slater did her probe."

Ginny sat back, feeling springs poke her. The nauseating smell of fuel and old, male sweat enveloped her. There was also the scent of Katherine Slater.

As Manilla glanced out of the small plane's window, Ginny watched Slater.

She was so young — not much older than Ginny, herself! Dressed in pressed khakis and new jungle boots, hair primly cropped, nails well-manicured, lightly buffed, she hardly seemed the world-weary anthropologist Manilla was in thrall with.

This was a young Ph.D. candidate, frightened, knowing she was caught between this wild adventure and two men she didn't trust at all — that was clear. But she was plucky. The perfect word — Ginny watched Slater straighten her back, brush off the guide's hand as he slid it around her shoulders.

Sea-green eyes glared at him. Manilla also glared — to no avail. Ginny chuckled. Even in a dream time, Manilla was Manilla.

Nervous sweat began to pour off Slater's handsome face as the plane dive-bombed a strip of bright red mud. Ginny couldn't believe they were going to attempt a landing there.

Slater buckled the frayed seat belt. So did the guide. Ginny watched without amusement as Manilla did likewise.

Going down sideways, toward the pitted wash, the plane clipped edges of tropical palms. A backpack fell into the aisle. A camera rolled out. Slater made a grab for it, but the guide grabbed her hand and wrenched it back.

Slater again shook him off.

Ginny took a hard look at the man. Grizzled but not older than thirty-five, he was huge. His hair was cut closer than his beard — or what growth he'd accumulated on his face; perhaps identifying it as a beard was being too kind. Both facial and head hair were red. So were the whites of his eyes. In their centers, though, a deep, deep blue. Manilla, Ginny was sure, would identify it as "azure." His teeth were tobacco-stained and he smelled — cheap soap, whiskey. Maybe rum. Ginny was unsure. Her inventory was cut short when the pilot announced: "We're here!"

Ginny watched as Slater made a grab for the camera. "Where's the village?" she demanded.

"No village around here, lady. Who told you there was a village?" the pilot answered, laughing at her.

Slater turned toward the guide, who was picking through the bags in the overhead rack, "Johnston — you said — "

The guide stopped doing whatever he was doing and turned on the anthropologist. "Look, Professor, you wrote and said you wanted a guide to show you possible sites of the Maneatos Indians. There ain't nothing close to where you're going to find Maneatos — that is the point, isn't it?"

Ginny watched him remove two packs and open the door.

The pilot interrupted: "Closest town is Tefe, lady, and that's uh, maybe two hundred and fifty, three hundred miles, right on the Amazon proper."

Slater's face dropped the professional facade. She was clearly shocked. "The Amazon PROPER — aren't we supposed to be on the Amazon now?"

Ginny glanced outside. Green — maybe a hundred different shades of green. Even the air seemed tinged with it. No sign, far as she could see, of any water. Slater had been had. Shivery tingles went up and down Ginny's back. Manilla, however, merely shook her head. Manilla knew the plot already.

The guide headed out the cargo door, explaining, "Well, the river to your immediate right is the River Branco and it forks into the River Negro about seven miles down."

Ginny noticed the pilot checking his instruments nervously.

He turned in his cockpit seat and barked, "God, they're all the same, you know? This is it — the real Amazon — just like the travel brochures say. Wild and wet — uncivilized. Isn't that what you wanted? Lots of wooly bully geeks dancing in voodoo masks?"

The guide jumped out, scaring the resettled macaws, making them screech as they broke from the trees. Ginny couldn't believe the smell of the air — it smelled as if it were teeming with life. The heat hit her like a fist. Manilla, too, was perspiring. Manilla had told the truth. They were actually there, in the Amazon River Basin, with these people. There was nothing to do but to keep up, to follow. Ginny let Manilla jump in front of her.

Slater was already outside pulling on a pack. Her voice was shrill as she turned to the guide, "Johnston, I know where the River Branco is — these are tributaries. I wanted the actual, main river. If I'm going to test my theory, I need — "

"Oh, I know what you need, Professor — now let's just haul ass out of here — or, don't. I get paid either way. No refunds — check your contract. I ain't going to lose my license just because some damned Yanque cunuo goes soft." Johnston's voice was threatening.

Ginny reached over to Manilla's arm, brushing it for reassurance. Manilla didn't respond. Her whole being was focused on what was transpiring.

From the airplane's window, the pilot called, "Ma'am, look, we all get a little bushy out here. Between the fucking revolutionaries, the Indians, the scorpions — it's a bit of a hell, you know what I'm saying? You professors come out here, flash a lot of cash, make men greedy, come out with your film crews to do your National Geographics, then you get out, leaving nothing — so, no disrespect intended, but, fuck you, ma'am, and your damned University. Listen to your guide and I'll be back for you both in three days."

Ginny watched Katherine Slater bite her bottom lip. Chuckling, Johnston lit a cigar. If only Slater knew she wasn't alone! Ginny turned to Manilla, wanting to do something — Manilla simply shrugged. All they could do was watch — and follow.

The plane barely waited for the guide to slam the cargo door shut before it revved its engines for take off.

"That's it, we're home." Johnston shouldered his pack and a smaller bag. Then he started for the jungle.

It was hours before they burst from the emerald and olive of the forest. In front of them was the reddish-brown River Negro.

Ginny watched Slater drop her pack, sit on it and pull off her already mildewing boots. She took off the shredded socks and neatly tucked them into the boot tops — probably protection against the scorpions the pilot had warned them of. Under a banyon tree, the guide was already opening a bottle of cheap whiskey.

Slater's feet looked like raw hamburger. Still, she approached the water, watching the banks and the surface — looking for what?

Manilla leaned toward Ginny: "Piranha, eels, giant catfish, kaman . . . "

Ginny almost smiled; Manilla had recalled everything.

"If you got any open blisters, best watch out. Botflies — they'll take a chunk out of you and leave their eggs — then the little buggers eat their way out. You wake up and find your arm gone and your skin crawling with the little darlings. Black flies are bad, too — but you know that, don't you, Professor? Worst is sand flies — leishmaniasis — kinda like leprosy — all your best parts drying up and falling off . . . "

"You just love it, don't you? Look Johnston, I'm no White Princess. Do your job and leave me alone!" Slater was shaking with fury. Her fists were clenched at her sides.

"Well, since you're so prepared, I'll just catch a quick forty winks while the air cools. We'll travel till nightfall. Pitch camp. Can't go in the dark, now, can we? Even with a good moon, it's the fastest way to somebody's dinner, no matter what we think we know, eh?"

Ginny noticed Slater stood by the water until the loud snores of the guide were clear. Then, moving away, quietly crying, she sat down by her pack.

Time moved, the air shifted, colors began to deepen. They were at the night camp. Johnston, a toothpick between his lips, was pulling out pistol, machete and bourbon.

"You told me there wasn't anything or anyone around for at least two hundred miles — so why the arsenal? You'll burn us down with that forest fire you call a campfire, Johnston." Slater moved her sleeping bag and the fine netting it was swathed with farther from the flames.

"Look," the guide answered, "I've been hearing things all day. Someone's following us. Didn't want to spook you. It's most likely a damned Indian wanting some booze or my gun — so I'm just letting them know I know, and we don't need any trouble, all right?"

"I'm beginning to think I'd be safer with them! Don't lose it on me, Johnston. I don't know my way back to that airstrip — not totally, anyway. Please try to keep it together." Slater's voice was almost even.

Ginny saw the effect on the man. He settled down.

Maybe he could protect her, Ginny thought. Maybe they would survive the evening without attack.

Again, the air shifted, almost shimmered. Light went from cobalt to mars black — colors Manilla had introduced to Ginny. In this living palette, they seemed like words from a survival manual. With the change in light, Ginny noticed that a silence had crept around the camp. She couldn't see the guide because of the blackness. Actually she couldn't see Slater, either.

Slater's loud whisper identified her position. "Johnston?"

Three times the woman called and received no reply. The sounds of struggle, of ripping and finally, of a zipper torn in half came from Slater's sleeping bag.

"JOHNNNSSTOOOOOOOOOONNNN!!!"

Slater's scream was joined by the howling of several monkeys. Her flashlight poked circles of light into the canopy of black, but not much more. One sweep revealed a spider the size of a baseball, mashed flat. Another found the remains of the fire — less than embers. Slater made her way gingerly toward the coals. Desperately she blew, then waved her hat stirring a small wind. One or two tongues leapt up and she gradually fed the fledgling flame. Clearly she was trying to keep the panic back by attending to the mundane chore.

As the fire began to roar once again, footprints, booted and not, came into focus in the area surrounding their camp. No sign of struggle, though, no stolen pack, not even an empty whiskey bottle. Slater moved to the edge of the bush. A nocturnal monkey screeched a warning. She moved back.

Ginny and Manilla sat with the woman: in silence, until daylight.

It was high noon. Toucans yammered above them, dropping twigs and leaves on their heads. A bird Ginny couldn't identify flew almost in front of them. Manilla whispered: "It's a kingfisher. It will lead us to the water."

They followed behind Slater as she thrashed through the creepers.

Macaws, parrots, giant herons, blasted up and away from her as she slogged through the mud. Everything seemed etched in green. Everything seemed alive, growing. Nothing stood still. The air, rainbowed, itself seemed to be breathing. Slater began to lose the panicky pace she'd set. Something in the energy around her began to fill her, made her part of it. She stopped hyper-ventilating.

Ginny felt her own lungs ease.

Slater got to the river's edge. She filtered some water into her canteen. Took a few swallows, checked her compass, then began to hike.

It was late. The sun had gone down like a dying animal. Slater would have to make camp soon. She checked the compass for another reading. The crystal showed spidery cracks in all directions. It must have hit her knife or camera in the pack. Slater swore, then hurled it into the woods. She again struck out in the direction of the river.

Coming around a large tree trunk, Slater saw the old footprints and deserted pack of her guide! She'd walked in circles all day! She stooped to gather firewood, directing the rising fear and anger into the chore.

Ginny realized the guide hadn't been back. Surely Slater knew.

The moon began its rise. Lighting the woods as brilliantly as the fire, itself, it was fuller than the night before. For one swift moment, a cloud obscured the silvery light. In that minute Slater gasped. She looked toward a clearing, just beyond the firelight.

Grasping her knife, she called out Johnston's name.

Ginny squinted, tried to see what Katherine Slater had seen.

The moon slammed from behind the clouds. The light was dazzling. There was no one in the clearing. Nothing in the shadows.

Slater sat up all night, her knife in one hand, a burning torch in the other.

At daybreak, she put out the campfire. She rummaged through the guide's pack, taking what she could salvage to stuff into her own. Slater discovered that Johnston's pistol, machete, compass — even his flares — were all missing from his pack. She was on her own. He was not going to find her.

Ginny and Manilla walked beside the struggling anthropologist as she went down, four times. Armies of ants went scurrying as she hauled herself from the rotting vegetation. She seemed to feel nothing, save the blind panic which pushed her on.

Over and over she made poor decisions, crashing into trees, turning her ankle in animal holes, slipping as she came too close to the river's edge. Every so often, from sheer exhaustion, she collapsed, and then, breathing heavily, fighting tears, terrorized she watched the shadowy bush — waiting for whatever had been in camp to make its move. Finally, as the sun fled a second time she made her stand.

It was clear to Ginny and Manilla, that this was the final testing place. The pack had torn on a thorny creeper hours before. Now, she was strewing matches, knife, camera even canteen, behind. Too late, Slater had discovered the rip. She was without defense, now. No fire, no weapon. Only the cold fury that comes from absolute desperation. They knew this woman, bloodied, feverish, crazed with fear would fight using only her teeth and nails. She would fight because it was all she could finally do.

"Manilla, I'm so sorry." Ginny broke off as the moon rose, full and round, an awesome witness to the battle.

A tall, lean figure moved from behind the veil of trees. As it approached, ruby eyes glittered madly from the face.

Slater saw it. She screamed.

A voice so suave and quiet that it was unmistakable called out to the young professor. "I am here," it said.

Recognizing the voice, Ginny recoiled.

"Come to me."

Not Johnston or an angry Indian, not even a jaguar, but a human — another woman! Slater, sobbing, limped forward.

Slender arms extended, ruby nails, like so many tiny flames in the moonlight, sparkled at the tips of the fine hands. A European woman, dressed in dark clothing, emerged from the bush smiling.

"Thank Goddess." Slater slumped into the open arms.

Shocked, Ginny watched. Darsen did not crumple under the weight of Katherine Slater. She merely lowered her to the ground. Almost tenderly, Darsen raised a canteen to Slater's cracked lips. She bathed a cloth with more of the water, wiping the grime from Slater's cheeks and forehead. Then, she touched the filthy cloth to her mouth.

Ginny and Manilla found themselves trembling.

Darsen carried the unconscious Slater through the jungle.

They came to a break in the forest. There was a house, two stories brilliantly lit from the inside. A porch swing moved in the humid night air. The screen door opened. A toucan on an ironwood perch screeched at the prone stranger. Darsen silenced the bird with one glare. The room seemed golden. Orchids and incense hung on the air, added to the unreality.

Lying Slater upon a rattan couch, Darsen began to loosen her clothing. Coming from her faint, still weak, Slater tried to protest. But Darsen's sea-blue eyes burned into her and all struggle ceased. Darsen fetched a basin of water mildly scented with peppermint. She began to bathe the quiet professor.

Unable to watch the intimacy, Ginny turned away.

Manilla couldn't stop staring.

Even knowing what was to come, in that moment, Darsen, so tall, so dark, so elegant, so powerful underneath the fine facade, ministering to Katherine Slater — absolutely vulnerable, absolutely open — the scene was breath-taking. Around them the jungle seethed and sung; the colors danced in brilliant halos around them. Even Gauguin could not have captured such radiance, such splendor.

Then, almost as if she could sense Manilla's stare, Darsen glanced up. In that second, the nightmare came back.

The illusion was broken.

It seemed to Ginny an endless round of sleep, ministrations to Slater, rain, sleep. But she and Manilla stayed by Slater's side. Neither of them dared to follow Darsen, to abandon Slater.

Once, Slater awoke. She called for Darsen, but there was no answer. Rain beat on the little house. Shutters had been pulled tight. A single candle burned, attracting moths. The scent of their singed wings laced the air. Again, Slater called for Darsen.

At the end of the hall was a door Slater had not noticed. The mahogany was stronger than any of the other wood in the house. Slater knocked gently.

Suddenly, it opened, and Darsen was before her.

"I, I didn't hear you, didn't see the door open, I mean," Slater stumbled.

Darsen only smiled. "It's probably the malaria — you've been through a lot these past weeks. It will never be fully out of your system. You must always be careful. Come in, Katherine, please, there's something I've been wanting to share with you." Darsen held out her hand.

Slater noticed a small, silver ring on the left, pinky-finger. The silver was hammered, shining like moonlight. In its center, like a single drop of blood, an intensely red stone.

Katherine Slater grasped that hand.

The room was half again the size of the original cabin. Dozens of cages lined the edges. In each cage: bats.

"My God!" Ginny shuddered.

Darsen escorted Slater to a high-backed stool. "We haven't really had a chance to talk — for me to explain to you why I'm living here — what my work is. Tonight, the time has come, Katherine." Darsen moved away and closer to the stirring animals.

"You know, the Finnish people believe that our solid bodies let go of our souls at night and those souls turn into bats flying till morning, when once again, they return to us. Egyptians used different parts of the bats for medicinal purposes — their

Indian counterparts still use bat skin for the occasional poultice. But why I am truly here is for these. Do you know that two thousand years ago the Mayan god Zotzilaha had a human body but the head and wings of a bat? He demanded human sacrifice — no mystery to the Mayans — and often appeared holding a human head in one hand and a knife in the other? To this day, in Mayan Guatemala, there is a bat-worshiping tribe. The bat has long been admired. Its bastardization came only in recent years. Your culture, my culture — our silly fears and fictions. I'm studying these South and Central American bats. I'm an artist, Katherine. A painter. I'm working my way through the Amazon animal kingdom.

"Generally I like to do only field studies, but, with the bats, it's a bit difficult, as you can well imagine. I was actually attempting a night study when I came upon you. It seems bats do not want to soar with my soul." Ruby lips slightly parted, her hand touching the edges of Slater's hair, Darsen smiled.

Ginny was mesmerized to see that Slater allowed the touch.

Darsen continued, "Now, would you like to see my work?"

Pulling back a cloth covering, Darsen revealed a huge canvas panel. It was as if she had simply cut a window into the jungle outside.

"Manilla, I've seen those paintings! She still has those paintings!" Ginny whispered.

"Do you like it?" Darsen was again by Slater's side.

"I don't know what to tell you. I've never . . . never seen paintings like these before." Slater's face began to grow pale. Sobs wracked her body. She slid from the stool, ran into the hallway, ran away from the haunting paintings.

Darsen took her to the living room. Lying her on the couch, she gently wiped the woman's forehead, crooning, "Katherine, don't try to sit up. It was another spell. I've radioed for help. It will be another week before bearers can get here, maybe more. The only way in is up river and the rains have come early this year. I'm afraid it's all been too much for you. The animals, my studio, it must seem so strange." Darsen knelt next to the woman, running slender fingers along Slater's cheek. Occasionally the ruby ring caught the firelight and gleamed, like a silent animal, between them.

Slater struggled to sit. "Darsen, your work is magnificent. I don't know what to say. You've been so wonderful, but I have to get back to MY work. There must be people looking for me. And my guide, Johnston — never any sign of him. I am confused. This entire trip started so poorly. I had to fight with so many of them to trust me, the dead-ends, so little belief in the Amazon reality, always, those men, laughing at me, my theories."

"Katherine, I understand. When you were delirious, you spoke of the expedition. The radio confirmed who you are. Please, don't worry, my sweet, sweet woman. It seems we are closest to truth when it seems we are closest to difficulty. Maybe I can help you. There are certain things I've stumbled upon, out here, but, later, later for all of this." Darsen stroked Slater's head.

"Manilla, she never radioed anyone. I've seen no radio here! And Slater didn't talk in her sleep!" Ginny's outrage was rising.

Then, Ginny grew silent. Darsen was hovering over the quiet professor.

"Oh, no, no!" Ginny stepped back, but was unable to stop watching.

Darsen began to undress Katherine Slater, slipping off the simple frock, letting it fall to the floor as gently as a flower petal. Katherine's eyes closed. She grew limp at Darsen's touch.

Slater's skin glowed like molten gold with the light reflected by the fire. All was hushed, even the raucous toucan, still perched in the corner, watching. Only the rain on the leaves and the house itself — only the rain and the rising moans from Katherine.

Ginny could not pull away.

Manilla moved as far into the shadows as she could.

Darsen let her blue-black hair trail over the face and throat of the swooning woman. Each tendril looked like a line of blood dripped over Slater's white-gold flesh.

Slater's hands slipped Darsen's black blouse from the strong shoulders. The immediate release of the full breasts caused Slater to sigh deeply. Nipple to nipple, the vampire moved over the prone woman, her lips beginning their terrible descent. Darsen traced the shell-like ear, then moved lower, finding the great vein and gently sucking there. Slater did not cry. She only exposed her neck more fully, thrusting the tempting stem toward Darsen's lips. Again and again Darsen lit upon the neck, stinging quickly, lightly, like some bee maddened by the nectar it sipped. With each nip Slater moaned.

Darsen's hands caressed the ribs and belly of the anthropologist. Tracing abstract patterns, scratching only lightly, their touch caused their own fire. Slater began to undulate beneath the taller woman, her legs splayed, allowing Darsen full reign, full ride.

Darsen's mouth descended again, lighting on the dark nipples, teasing and tugging at them, using her teeth, this time less tenderly than her love bites at Slater's neck. Slater cried out but didn't push Darsen away. Again, she thrust her breasts higher, seeking the probing mouth, the insistent teeth.

Darsen began to thrust against the pelvis of Slater, her own center becoming heated, own lust beginning its uncoiled fire. Slater met each movement, bucking and begging Darsen to go on, to go inside, to go down upon her.

Slater's hands began to tangle in Darsen's mane — soft sounds came from the writhing woman. Sweat bathed her, maddened her with its tickle and burn. She called that she needed Darsen, now, now, to take her. She couldn't wait, had been waiting since the first night she'd come to the jungle, had been waiting, maybe, all of her life.

She cupped the back of Darsen's head, moving her from her breasts, moving her lower, lower, past belly and mons, to that lush center already made liquid by Darsen's touch.

The vampire allowed the direction — reveled in it — followed the insistence. Down, down, it was as if she became watery, flowing over the sobbing Katherine Slater, flowing even as the great river flowed outside.

Ginny's heart began to feel strange — as if it had caught the rhythm of the women in front of her, as if it had begun to strain and pound, heavy with its own remembered lust. She knew Manilla was watching her, watching all three of them, silently, in the corner. Manilla felt no pull, no lust — only revulsion. But Ginny couldn't get free!

She watched as Slater threw her legs over the shoulders of the vampire, exposing her very core. So wet, so swollen, Ginny could feel the ache in her own vulva. Then, in a millisecond, something changed.

Faster than even Ginny could see, Darsen was between those legs, her mouth not the exquisite flower, pleasuring her love, but something cruel, something sharp and evil. The lips drew back, revealing the slit tongue and the long fangs. Slater couldn't see but she could feel the transformation. Her cry of passion curdled into a scream of pain.

Ginny moved backwards, revolted, cringing, seeking Manilla.

Ginny remembered the night of the fire, in the loft, the same spell Darsen had cast on her — the same horrific shuttle from fire to ice — the piercing sting of the vampire's bite and long, aching drink.

Again and again Darsen sought out the artery, the tender flesh of the labia, the clitoris itself, her sounds inhuman, her suckling monstrous. Slater finally fell unconscious.

When it was over, Ginny approached Slater's unmoving body. She was still breathing. Her color was deadly. Upon her finger, Darsen's ruby ring glowed.

When Slater awoke, the hunger was moving through her. Darsen watched, emotionless, explaining to Slater that she would need to learn how to hunt soon to go after living blood. Time and again Slater covered her ears, screaming for the monster to get out, to leave her alone. The suffering was agonizing to watch — more so because Slater wouldn't give in. It became clear to Ginny that Slater was attempting to starve.

Then, Darsen brought a still-breathing child from the Indian village, for Slater to finish off. In the midst of her anguish, Slater, yet again, refused to drink.

Infuriated, Darsen slew the child, then slammed out of the cabin.

Again, how long? Light came and withdrew. Slater was dying. The pain wracked her body. The hunger was destroying her.

Ginny could do nothing but bear witness. She stood beside the suffering woman while Manilla stayed in the shadows. There was nothing to be done.

Then, in the middle of one of the nights, sounds from outside drew Slater from her torpor. She dragged herself to the door. She tried to get out but the door had been sealed! Mustering what remaining strength she had, she tried the windows. The shutters, too, had been barred from the outside. She was being entombed. It was her own fault. Why had she been so weak? She howled her questions to the darkness. The only answer came from a sudden crackling. Smoke began to fill the room. Flames began to show through the cracks in the walls. Darsen had sealed her in to burn her alive!

"Manilla, we have to stop this. Get me out. I want to stop the probe. I can't watch this!" Ginny screamed at the silent Manilla.

"No, Ginny. Just a little longer. We owe her this, to witness this. Just a little longer," Manilla whispered.

Slater's skin began to blister. Spiders and scorpions dropped from the ceiling. The walls began to sizzle and hiss.

Then, Slater spotted the fireplace. Laughing hysterically, she began her hellish ascent. Smoke coated her lungs. Her skin was peeled back by the rough stone. Her eyelashes and hair were burned off. She tasted the roasting of her own mouth. Up and up she climbed. She bent bones and sinew, straining, knowing if there was any hope, any revenge, she had to escape the inferno.

For weeks she had prayed for death, tried to die, but now, faced with this end, she was unsure. What would her death be like? Had she left her soul to Darsen? Had she given her very essence, her spirit, to this demon? No, she couldn't die, not until she had answers. Darsen must be stopped! Not allowed to do this to another human — not allowed to keep killing. Whatever happened, Katherine Slater must try to finish the greatest demon that had ever visited Earth. Darsen's death would give her her life.

Manilla and Ginny watched the final seconds as Slater emerged on the roof. So much skin had been destroyed she looked entirely black. Hairless, bent over like a hag, she fell from the flaming house, crashed into the wet and waiting arms of the jungle below her.

"It's finished." Manilla touched Ginny's hand.

Ginny let go of the probe.

Shaking, holding Manilla in her arms, Ginny couldn't speak.

They were back. She now knew more than she had ever wanted to know — about Katherine Slater, about Darsen and, about herself.

———

Peach and mauve from the morning sunrise bled into the room. The pale illumination was enough to waken her. Manilla pulled on her hiking boots. Quietly, carefully, she crept from the bedroom. Ginny was still asleep. She'd caught a rabbit, in the yard, after the experiment with the probing. It was enough. The probe, itself, had exhausted her. They'd barely gotten her inside, after she fed, before she fell into the coma-like sleep.

Manilla put on her jacket and began searching for the car keys. She needed to get her ass back to Weston. She needed to get to the library. There had been things, this time, that she'd forgotten. Things about the Amazon, the Indians — and maybe, even a clue about the ring.

She touched her breast pocket. Still there, the familiar lump. She didn't dare take it out while Ginny was in the same building, not until she could be sure Ginny's theory of its being dangerous only if Manilla were in danger, was true.

She could use the computer at the library. She could find some of the archaic texts on vampires, maybe even the books themselves, not just the computer text. Weston was big on actual volumes in the permanent collection. The anthro department might finally prove useful. She smiled grimly.

Grabbing the last apple in the refrigerator, Manilla paused only long enough to leave Ginny a note. Then she headed out for Weston College.

———

It was late afternoon when Ginny finally awoke.

She grinned through a mouthful of toothpaste. The mirror held no bloody monster. Banished now, the probe had shown her horrors but it had removed the stress of many unknowns. Slater had refused to become like Darsen. She, too, could fight this . . . this disease.

She rinsed and spat and looked, again, at the clean face in the mirror. Grotesque as it was, she had to admit, the animal blood had done something to her. Her skin, her eyes, even her hair — almost shining. She looked, fresh, younger.

Also, she felt amazingly healthy. Not since before the fire had she been so alive. No depression. No lethargy. Not even a dark circle or tiny line around her eyes. Virginia MacPhearson, last in the line of MacPhearsons, was back!

She found Manilla's note in the living room. It pleased her. It was rare that Manilla accepted the offer of the car — it was so difficult for Manilla to accept anything material. Besides, the day looked inviting! The light outside was brilliant. She felt like getting the kinks out, walking to class would be just the thing. She pulled on boots and coat and then headed out, locking the door behind her.

———

Stretching Manilla pushed back from the library carrel. Surrounding her were fourteen or fifteen thick volumes, none of which could be checked out overnight. Thank God the library didn't close on week-days — or week-nights. Sequestered in a special study room, she was free from prying eyes.

Her computer had offered literally thousands of vampiric references. Most were fiction or, to be accurate, fictionalized.

It was as if authors all knew some bit of truth, but, for whatever reason, held back. Cross-referencing and double-checking, she found all had similar information. The general oogie boogie lore — no help. It bordered on what she and Ginny were experiencing, but it was so full of untruths it was ridiculous. The cross, the sunlight, the sleeping in coffins crap. She understood about the sunlight — if you had to find blood to stay alive, better to do your stalking in the dark, especially if you needed to suck the blood from your kill quickly and then go to sleep. Couldn't very well join a fox-hunting party and go off merrily with polite society, expecting understanding at lunch. As for the coffin routine — all that death stuff could be easily accounted for — superstitions around predators. Besides, if Darsen were any indication, a lot of early deaths were caused by her kind. A lot of cemetery time could be attributed to the vampire. Or maybe, in times of plague, in times of war, when bodies were hastily gathered together, grave diggers over-taxed or just not around, easy pickings could be had in the burial places. A vampire who had just fed greedily might be overcome by the sleep — some kind of quick cover was necessary. Manilla had seen Ginny's fast spiral into that sleep. Maybe, if one wasn't too choosy, a coffin could offer protection. People observing the monster arising from its nap would mistake that for a life-style choice. It could happen.

The other myths were more problematic — the flesh-eating ghouls. As far as Manilla could see — even observing what Slater had given her of Darsen — flesh was definitely NOT what Darsen was after, unless you read "flesh" as a metaphor. What if all the sexuality that seemed to be right on the surface of every vampire notation was just too much to deal with directly? The eating of flesh could be a simile. After all, Darsen had taken bites of both Slater and Ginny!

Manilla smiled, a wee bit disgusted with herself and her own sick humor, but it was a wonder she had any levity left after this immersion. Cannibalism, Black Masses, human immolations, crucifixions — every torture device she'd seen in scary movies — recorded with a blase hand. It wasn't just the vampire hunters who employed these devices, but people accused of vampirism! Women and men, so often aristocracy, feeding off the people directly. Not enough to simply tax them to death: the humans were like private herds of cattle.

No wonder the Church and its counterparts in other religions all had myths and methods for dealing with supernatural events and people.

Not many of them were that open, surely, but the few who were historically recorded were enough. How many other crawled the night, hidden, choosing a closeted existence, learning what too much arrogance had cost, in the end? For, it was true, all the public monsters had been done in. Their deaths usually as horrible as the ones they'd inflicted.

Then, of course, the muddled records — mixing everything from great martyrs to alien grays — all the unexplained phenomena blamed on these creatures. Clearly, the vampire was the most feared of any mythological beast. The simple literature far outweighed anything similar. There was a distinctly adversarial relationship between humans and vampires that went through recorded time. Of all nightmares, the presence of vampires seems to haunt human dreams the most deeply.

Also, their promises. That was another linkage. Their unappeasable sexuality, their connection to Spirit — be it Dark or otherwise — their longevity, their strength and intelligence, their raw power. Each gift a total package in itself, but combined. No wonder there were periods on all continents when people lined up to give their life's blood!

Blood. It came down to that. Something in the crimson currents, something which carried more than even the vampire itself could create, for, if you thought about it, a vampire was the antithesis of creation. That was a key. Manilla noted it, underlining it in neon yellow: CREATION-BLOOD.

How often had Slater and Ginny used metaphors of the blood in describing Darsen's hold on them? She entered their lives, their hearts; she ruled their rhythms, touched their pulses for power, made their hearts change beat, brought their hearts to a halt. She made their blood race hot or she made it frigid. She was not only drinker of their blood, but ruler, too. Darsen was in their blood. She entered them through the veins. Once there, she could then enter their souls.

But while she could visit their dreams, walk in their spirits, she didn't rule their souls — only their bodies. The soul had its own life. Slater had said that. Before and after her death. Darsen didn't send Slater's soul to that dimension. Had Slater believed that it was a consequence for allowing Darsen's temptations, a karmic law? So, Darsen was stoppable, on some level not an earthly one. She could not follow nor could she rule there. SOUL was the next word Manilla wrote and underlined.

CREATION-BLOOD-SOUL

Or, shades of catholic girlhood, it was becoming a biblical obsession, wracking her dreams. Darsen was simply a serial killer and a genius — like those in power who could afford the luxury of their madness played out, those who had come down through history. And Slater? Slater had been involved with lots of weird South American Indian phenomena. Who knew what drugs or hypnotic suggestions she'd planted? Ginny was also under some kind of drug administered by Darsen, the bite not a bite at all but a kind of transfusion of an archaic drug — one that made her act out — even as with Slater. And Manilla's heart-connection to them both had allowed the hypnotic suggestions. As with the literature, Manilla had "invited the vampire in."

But it held, even in this scenario, even with the serial killing theory; CREATION a creation of the further madness, of others falling under the "spell," a creation of an altered, illegitimate reality by the killer; BLOOD, always, with these kinds of killers, blood was at the base of it. It was life. It was the final mystery; SOUL, the metaphysical accouterments and phenomena, the dark age fears manipulated and played out. And the sexuality — didn't that just about cover all three issues? Jesus!

Manilla shook herself. She stood up, wringing her hands through her curly mop of hair. She paced the study room, stopping only to gaze out at the trees beyond the library lawn.

No.

Like the trees, there was more than the obvious, the easily explained.

She was missing the wider reality.

These mundane theories, as plausible as they might seem (with a little stretch) were comfort food. Too easy to see, to understand. Too neat. Too digestible.

They hid the more far-reaching truth. In that truth was the fear that must have stopped all vampire hunters since the beginning of time. Drop the accessibility of the friendly landscaping and confront the wildness beyond its first ring of growth. There was a mighty forest there. In its midst were secrets and dangers and darkness and life. There was also death — and blood. There were energies and spirits and dimensions moving throughout the canopies of woods — all the way to the sky and back to the earth, herself. If one just believed in the human eco-system and its selfish view of a tree, one was blinded to all the other life-forms dependent and thriving in the forest — visible and invisible. Fuck, it was simple science!

Manilla stopped pacing.

Darsen's being a serial killer who used mind-altering drugs and hypnotism didn't account for Slater's body falling to a handful of rising ashes after the fire in Ginny's loft. It didn't account for a wound so gruesome it was whispered along the corridors of the hospital the night Ginny was brought in — a wound that, in a matter of hours, healed over completely.

More than anything else, if Darsen had been a mere madwoman, why wasn't her body discovered in the rubble? Why hadn't anyone seen her escape? The building was ringed with fire trucks, ambulances, pedestrians. All that was seen was that fireball, the fireball that exploded out of the loft, over the heads of the hundreds of people below. The fireball which went careening into the night, like a small comet. It was even written about in the papers. No explanations given — theories of ignited natural gas, chemicals, but nothing confirmed.

SOUL.

BLOOD.

CREATION.

The forest for the trees . . .

Manilla left the study room and sprinted downstairs to the computer labs.

What if every person who had come up against the monster was prevented from writing the whole truth? What if each were only allowed bits, pieces remembered, shards of experiences? Or what if the experiences had been scrambled, shunted by convention and superstition and organized religion, even as her theories were being re-ordered in her own head? Or what if something even more heinous had happened through the ages? These brilliant, disgusting, manipulative beings, couldn't they allow just enough dis-information to keep humans off their backs, at least for the most part? Clearly, they still enjoyed the gaming involved in their hunts. It would be horrible to live eons with the same pattern, never changing, so they allowed certain writers some minutia, some simple truths and then, sat back, laughing, knowing the human imagination and human fear would distort the crumbs they'd scattered.

Vampire lore was the wrong track — even with the computer's aid.

No, it was about the creation — and the blood — and the soul.

Where did one find these things packed together so tightly that there was no separation, no space between the elements? Where do layers and layers of life, dimension upon dimension engage with our own? Where do the air even seem to be breathing? Where had reality lost its previous hard-edges for her?

Manilla flipped on one of the computers. She waited for it to warm up and then punched in the place where she had to go:

THE RAIN FOREST

Which rain forest had both Slater and Darsen been most intrigued by? Which rain forest had Darsen been painting for decades — paintings that even Ginny had described as "alive"?

Manilla sat back, knowing it was going to be a long, long night. She typed in one word: AMAZON

———

"Unnnhhh!" The doctor rolled off the hustler. "Damn, kid, you ARE a pro. That was great. But I have to get back to the hospital. I'm on call tonight. You want to stay or you want a ride in?"

"Take me back downtown." Joey wrapped the yellowed sheet around his chest. He despised the tacky room the intern had rented.

"Don't even have time for a shower. Well, the water's probably hotter at the hospital anyway. Get a move on kid, if you want a ride." The intern pulled on his khakis and denim shirt.

Joey stood. He hated the way he smelled. But he needed the ride. He didn't want to meet Darsen here.

The man threw a crumpled bill at the boy.

Joey caught the twenty, stuffed it into his jeans.

The doctor scanned his watch as Joey finished dressing.

The boy finally picked up his parka, began fishing around in the pockets for cigarettes. "You got one?" Joey asked.

"You know, those things can kill you — " the intern stopped himself, blushing wildly, muttering something under his breath. As he opened the motel door, a blast of icy air filled the room.

To Joey, it was refreshing, clean. He breathed deeply, smiling.

There was more than one way to skin the proverbial cat.

The light hurt his eyes as he awoke. He was sweating again. The sheets were soaked. His hair was plastered to his bony skull. He rubbed swollen, sticky eyelids and sat up, shaking.

Darsen held the lamp close to the boy's face.

"You let him go?" Her voice was like a Styrofoam cup being torn in half, screechy and artificial.

"What're you talking about?" Joey mumbled, feeling hot and cold simultaneously. It felt as if she'd driven a stake through his eyes.

"You know who, Joey. What did you do?" Darsen was apoplectic.

"You mean the john? My trick? Shit, he was a doctor! Can you believe it?" Joey managed to giggle through his sore throat.

Darsen shifted the lamp from its place in front of the boy's face.

Suddenly, she had him by his hair. She bent the skinny neck back, exposing the throat, the sunken chest. He trembled like a fawn caught in the jaws of a puma.

"Open your mouth," she spat the words as if they burned.

The boy let his jaw go slack. It was all he could manage. He was merely a marionette — they both knew it.

Darsen screamed and let him go, "NO!"

Joey's body fell against the reeking pillow. His neck crashed against the headboard with a thunk.

"How long?" Darsen eyed him from the shadows, her gaze filled with garnet light.

"I got tested at the clinic, when they sent the mobile unit downtown. Just found out, for sure. Guess I've known a long time, though. It's kinda funny, don't you think?" Joey closed his sore eyes. He didn't want to really see her answer.

"So, that's why you let him escape?" Darsen's hiss was evil.

Joey still didn't look at her, but answered, "Don't you think it's better like this — I mean, for me, anyway. He won't know till it's too late — then, who can they blame? How they gonna trace me? It could be anybody killing them, don't you see? No more ghosts grabbing me in my sleep. No more cops to look out for. They all get what they deserve. All of them." He rolled over. He wished he was alone. He didn't want to deal with her anger.

"Joey, this isn't our arrangement. You're breaking your promise to me." Darsen kept her fury in check. Her tone was low and dangerous. She sat on the narrow bed, laying slender fingers upon the skinny chest, drummed delicately as a cat.

Joey turned on his back. He put his fists to his eyes. He didn't want her to see him cry and he didn't want to see her face.

He felt something around his heart give a little squeeze.

He knew he'd fucked up. But just once, he wanted to do something just for himself — to try his own revenge. This was so simple, it had come to him in a flash. Really, a kind of sick joke. When he found out the john was a doctor, he didn't think she'd mind, just one, just one for himself, this way . . . just one.

Darsen's hair came down over his face in a black wave. He could smell the lily - scent of her. So sweet, so deeply sweet. He liked looking at her. She was so beautiful. She could be a movie star, so beautiful.

Purged of its angry edge, her voice caressed him, "Joey, you must listen very carefully. When you wake up we are going to talk about this some more. Right now, you need to sleep. Are you listening to me, Joey?" Darsen increased the rhythm of her nails against his chest. Five ruby daggers tapping upon the stretched skin directly above his heart.

Joey was absolutely still.

There was a rushing tide, a quickening, the blood in the midst of its own song, in thrall with its own journey, careening through his body and back again. His face flushed with the listening. It wasn't just his fever. He wanted to tell her he understood. He wanted to tell her he could hear the music his heart was making—making for her. Because of her. He wanted to say these things, but words were useless. His breathing began to keep pace with his pulse.

Again, Darsen sped up the tapping.

Joey began to panic. Couldn't catch his breath. Felt that the machine in his chest was going amok; his heart would destroy itself if it didn't begin to slow down.

Then, mid-tap, as gently as she'd begun, Darsen stopped.

It was over.

Joey gasped in his damp bed.

He closed his eyes, hard.

She wanted him to go to sleep.

He would sleep.

She would watch him while he slept.

He knew this and was terrified.

━━━

Gunner flipped through the tattered three-ring binder. His address book. He smiled, cracking open another can of Rolling Rock Beer. He'd never so much as owned a little black book. Running large fingers over a column of numbers, he came to the Malibu office.

"Love time zones!" he chuckled, leaning back in the desk chair, feet propped up on the kitchen table. He noticed he needed new heels. Hard to find a cobbler in Syracuse who knew shit about cowboy boots, let alone the difference between a walking heel and a riding one.

"Howdy!" he answered, surprised the call had gone through so fast. "This is Gunner. No, still upstate. Yeah, well, I figured it would be you or Mikey on the desk. How's it hanging, man? Look, I got a special favor to call in, okay? You ready? Would you fax the files on the Slavin case? I know, I know, but, like I said, man, I'm calling in a few — dig? How's the wife? The kid? Dog? You're a real mensch, Georgie, what can I say? Right. I promise. Nobody will know it was from you, man, you got my word. No lie, bro. Okay, the number is — "

———

"MacPhearson, who would have thought?" Minx slumped against the mirrors. His back left a sweaty swatch against the glass.

"Vitamins!" Ginny laughed, toweling off.

"Tell me what brand, kid. Where did you learn to move like that?" The instructor watched his student carefully.

"Guess I've always danced like this, maybe nobody noticed before, is all."

"Well, I'm noticing. Look, this is your first year in the program. You don't know me from a tube of Ben Gay, but, listen. There are a lot of good kids in dance and most of them are going no farther than the local company. But you, Stretch, you and those legs. You promise to work hard for me, Ginny — and I mean very hard, no whining, no complaining, no prima donna scenes — you get an audition, in the City, come summer. But, I'm the boss, got that? I think we have something very special between us, chemistry, kid, very hot." Minx moved across the floor playfully, coming to rest at Ginny's feet.

Ginny laughed, moving away.

Reaching for her ankles, Minx grinned, motioning for her to come closer, to come low.

"I really have to get home. Thank you for staying late, with me. I appreciate it," Ginny tried to get free.

This time the man held her hard. He rose, moving his fingers along the sinewy insides of her calves, past knees, higher.

"Why don't you show me how appreciative you really are, Ginny." His voice was sure. Too smooth. This was no new routine.

"Please! I'm really flattered, but I'm in a relationship — " Ginny cautiously pushed the man's hands away.

No good.

The beefy fingers began caressing her inner thighs.

"Honey, this ain't about relationships. Grow up. This is business." Minx pulled her closer, still kneeling.

It was one long move: Ginny kicked out. The man never saw it coming.

Minx was across the studio floor, smashed to a rude halt by one of the pillars in the center of the room.

"Dammit!" he moaned, nursing a bleeding head. "All you had to do was to say 'No'. "

Ginny gulped the air outside the studio. It tasted clean. She slowed down the adrenalin coursing through her body. Her heart was in the midst of its own mad dance — not from the threat of Minx, but from her new power. She had stopped him with this power!

She wasn't worried about retaliation. All that mattered was the fact that she'd stopped him! Not by running away or screaming for help, not through bargaining or blackmail — but through her own strength!

Freedom.

Absolute freedom.

Even her dance had become stronger, more sure, more passionate.

Ginny hadn't thought the changes through, never guessed what they might mean.

Here was safety. Here was delight!

She actually began whistling as she walked back from the studio toward her cottage. She was no longer afraid.

———

The lights overhead seemed to crackle every so often. Manilla's neck was stiff, her eyes blurring. She'd have to quit soon. But just a little more . . . so close . . . she was coming so close.

> " . . . the Hekura is a medicine man with great power. His is the realm of healing; spirituality, emotions, physical ailments, mental problems. When he spoke to our group of the lost Amazons, the tribe of women, we took it as his absolute truth. He was a man who added no personal embellishment to any of his

communications. He was well -respected by all the members of our research party . . . "

Manilla kept reading:

" . . . The Hekura informed us that the Amazon Tribe lived in a part of the jungle miles from the river's main flow. These women, he translated, live without men. They live together by choice. Long ago, many, many years before his own time, their men abandoned them, out of fear of the women's rising powers and increasing knowledge of dark magic. Ashamed of their cowardice, the men wandered, always emerging just on the edges of other tribes' camps, begging shelter, food, smoke. It happened during the grandfathers' grandfathers' time. But even today, men who stray from their hunting parties or who get too drunk and fall asleep in the jungle at night, sometimes fall prey to these devil-women. They go missing for weeks, are believed to be dead. Sometimes they come back, emerging from the jungle, returning to their villages, silent, moody, almost shrunken. They return but they are unable or unwilling to divulge details of what they have seen, they have lived through.

Never again do they have relations with the tribal women — their wives, their lovers — it is given up willingly. No one tells them to do this thing. No one enforces it. It is their choice and they do not explain why. They even stay away from their girl children, their mothers, their aunts and cousins and grandmothers. It is cause for much sorrow, much pain when these men come back home in this condition. Luckily, few are foolish enough to be careless in such ways as to endanger themselves. But still, it does occur.

When these men die, their bodies are always closely examined by all the tribal members. The Hekura has a special ritual of cleansing and purifying that must be performed before cremation of the body can happen. During this ritual, our Hekura *had looked for signs of illness in the men, but their bodies betrayed nothing that would account for their shame. Yet, he could sense, that they were not whole men.*

The youngest ones, the unwed ones, they never returned.

There is a story, the Hekura said, that tells of the power of these Amazon women. It is told that they have acquired the power to strip the souls from their enemies. Once taken, the soul is changed. It is transformed into a small stone. Sometimes these stones are the size of fists, other times they are as miniature as teardrops, but always, always they are the color of human blood. When these souls are stolen, they are then thrown into the water of the river. It kept the dead from retribution. It hid them from their families and their medicine people. No one knew how to change the souls back from stones. But many people had heard these stories. All the tribe believed in them as truth . . . "

Manilla sat up straighter. Christ, it couldn't be? She took the ring from her pocket. Holding it up in the fluorescent light, the color seemed deeper than ruby or garnet, but it might only be the lighting. It was small — the size of a tear — and it seemed, even in the library's artificial atmosphere, to have some kind of inside illumination. Gently, Manilla shook it.

"Slater, Slater, can you hear me?" She whispered to the stone. "God, Slater, is that what this is all about? Did Darsen steal your soul, when she put that ring on your finger, was it some kind of sponge, just bleeding your spirit in there? Are there others inside with you? Was that why you wanted to keep Ginny away? Are you afraid her soul will be taken? But, dammit, you said Darsen didn't have your soul — remember? Or was that dream just a dream, after all? Slater, you've got to help me with this! Please!" Manilla slipped the ring on her finger. No answering bolt of light, no flame-on power.

"Shit!" she muttered, going back to the screen:

" . . . one day the Hekura took us to his home. There, he removed a bag made from the skin of a squirrel monkey and hidden under the mats on his floor. He sprinkled in a circle on the floor some flower pollen, which he took from a separate, woven bag. The circle was approximately one foot in diameter. Then, opening the squirrel monkey parcel, he dropped a handful of brilliant, ruby-tinted stones into the center. They resembled nothing so much as crystallized drops of blood. Each seemed to glow with a fire from within its core. One of the men clumsily reached for the stones. The Hekura gasped. The surprising reaction of the medicine man was enough to stop our comrade in the middle of his faux pas. We must not touch the jewels, the Hekura warned. These were recovered souls, rescued from the river. They had the power to destroy anyone who handled them without the proper reverence. They had the power to destroy their known enemies. They also had the power to protect. After the abrupt warning, he retrieved each individual stone and placed it with infinite care, into the monkey pouch. The Hekura's two apprentices asked us to leave. Every apology made on behalf of our blundering colleague and our group, as a whole, was ignored. We never saw the medicine bag again — nor was it ever alluded to. Eventually, we were back on friendly terms with the Hekura and the tribe and remained so for the duration of our stay.

To admit it was unnerving: to hear the story of the hidden tribe of fierce women and the stories of abduction of unwitting men, then to see physical evidence that matched the legend is to only admit the truth. We never came into contact with the lost tribe. We never found similar stones, though at various points, we did pan the river. However, the legend came to our attention in village after village up and down the Amazon. And, whatever they were, we did see actual stones in the Hekura's home, that one afternoon . . ."

It was very late. Too late to try to reach Ginny with what she'd found. Again, nothing clarified. It seemed as if an unseen hand were clouding the clues. All the new information did was to strengthen the mystery. If the stone in Slater's ring were the stone capable of capturing a soul, was it empty when Darsen had given it to Slater? Did Darsen give these stones to all her lovers, knowing, sooner or later, that's how she'd control them? Yes, that would match the other stories — and was logical, given the sequence of events Manilla had observed. But why had Slater given HER the ring? If Slater's soul was inside, why didn't Slater answer her calls? Was it Slater's power, lashing out at Ginny, the other night? Why couldn't Manilla control that, either? If Slater couldn't hear her, then as long as the ring was around Ginny would be in jeopardy. Should she throw the ring away? Maybe, maybe, in the lake? Cayuga was no Amazon River, but it would protect Ginny from harm. But would that mean she could never see or hear Slater again? Would that mean she was throwing Katherine Slater into oblivion?

Too tired. Way too tired to figure it out alone.

Besides, she had to get some time in the Art Studio. Too much time away from there, and access to all Weston's resources would be denied. She'd flunk, for sure. Had to find a way to continue the research, to support Ginny, to do the painting . . . to . . . . She pulled the sleeping bag over her aching shoulders. It was too hot in the tiny room when she left the radiator on, so she simply slept in the down sleeping bag during winter. The bag was also like a warming hug, a sweet cocoon. She felt safe, there. So few places were safe, anymore.

Manilla snuggled deep into the depths of the mummy bag. Her eyes were still burning from the reading and the hours in front of the computer screen. Thousands of words to sift, to digest. How to pull spare facts from fantastic fiction? No guides. No guides. What had Slater said? To trust her heart? Ha! She began to drift off.

The zipper was being peeled from beneath her chin. Manilla was suddenly wide awake! Cold air rushed against her skin as the bag split apart. She tried to protest, then realized she couldn't speak!

"Manilla, don't be afraid."

In the night shadows, all Manilla could make out was something tall and dark above her. It was standing next to the bed, reaching down, reaching for her! The sleeping bag came apart like two halves of a giant fruit; Manilla, the tender flesh lay at its center.

The only sounds between them were the sounds of breathing — hers — and the metallic "zing" of the zipper. The shadow moved over her. Manilla felt smooth, cool flesh come down upon her own. An involuntary sigh wrenched itself from between her clenched teeth.

"I've waited for you, Manilla."

The voice, so familiar, so longed for — outside of her head coming directly from the figure moving against her. Then, Slater's tongue filled her mouth with its heated desire. The force of it shocked the student. Hard, stabbing, then suddenly softer, flooding her with hunger.

Manilla could scarcely breathe. For long moments, the image of Darsen, a disguised vengeful Darsen, played in her mind. Darsen coming to kill her, taking the form of Katherine Slater, but the image melted. This scent, this touch, this voice, it could be no one else. Slater was with her, within her, making love!

The strong arms held Manilla down. The lithe body pressed and rested, belly to belly, open sex to open sex, taut muscles moving between her legs, opening Manilla in a way Ginny had never imagined, commanding Manilla in a way Manilla had never allowed, never allowed anyone, until this night.

Wet.

Both so open, so wet.

Liquid fire, molten, hungered. The only facts she had. The only answers she knew. "I want, I want — " Manilla gasped, moaning at the press and pull of Katherine Slater's hands as they sought her, opened and entered her.

"Shhh," the older woman hushed her. "I know, I know."

Then, she was awake.

Outside the dorm room door, Manilla heard the clatter and clang of the cleaning women as they began the days ablutions.

Winter sun filled the shadows Slater had come from, the night before.

Slater?

Manilla sat up. She was still enmeshed in the sleeping bag. The zipper was zipped tight. She thrashed her way out of the bag.

On her finger . . . the ring was missing!

Manilla unzipped the mummy bag all the way.

She held it upside down and inside out. She shook it like a child in a tantrum shakes a stuffed animal or a rag doll. Something shining and heavy fell to the rug on the hardwood floor.

Manilla sat down next to it, afraid to pick it up, afraid, now, of what it contained.

"Slater," she whispered, trying to keep the tears out of her voice.

It had been just another dream.

██████

It was dark when she came to him. This time Joey was awake. Fully awake.

"Good evening, Joey," Darsen purred, her breath cool and sweet.

"Hello." Joey was desperate to hide the anxiety. Still, glad she was there. Terrified she was there.

"Have you had time to think about our arrangement?" Darsen sat in the straight chair opposite the television. She was wearing a black, woolen poncho, black tights and high boots. Even her hands were sheathed in black calfskin gloves. Her hair hung loose and silky around her exquisite face. She was the most beautiful human being, with her piercing sapphire eyes and jewelled lips — the most beautiful person Joey had ever seen. She knew it. Knew it mattered terribly to the boy.

She leaned forward, "So, then, you understand? I need you, Joey. Isn't that the most perfect relationship of all? Each party needing the other? Do you feel that, Joey? Do you feel your need?" Darsen folded her hands in her lap.

The gentle clenching of Joey's heart began again. As if something were in his chest, encircling the organ, not tight enough for discomfort, but tight enough that he was aware of the trap. Joey nodded stiffly. Indeed. Yes. Of course.

"You know, Joey, there are examples in nature, just like us. The difference here is that my need is less. Joey, you are like the tiny fish who school around the shark, feeding off scraps that float from the shark's unforgiving jaws. Like these fish, Joey, you perform certain services. I could find other, equally insignificant fish, or, I could do without those services. The tiny fish keep the shark's teeth clean. They swim in and out, between the razor edges. They are tolerated only because what they do is pleasant for the shark. Pleasant, Joey. And convenient. But not necessary.

You see, unlike other animals, the shark doesn't NEED clean teeth. The shark has an endless supply, row upon row. They continue to grow, fall out and be replaced, as long as the shark lives. If those little fish were not there, it really wouldn't affect the shark's longevity, Joey. It's simply a matter of ease. Of comfort. A little diversion. Are you following this line of reason, Joey?" Darsen leaned forward farther, her face was now mere inches from the pale face of the boy.

"A diversion," Joey repeated, feeling the hand on his heart squeeze again, ever so gently.

"Exactly. And what do you think the shark does if it doesn't get a meal for a few days? All those tiny, tiny fish, swimming, without fear, in and out, between the razor teeth, directly in the mouth of the beast, in their fishy minds, this is how it should be. They are totally unaware that their good fortune is based solely on the shark's mood. And, a shark's mood, Joey, is entirely dependent on its dinner. What do you think a shark might do if, for whatever reason, there was no dinner for a number of days?" Darsen smiled. The smile was quick and horrible.

Joey was silent. Couldn't summon enough air to form the words. The image, though, was clear in his mind.

"Correct, Joey. Perhaps only a single mouthful for the shark, but surely better than nothing. Better than starving, eh? Lucky for those little teeth-cleaners that it is rare for a shark to have a bad day, to miss more than a single meal . . . ."

Joey was perspiring freely. He felt he might vomit. Yes. It was absolutely clear. He would never risk displeasing her again. Never risk damaging their promise to each other, except by her permission. Yes. He did understand.

Darsen leaned back in the cheap chair. She clapped her hands. The muffled sound reminded Joey that the gloves were simply additional skin, yet another animal in her service. He closed his eyes. The strain upon his heart eased.

"See, my friend, I do know you. I know what happened to you with your older cousin — yes — way back when you were just a child. I know all about his dirty ways. I know about that high school football player you were in love with, too, Joey. The hike in the woods that Sunday, when he told you his deep secret, that he liked boys, too. You couldn't believe the star quarterback wanted to be with a boy like you. Could you, Joey?"

"Don't, please!" Joey felt the hot tears as they tore down his face. A flood. No one knew these things. How could she know?

"You were lucky, weren't you, Joey? Until his family found out. They came looking for you with a baseball bat, didn't they? Upset your parents, your sisters? Only your dirty cousin wasn't surprised at the news — was he, Joey? He knew you liked boys all along didn't he? Yes, you are a lucky boy, indeed. But lovers leave. People disappoint. You've seen that for yourself. Even parents stop loving when their sons let them down, don't they? Isn't that why you're really here? Haven't you secretly prayed that just one person, one single person would stay with you? Stand up for you, Joey? Just one? Answer me!" Darsen hurled the chair off to the side of the room. Before he could utter a word of reply, she hauled the boy out of the bed,.

Joey was sobbing, flinging his fists against the vampire's chest, fighting to get loose. He couldn't stand her knowing, couldn't stand her touching. She'd raped his memories, made what was clean unclean, unholy.

"Enough!" Darsen's face had metamorphosized.

Gone the expected beauty, gone the elegant woman in black, gone the caring mother-figure, the mentor, the dark angel; instead, a hell spawn so alien he had no images to compare it to, no human words left in his sixteen-year old mind. Joey was on the floor in front of a nightmare!

"It's time to leave, Joey. It's time to hunt."

He blinked.

It was Darsen, again, the beautiful woman, helping him to his feet. A simple touch of her cool, gloved hands to his temples, stopped his trembling.

She smiled benevolently, "Don't forget your coat, Joey. It's cold."

The truck stop was nearly empty. Just off the thru-way, it was a last point before the city, a place to grab a nap in the cab, drop a dexie or two, finish off the coffee in the thermos.

It was also a place for boy-sex.

Pull in the rig close, toward the grass.

Turn off all the lights.

Quick hike into the trees.

Sometimes, if the night was clear, the air balmy, it was like a movie set. Sweet meat: chicken, beefcake, spring lamb. Boys in the shadows, whispering, waiting. Some would do it for free — the older ones, the ones out for dangerous adventure, the ones afraid of what harsh lights might reveal. They'd come to this rest stop, knowing they'd find others as hungry and desperate as they were.

Most hustlers steered clear. Too far to hitch and not an easy hike back. Besides with so much free action, truckers were growly about paying working guys. Might even beat up on you, after paying, just to prove something.

Joey had only been there once, on the way in to Syracuse. A trucker, hauling apples and other winter fruit, had picked him up. A blow job and then the trucker shared some weed. Easy exchange. The guy was kinda sweet, kinda nice. His first initiation to the city. The trucker took him all the way to the corner that became his new job site. Joey would always remember.

Darsen left him there.

Moving behind the pines, a man approached.

Joey showed his face, then pulled back into the shadows.

The man came closer.

Cold out. Spitting snow. But no other rigs around. No other cars. The man chose Joey because of the cold and because there was no other choice. Wanted action fast and then wanted to be on his way.

Joey hoped they'd get into the truck's cab, where it was warm. Though riskier, what with cops coming up and shining lights inside, it was still warm. In the cab, the guy would be less likely to hit him, not want blood all over his stuff.

In the snowy woods, anything could happen.

Joey couldn't afford another mistake.

He could feel Darsen, off somewhere, measuring his every move.

Little fish and razor jaws.

The truck driver was quiet as he sidled up next to the boy.

He smelled of sweat, leather seats and gasoline. He ran his lips over Joey's smooth face.

Joey could feel the stubble from a day-old beard.

"Cab's warmer." The man breathed cigarette breath into Joey's ear.

Joey nodded, his hand caressing the rising bulge in the driver's crotch.

"Follow me, kid," the trucker moved sideways, grinning.

As Joey did so, he could feel the light tap of the folded razor, shifting, inside the ankle of his boot . . . .

━━━━━

Ginny felt the first, stinging grit of the new snow.

Powerful storm, mean, threatening.

Moving faster, she wiped it from her face.

She wanted to find something to feed upon as quickly as possible. The cold in her gut had returned with a vengeance, making it impossible even to think. It would be the first real kill without Manilla there to help her. The birds didn't count. She needed to eat, to take suck, to find life. The pain inside was like another mouth, tearing her. Never had she known such agony. It seemed each time she fed the ecstasy was greater, her senses dramatically increased, her joy, her strength, her passion all flowering beyond her humanity — but when it wore off, the hunger was equally powerful. Instead of growing used to it, it was taking root, feeding off of her, killing her by pieces.

Clutching the knot that was her belly, she knew, with absolute certainty, she would forever have to hunt large mammals. Never again would rabbits, mice, voles sustain her. She was becoming a dangerous predator of the alpha type. How had Slater lasted so long? How had she learned to control this lust? She couldn't have run through Weston's woods every night. There would have been no time to hide all the carcasses. And the lab animals — mostly small monkeys, a few apes — they couldn't have provided all the blood she would have needed for sustenance. Of course, Manilla had caught her with the calf. Maybe that was the answer, to become a farmer or a rancher. Christ, how many ranchers were like her — like them?

Ginny had to laugh, though the sound was brittle and bitter.

She kept pacing through the woods. No wonder Darsen hunted humans, next to tracking game in the wild, humans were like fish in a barrel.

"No!" She stopped where she stood. She said it aloud again, "NO!" She wouldn't let the thoughts come again, not even creep in close. "Stay clear, MacPhearson!" she ordered herself. She held her face up, accepting the sting of snow as contrition. "Though it isn't like I've had much of a choice in all of this, not like I was given a fair chance to refuse."

She stumbled through the woods again, beginning the search all over. "Manilla would say we all have choices. Did I, with Darsen? Really? Did Slater?" She pushed the thought down. Had to get control, had to focus. Never mind torturing herself with these metaphorical quizzes. She had to be silent in order to hunt. Everything, from morality to mortality, was extraneous until she fed.

She sniffed deeply. Her hair whipped across her face. Her eyes watered from the pain. Ginny caught the faint essence of a doe, white-tail. The woods were full of them. Hunting in this area was prohibited. The deer huddled together, waiting out the storm. She would find more than one if she came upon their hiding place. This doe was alone. Must be sick or weak. Easy kill. Practically speaking, she was doing a favor for the genetics of the neighborhood — what did the hunters call it? Culling?

She began to move in earnest.

She knew she had little time.

The doe was a two-year-old. Confused by this human, realizing, too late, this was no human at all, it had gone down easily.

Ginny broke the neck in one graceful swipe.

Where had she learned this action? There had been no killing instructor, nothing she'd ever read had led her to the technique. But now, she was a master. A hunting machine. How? There had been no moment of hesitation. The animal had not suffered. Even the noise was negligible.

As consciousness melted, she drew the still-living blood inside, feeling the deer fill each dying cell in her half-human body. The tingling was intense, the warmth, thrilling. it built higher and higher, taking her over the edge, directly into the delicious, flying panic that said orgasm was eminent.

She tried to slow it, to keep the disgusting blood-suck from becoming pleasurable, but it was a useless lie. She could no more cease to feed than she could stop, mid-climax.

Raising her reddened face to the storm-filled sky, Virginia MacPhearson, last in the MacPhearson line, screamed in pure animal release.

The trembling subsided.

Ginny knew she couldn't make it back to the cottage.

Sleep came too fast to this new body.

Unsure whether she could withstand the brutality of the storm, unclear of her limits, she had no other choice. She would find shelter in the woods. Through the howling ice and wind, she came to an oak tree. Ancient, honed out by insects and lightning, too drafty for hibernating animals, it was abandoned, waiting.

"Manilla would remind me to say thank-you. So, thank you, tree." Ginny smiled crookedly, sleepily. Tucking her coat over her head, she stopped the holes above her as she nestled inside. There were dry leaves and brush below. She arranged these in a heap around herself. Too bad she hadn't thought of carrying the deer here. Hadn't people saved themselves in storms like this in the old days, by crawling inside a freshly killed animal? No, this was better. Cleaner. Not nearly as distracting as all that blood.

She fell into the deep and dreamless void.

Outside, all about the tree, the storm raged.

Close to sunrise.

The bluish light filtered in through the snow.

Ginny opened her eyes. Her mind refused to accept the place she'd spent the night. Clawing frantically, as if she'd been buried against her will, Ginny burst into the clear cold.

Huge snowdrifts were piled against every tree. They masked even the blood-soaked trail she'd left the night before. Wiped clean. Safe. All was blue and silver.

Dawn was coming upon her. Pearly. Inviting. Time to move quickly as she now knew she could, before anyone in the city noticed.

Ginny pushed open the cottage door, just as her next door neighbor left for work. He didn't see her as he picked his way through the drifts on his walkway. A snowplow came roaring around the corner. She slipped inside.

Exhilarated.

Free.

She need never fear the cold again.

For the rest of her life.

"So, what did you find out?"

"Well, Gin, there's a tribe in the rain forest — these Amazon women," Manila cradled the phone against her cheek. For once she was glad of the distance it offered. The dream of Slater . . . only a dream, but, her dream. Another white lie, a kind of betrayal just when Ginny needed all the support she could get.

"Manilla, Amazons — like those Greeks that cut off one breast so they could shoot their bows more accurately? You've got to be — "

"No, wait, listen, not those Amazons — but a tribe of women, in the Amazon Basin. Who knows where they originated? The indigenous people are scared stiff by these women; all the tribes have stories." Manilla tried to keep her voice even.

"Manilla, are they . . . like Darsen?"

"Vampires? I don't know, Gin. Something tells me they aren't. The stories the Indians relate don't mention that aspect, but they are connected. More importantly, there is a myth that says the women can turn men's souls into stones — red stones, Gin — and then, to keep the dead men's families from rescuing the souls — or to keep the souls, themselves, quiet — the women throw the stones into the River. Ginny — the Amazon, the red stones — "

"What do they do with women's souls?" Ginny didn't hide her sarcasm.

Manilla stopped talking. She cleared her throat. Her guilt was rising. Maybe, even over the phone, Ginny could read her mind, see her dreams.

"Manilla, you still there?"

"Yeah," Manilla answered.

"I'm sorry. It's just that this is all a long shot. Even if this ghost tribe exists and they are all women and they do this mumbo-jumbo with the stones, say Darsen even made them all . . . like her . . . it doesn't tell us a single thing about YOUR stone."

"Not my stone . . . Slater's stone. Gin, what's up, what's wrong?" Manilla couldn't stand the place they were headed. The fight loomed large.

"Manilla, I don't need to know this archaic theory. I don't need to know the history of the Amazons. Something more powerful, more wonderful is happening, right here, right now! These changes. We never thought it through, but these changes! My God! Do you know how it has affected my dance? Or the other day — Minx — my primary instructor, he got a little pushy, you know? But, did I cause this big scream-scene or run away like some scared rabbit, or even swallow it, like I used to do? No way! Manilla, I knocked the jerk across the studio! Today he wasn't even in class. But I'm still in the program. He's the one scared. I like it, Manilla. I suddenly understand what guys have, naturally, this enormous edge of physical power over anything smaller or weaker, why they walk all over us — because they can. Now, I can. So, you did some wonderful research, love. Some wonderful work, for me. You can't know how much that means. I know how awful this has been for you. I apologize about the crack about its being your ring. I know Katherine Slater was important. I'm not forgetting. It's just that, whatever was in that ring, I truly don't think it can hurt me now! Manilla, I'm changing. Every hour, something new, something stronger. Oh sweetie, if we approach this not in some negative way, some victimized way, but positively, we get a whole new insight. This isn't a curse. It's my destiny! Maybe it is the best gift I've ever been given." Ginny's voice was bubbling, high.

"Ginny, stop it! Do you know who you sound like?" Manilla was nearly screaming.

"No, but — "

"This is exactly what Darsen told Slater — the greatest gift — a blessing — her destiny! It's what Darsen always tells people — down through time — its in the books, Gin! She chooses you and changes you but doesn't give you the downside: that, you have to find on your own! Gin, I'm so close to cracking this, to finding a way," Manilla was pleading.

"A way to what? Back to Katherine Slater? Manilla, I know about your dreams. I haven't said anything because, well, it isn't right, asking you to give up sex just because I'm going through these changes. But I know you've been fantasizing, I know you've dreamt about her. Maybe you wish it were her, here, outside and my soul caught in that rock on your finger." Ginny's voice was electric, cutting like a power saw.

Manilla gasped, nearly dropped the phone. She was wearing the ring, right then. Could Ginny see that? And the dream. "Gin, how?"

"Fuck you, Manilla! You are so transparent! You've been dreaming about Katherine Slater since the first day she walked on to campus."

"It's not true — not like that! Ginny, damn it, we've gone through too much together for you to say these things to me! You know I don't want you anywhere but with me. Why are you acting like this?"

"I called to see how you were doing — and on the slim chance that you actually found some useful information about Darsen. I find you've been up for days, tracking down lesbian witches in the Amazon and aren't any closer than when you started. You don't even ask me how it's been — how I managed to . . . to hunt . . . and get back by myself. Didn't it cross your mind, once, that, if you weren't with me I might get caught? Or lost? No, of course not — too involved in the Gothic details about Slater's precious Amazon adventure! Well, I'm telling you — I have gotten along just fine. I don't need what you are risking your time on. You should either be here, with me, going through this with me, celebrating with me, or in the Art Studio, painting. That's how you can be supportive. That's how you can prove you're really in this relationship, Manilla. Take care of what is in front of us, here and now. Not the past. They are all dead, whatever occurred back there, then, all dust. It's now we have to deal with. Right now."

"Gin, why are you so angry?"

The phone was silent. A click, a buzz. An empty line.

"What did the autopsy prove?" Gunner threw the file across the D.A.'s desk.

"It proves you were right about the missing blood. How you knew, that's another matter, Gunner. Right now, it's one for one. We didn't think to check the oil levels on the others." The D.A. stubbed out her cigarette. She reached for a fresh pack. She offered it to Gunner.

He shook his head. She peeled the cellophane, then struck the box against her palm, deftly releasing a single, white stem.

"Nancy, you're going to have to trust me here. I know it's out on a limb, but I know I'm right. Bone right. Seriously. There is more than this hustler involved. I mean, the kid IS involved all right, but he isn't traveling alone anymore." Gunner spun the loose watch on his wrist.

"Gunner, what are you saying?"

Gunner didn't answer right off. He was watching how she held her cigarette, how she smoked. She was a looker — had been since they'd gone to elementary school together. Close to fifty, still the best legs in town. He'd always been a leg man, maybe she was the reason.

"Wipe that stupid grin off your face, Detective!"

Gunner coughed, embarrassed at being caught. "Uh, Nance, I called Malibu. A few years back, while I was working that beat, the Slavin case — remember? Didn't hit the media, lots of quiet money spread around, but it circulated in-house. Real sicko case. Cults. Hollywood wanna be's. The whole enchilada of La-La Land."

"Yes, vaguely, I remember. Not my cup of tea. Something about these cult cases gives me the heebie-jeebies. Can't even watch them on 'Geraldo.' " The D.A. blew smoke over her littered desk.

She liked Gunner. Had since they were little. Known him long enough before Viet Nam to like him still. Tough. Honest. Big heart. But, like they said on TV, he'd never let you know. Not anymore. Kept to himself too much, not that it was any of her business. Not anymore. Fine work — when he wasn't haunted.

Trouble was, he never let it go. Carried bodies around like ballasts. Especially the kids: Viet Nam, L.A.

"Nance, the night before I came back, two homes in the Malibu Colony, right after each other. First, a major party, drugs, call girls, party boys, the works. Somebody goes ballistic. Hunting knife. S/M. All through the house — while folks were passed out from the party — real cowardly — even took a senator's kid. Nothing in the house was stolen. Damn, I was so fucking cocky by then, thought I had the overkill cases figured out like Math 101."

"Blood missing?"

"Nance, you are so brilliant — yes! I didn't realize that, then, though — not till the following night's blow-out." Gunner reached for his own cigarettes. She didn't smoke menthols.

The D.A. leaned across the desk, holding out her lighter.

Gunner took the chocolate-brown hand, covering it with his own paw, pulling the tiny flame to the tip of his cigarette. Just like old times, in high school, behind the gym. He had to laugh.

"Gunner, go on with it," the DA sat back.

"Ah, Malibu, right. Bodies, or what remained, were being pieced together and we found significant parts missing. I don't just mean hands and heads — other parts. Twenty-four hours to the minute, later, Nance! Three houses down from the first hit! Fuckers pulled it off right under our noses!"

"Not your fault, Gunner. Sometimes, In these cases, you can't know what to expect. Look at the children in Atlanta." Nancy sat, swiveling in the office chair, shaking her head in disgust.

"Yeah, but this wasn't Atlanta. It was Malibu. We had enough cops. The place is dinky, Nance. You know what I mean? High profile clientele — the best equipped station. Those movie folks wanna feel protected. WE messed up, got lazy — or so I thought."

"You didn't mess up, Gunner. It WAS a hustler involved. I remember the outcome of that case. Became textbook. It was a kid the gardeners knew. You figured right, Gunner. The kid had been invited to both parties — recommended by the gardeners, correct?"

"Yes, yes, but the report kept a lot of stuff secret, Nance. See, we shook down the gardeners, early. We tracked the kid, easy. He was a hanger-on with this Venice Beach cult. Satanic thing. Wanted to be a big man with them. Our scenario was that after everyone got good and loaded at the parties, they all passed this kid around a bit much. He went nutso. They raped him, made him do things he wasn't ready to do on the job. When it stopped, he went crazy. After the murders, guess he decided to bring back a few trophies for his friends in the cult. Get some kind of payback for his rough trade. We shook the cult down, caught them with the treats. Put them all away. Course right off, they plead innocent. Said the kid arrived at the commune with the body parts and they never thought to ask him how he'd acquired them. Acquired them — good line, huh?" Gunner stubbed out his smoke.

"So, it wasn't the cult that did the killing — it was the kid —" Nancy was struggling to keep the story straight without letting the images nauseate.

"That's just it, Nance. The kid admitted to being at the Malibu parties, doing what he'd been hired to do. But he claims he passed out, like everyone else, right around dawn. When he woke up, most of the others were dead meat. Not all, but a lot. The killer had a decided taste for the more well-heeled guests. The scruffy ones were left alone. Anyway, the kid claims he was still high when he came to. Everything quiet, but blood was everywhere. People all hacked up. He was out of his mind, he said. Then he gets this vision to round up the various pieces already dissected — take them to his Black Mass friends in Venice. Score mega brownie points with the little devils if he does this. What's the harm — everyone's passed out or already dead — who's to notice? Right? Charming bugger. I told you, Nance, a real sick case. Anyway, he swears he's the victim as much as anyone at the party. We check all the alibis, of course. The kid's sucks. But it wasn't till the second investigation, day two, I notice something familiar. I know what missing body parts look like. I know how much blood gets lost when you cut those parts off. Viet Nam in full playback! I tell you Nance, there wasn't enough blood in those houses for what went on! I told the coroner. Unless the kid carted bucketfuls off, we were missing more than a few pints. Where were they? Damndest thing, Nance, never did figure it. And the kid — he was no help — his story had so many kinks in it . . . ."

"The gardeners?" Nancy watched as pain flickered over Gunner's eyes.

"Course. They turned out to be cult members. We hauled their asses off, too. But we couldn't pin the actual killings on them, either. All eventually released."

"Gunner, did you talk to the kid again?"

"Never got the chance. Hung himself in his cell. Second night inside the joint. Old enough to hold as an adult, but you know, he was still a kid. Found him at the end of his bed sheet. Shit. Shit." Gunner stood, began pacing the office.

"So, you think these killings might be related to that cult? You think they've moved East?"

"Course not. Not even close. Call it a hunch, call it saving face, it's just that I've got this wild hair up my ass when I walk into those motel rooms and find missing blood. It's such a warped thing. It can't be spreading out here! There should be some safe places left, Nance. You know? Maybe that's why I came back. I just want to believe that for a little while. I know there's more here than just the hustler. If the kid were the only perp, I'd say, let's nail him, now. But, what if it's like the Slavin case? What if we nab the kid and there's a whole lot more to it? We just scare the others off. For a little while. Then it starts up again. Then what? I don't need any more bodies on my conscience. I want to pursue this thing a little deeper than the locals do, Nance. I need you to help rein them in. Just a wee bit. No rousting kids off the street, not yet. No scaring off anybody. I'm not in the business of asking for privileges or favors, Nance. You know that. It's just so frigging weird to come across this MO out here. Especially here. I mean. What are the chances? I think I have an edge over the uniforms is all. I've seen this before. I've walked through this. I've made those mistakes. Let me try using what I know, just for a few more days?" Gunner stopped pacing.

"Gunner, this is a very slim line of reasoning. I don't know. What if you're really off? What if I do hold the rousting and some kid keeps killing while you're checking your pants for a wild hair?"

"Then some stupid ass john gets it and I'm a jerk for asking and I'll hand you my badge, Ms. D.A. I could live with that. Murder — it's always around, Nance. It will keep circling. What I can't live with is knowing something and not being able to use it. The uniforms already think I'm too cocky to live with. If I thought it would do any good, I'd tell them about the Slavin investigation in total. I bet the fuckers haven't even read the abridged report. So, what do you say?" Gunner was actually chewing on the inside of his cheek. He couldn't remember the last time he'd asked a woman for a break.

"Three days. That's it. Then I want you to report back here, to me, personally. Meanwhile, the police continue the investigation. I'll hold them off from shaking down hustlers, but I swear, I swear, Gunner, if, while you are gone, we have another incident I will keep more than your badge in my drawer. You got that, Detective?"

"Yes ma'am. I won't forget."

Gunner walked out, pulling the door softly closed, behind him.

———

"Manilla, sit down, please." The Dean of Weston College motioned to the open chair.

Manilla sat. Staring directly in front of her, focusing on the window behind the woman's head, fingers wrapped tightly around the lion-paw armrests of the chair, she sat, knowing what was to come.

"Manilla, when you first arrived at Weston, there were high hopes, all around. You were an honor student, the top one-percent of the incoming class. Your proposed major was cause for great interest and anticipation. It seemed to shine a beacon directly at the heart of this institution; individual advancement, deep, intellectual pursuits, self-tailored courses of inquiry. It typified the personalized approach we, at Weston, pride ourselves in. You knew our expectations, too. Along with some mandatory courses there were clear rules. There were acceptable rules of etiquette and conduct that all Weston women agree to adhere to. Perhaps that is the crux of the problem: rules. You seem to have a positive abhorrence for any type of restrictions applied to your behavior! Manilla, this is a very serious problem. Do you understand?"

"Yes." Manilla bit the inside of her cheek. She would be a stone. She would be cold and hard as they had made her.

"You aren't making this any easier, Manilla." The Dean rose, exasperated, depressed. Manilla had been one of her favorite students, one of her hopefuls. Manilla had turned into one of her biggest headaches.

"I hadn't realized it was my job to make it easy," Manilla's voice trailed off.

"Do you realize, young lady, that you've backed this institution into a corner? We have had more faculty meetings about you and your predicament. Well, never mind. Needless to say, as your Dean, I've gone to the proverbial mat for you. With your advisors, the president. You were given the chance to receive an exceptional education at Weston. So many women of your — "

"My 'background'? " Manilla stood, her anger fueling her. "Contrary to the lip service you all hand out, Dean, this is not the land of equal opportunity. It's not what the glossy brochures make out. I've been a token —like the few other women of 'my background' are, each year, in your private club. Playing that role should have more than made up for any pressure the president has been applying. It isn't just a race thing, is it? It's always come down to the class war. As long as you have enough bucks in the bank, ..."

"I resent your tone, Manilla. I also find your attack uncalled for — and quite preposterous. Weston offers qualified women from all backgrounds the finest educational opportunities. Why, do you know what percentage of our students receive financial aid?"

"Not enough. And those who do get shunted to all the shit jobs on campus, doing full time work no one else wants to do, then trying to keep pace with the jet-setters. It isn't like other places where you work your way through school and everybody does it and it's kind of like a rite of passage, kind of like a hoot, really. Nobody snubs anyone else cause they work in the kitchen or mow the lawns or work on the switchboards. Everyone is on equal ground, working their tails off and understanding that they are all in it together. Here, you have some finite group of students you can point to, who get all sorts of aid because you 'don't discriminate' or keep the needy, brilliant scholar outside your doors. You point to your fine traditions and hallways of honor where any woman who has the mind and heart can come and find enlightenment, can join your girls' club when she's through. But the truth is, unless we can summer in Europe or spend winter break in Key West, we aren't offered membership. What about internships? Aren't the best ones negotiated abroad, during winter break? Or over huge holiday celebrations on Beacon Hill or the Berkshires or wherever the hell those parties are held? Don't tell me openings in daddy's firm miraculously fall to the most qualified Weston graduate — or grad school doors fling wide, not to the Ivy Leagues, not just because of good grades. Don't tell me any more of that garbage, Dean! I've been here for three-and-a-half years and I've worked day and night during most of that time. I see what is going on, the grooming and coddling and 'handling' of the most well appointed and the scraps thrown to those precious 'scholarship recipients' you so like to point to at fund-raising time.

"Better for both of us if you cut to the chase and not try to tell me the truth. Because I can't donate a room or a wing when I graduate. It would be better for all the incoming tokens to know, up front, what they are getting themselves into. I believed your crap when I came here. I took your sanctimonious money. I admit it. But I didn't know about the hidden prejudice, or that I would be some kind of lawn jockey."

"That is enough, Manilla! I am shocked! This diatribe is uncalled for!"

"Uncalled for? Give me a break! It's long, long overdue! Yeah, you all offered me a spectacular education, but not the kind I'd envisioned. Don't worry, Dean. I know there is no 'leg up' for 'my kind.' I'm not even going to be one of those grateful few who leave their alumnae magazine on the coffee-table so all my friends can see who I once was, how I once got to rub elbows with the rich and famous. No doubt, whatever I've learned, whoever I've become, Weston is largely responsible. I guess I'm supposed to thank you all for that?" The bitterness of the last years, of all the misplaced judgments, of Ginny's own fierce battles, the losses and confusion of the past months, all welled up, spilling over, ugly, cutting, unretractable.

"Are you quite through? I thought we might have a civilized discussion this afternoon. One which centered upon your future with this college. Now, I see you aren't going to allow either of us to leave unscathed. So be it. If that is your decision. Just know, I have been one of your staunchest supporters, Manilla. Even at the onset of your peccadillo with Ginny MacPhearson's family."

"Don't!" Manilla spun around, her hands balling into fists at her sides. "Do not bring her into this!" So, this is where it would come to rest. There was truly nothing left to salvage. Except, perhaps, the public humiliation of having Ginny used as a weapon against her.

"Manilla! All I am saying is that I am not your enemy. For what it may be worth I do concede that traditional values at Weston are . . . rigorously safeguarded. I believe you have a fair argument when you bring up concerns about class differences — but not in the way it affects educational opportunities for the women here. Each woman must face her own choices — and chances. What would the kind of 'warning' you seem to imply necessary do for young students entering here? Perhaps some few would come in less innocently, less vulnerably, but do you think such a warning would have dissuaded you? You have not been victimized by this institution. At any point in your career you could have chosen to leave. In fact, you have done well, made friends in both the student body and on the faculty. People have over and again pointed out the great promise in your work — "

"Once, maybe . . . ." Manilla faced the lake, defeated.

"Perhaps that is true. Many of your closest allies have graduated or left Weston. But, Manilla, surely you cannot blame a single member of this community for pulling you into the pit you've dug for yourself this year. Even with the fall-out from the MacPhearsons, there was no reason to let your studies falter. In addition, you cannot imagine the notes and memos I have received concerning your absences, your unruly outbursts, your total disregard for others — "

"Lies! What disregard for others? Maybe I've missed classes or even been rude, on occasion, but what of all the things that have been hurled at me? The way I've been treated?"

"Manilla, as I've said before, so much of this you brought upon your own head. The choices you've made haven't always been the best."

Manilla laughed bitterly. "I can't believe I'm hearing this now, after fighting so hard to just hang on." She dropped her head into her hands.

Trying to regain control, she ran both hands through her curls. She wouldn't let this woman see her pain. Ginny had been right all along. She'd predicted her father's reach wasn't through. He and the president had been buddies at Oxford — the old boys' club — exactly the point Manilla was trying to make to the Dean. She was an outsider, the kind Ginny's family needed protection from, so strange. All along Manilla had simply been worried about Darsen.

"Perhaps it isn't as bleak as it seems today. Weston hasn't given up on you, Manilla, though you seem to have given up on us. Your record for the past three years is strong. You have some excellent recommendations, along with the notes of concern. Your painting shows promise. For now, however, until you rout whatever demons are tearing at you, whatever distractions keeping you from your obligations to this institution, we think it would be better for you to take an extended leave of absence. Later, perhaps next year, we can re-assess the situation. Until then, I want you to know, my office will be ready to assist you in whatever way we can; my personal door will always — " the Dean never finished.

Manilla left.

The Dean didn't stop her. She hated the drama. It was particularly unnerving when a system which supposedly was in place to support the causes of women pitted them against each other.

The door shut.

Outside, the secretary, a coterie of waiting students, a pair of visiting parents, all witnessed the disheveled retreat.

It was finally over.

———

The Volkswagen's door was propped open by Manilla's largest easel. The trunk and back seat were filled with clothes and painting supplies. Manilla was leaving the rest. Haunted objects. She didn't need the memories.

Furiously, Ginny roared up and down the corridors. She scowled at any underclass woman daring to cross her path. A few were brazen enough to peek from half-cracked doors.

Of course, they knew exactly who she was. None had expected the anger behind those famous features.

"Is this the last of it?" Ginny stopped Manilla outside the front dorm door.

Manilla shouldered the canvas backpack filled with brushes and palette knives.

"This is all of it."

Ginny grabbed Manilla's shoulder, pulling her in tight. "Sweetie, I'm sorry. None of this is your fault. It never was. This shouldn't have happened to you. I think this is going to be for the best, though. Fuck them, fuck them all. It will be easier between us, with you in Ithaca with me. Believe it, Manilla. Believe it." Ginny kissed the top of Manilla's head, then helped her into the VW.

Never had she loved the young artist more fiercely. It was her father, yes, but it was more. This very ground was corrupt. Evil had walked here. It had dared to touch the one she held closest to her heart. Manilla was paying for debts she never incurred. Never had Ginny felt such a mixture of tenderness and fury! Ginny got into the driver's seat, slammed the door.

"Are you in?" she asked Manilla without looking.

"Yes." Manilla's answer was quiet.

Not waiting for another word, Ginny tore out of the parking space, spewing wet gravel across the rococo doors of the dorm. Spinning the car in a half-donut, she gunned it backwards, then changed direction. Instead of heading out to the road, she headed up the hill, toward the science building.

"Gin?" Manilla was unsure of what was happening. She only knew that Ginny's anger from their fight had changed focus and was now directed at everything but Manilla. She had never seen Ginny so aggressive, so tight.

"Never got a chance to thank them all, did I? Would you mind waiting for a few minutes, in the car?" Still without looking at her, Ginny touched Manilla's knee.

"No, of course not." Manilla stared hard at the dancer but could not read her.

"I promise. I won't be gone long." Ginny slammed the door open. She jumped from the Bug and disappeared up the long walkway and into the building.

The corridors were deserted. A few lights in the basement, where the Coke machine stood guard, meant most people studying. The offices, on the higher floors, however, were empty.

Ginny could detect not a single human scent. Stealthily, surely, she climbed to the floor where the lab animals were housed.

She didn't need a light.

She passed the buzzing salt-water tanks, with their octopi and staring crabs. Down the corridor, past the rodent labs, beyond the rabbits, beyond the reptiles and insects, down to the pungent area that signaled the primate lab.

The sound of thudding bodies could be heard as apes and monkeys sensing Ginny threw themselves against the walls of their cages.

They recognized her for who she was. They had met with her kind before. These were the very monkeys Katherine Slater had drawn blood from so many nights, sustaining herself. These were also the animals whose memories had been ransacked by Darsen, who sent her probe out over the animal kingdom, pin-pointing Slater's whereabouts when the vampire realized the anthropologist was alive and hunting her down.

These were the animals that had allowed the evil to creep into Manilla's life, to pull her down and endanger her, forever changing her, without her permission. They had called the monster to Katherine Slater and Katherine Slater had taken Manilla with her. More, they represented the wickedness she associated with Weston. Her confrontation with her parents had taken place at the president's mansion.

Perhaps she could not destroy all the seeds of anguish in this place, but she could stop some of them.

Ginny picked up a scalpel.

From her night perch, Darsen heard the screaming.

———

The stench of the bile rushed back into Joey's face as the contents of the toilet whirled before they were sucked into the pipes.

He slumped against the bowl. His head was spinning; his stomach, sore. Between the shivering and the sweats, he hadn't slept for an entire night.

The clinic had warned him to get sleep, avoid stress, take vitamins, eat right, not to go anyplace he might be exposed to colds, viruses, anything contagious, avoid sex.

Ha.

Was it possible to bat a thousand? He didn't go in for baseball, but he was sure touching all the bases in this game.

Sleep. Fuck enough, he'd settle for some. Too fast, he was going down too fast. He knew the pneumonia had him. It hurt to breathe. Burned. He was beyond exhaustion. But every time he dozed off, the fucking ghosts were there — or she was there — no peace either way. He'd seen enough of his street pals go down. It happened fast. Just like now. Maybe the rich queers could afford all the mega drugs they had around, but they weren't for street trash, he knew. He knew how the game was played. People wanted his kind to get weeded out, to be taken away, out of sight. People said this was the new plague; they were all living in the days of the new plague.

Even the ghosts weren't smiling.

In the kitchen, Joey hauled himself into one of the plastic chairs. The cold toast and half-drunk glass of chocolate milk waited. If he only sipped the milk and gnawed a little of the bread, maybe, maybe he could keep some of it down.

His hands shook as he picked up the raggedy edges of the toast. Another wave of nausea washed over him. He barely managed to pitch forward into the sink.

———

Darsen sat at the foot of the reeking bed.

The room was lit by the blaring TV behind her. Joey struggled to sit up.

She moved so quickly he wasn't sure if she'd moved at all. "Are you ready?" Her voice was sarcastic. Awful. Joey shook.

"I told you, little fish. This won't do." Her nose wrinkling with disgust, Darsen sat against the rumpled blankets. "Remember?"

Joey raised his head a few inches. His eyes burned from the fever. His mouth was a mass of cold sores. He tried to clear his throat, "I'm really sick."

"I understand that, Joey. But it doesn't change anything. Get out of bed." Darsen stroked the bony forearms of the boy.

He shuddered at her touch.

Ice.

So cold.

So cold it burned through his fevered skin.

"Darsen, I'm puking. I've got the shits, can't stand up, I tried, really. I tried. Even if I do make it downstairs, who's going to pick me up, out there? I'm a walking billboard. No one's gonna stop once they get a good look!" Joey coughed spasmodically.

Darsen moved away.

The boy's breathing was raggedy.

She was silent as she stood over him, watching.

Her black leather pants and jacket molded to her like the second skin they were. Every inch was covered in the rich, oily texture. Her vibrant body was pure animal, existing only to mock him.

"Please Darsen. It's the nightmares — I can't sleep. The ghosts are back. You promised you'd stay, that you'd keep them away from me! I can't get better if I can't sleep!" Scabby fingers clawing at her immaculate hand, Joey reached for her.

She did not flinch.

"Joey," she purred, "how do you know they aren't the ones who sent me?" Her voice was like the great rumbling of a jungle cat.

"Darsen, please, I know what's happening to me. I'm not going to get better without your help! Maybe some drunk might pick me up, somebody who wasn't looking closely, but Darsen, if I do it tonight it will be the last time. Listen to me. I'll die out there, tonight! Darsen!"

Joey's cough kicked in, wrenching him into a sitting position, leaving him wrung out and gasping against his pillows.

"Darsen, if I died tonight, you'd be all alone. The game would be over. It doesn't have to be like this, doesn't have to end. I was thinking . . . I know who you are . . . I know. You could change me, make me . . . like you . . . Darsen. Then, I could stay with you, help you, forever!" Joey's face broke out with fresh exertion.

He lunged for her.

His shaking hand grabbed hers in a death grip.

Darsen allowed him to sob.

He couldn't look into her eyes. Couldn't face the countenance of such a cold-hearted god.

She peeled the skeletal fingers from her sleeve, pushed the boy back into his sickbed.

With sudden and surprising tenderness, she tucked the covers all around. "Darsen?"

It was the last word Joey uttered.

———

"Gunner, I think you better see this for yourself." The Sarge quickly pulled his rival aside.

Gunner jammed the note pad and pen into his bomber jacket. Men scrambled out of their path as the two crossed the studio apartment.

Behind them, Gunner heard the crack and the rustle of the body-bag. The boy was just a teenager. A kid. More missing blood. This time, though, all of it had been drained.

All.

The sergeant stood in the center of the tiny bathroom and pointed to the empty medicine chest.

"Pay dirt, pardner. I owe you one big apology." The cop poked the shiny object with his pencil.

Gunner glanced at his grizzled reflection in the medicine chest mirror. Just a flash, but enough to make him run a ham-sized palm along the unshaven chin. Syracuse was a hell of a long way from Malibu.

Inside the chest, third shelf down, next to an open can of weed, a stainless-steel straight-edge razor, the only missing item from his personal effects, or so the wife had identified. The engraved initials matched those of the first john. She'd given it to him on their seventh anniversary.

Without a word, Gunner walked out of the bathroom, crossed the apartment and was gone.

———

The secretary put down the receiver.

"Well, that was the oddest call I've ever taken!" She turned her chair to face the student intern.

"Really?" The student was by the water cooler. A bored senior, conned by her parents into doing volunteer work for the college, she thought it was crap.

"Yes, Holly, really. Some detective from Syracuse. Wanted to know if we have a record of Ginny MacPhearson attending Weston. I told him I could personally verify it. Hardly need to look up Ginny MacPhearson's records! But, if he wanted to know more, he'd have to come in person, with proper identification, and speak to the Dean. We've never had police inquiring about our alumnae before . . . not that I remember."

"How do you know he's a real cop?" The senior sat down, pulling a piece of distasteful lint from her angora sweater. She watched the ugly fuzz settle to the floor.

"What do you mean, Holly?" Nervously, the secretary rolled her desk chair closer.

"You know, sometimes these private dicks, detectives, they don't work for legit cops. They're just hired by people. That's why they're called 'private eyes' — get it?" The student rolled her mascaraed eyes in pure disgust.

"Well, of course I do!" The secretary snapped her chair back to her desk.

"Or, maybe it isn't anybody official. Maybe he's a psycho! He didn't actually ask for MacPhearson's number, did he? " The student watched in pleasure as the secretary squirmed.

"Oh dear, maybe I should speak with the Dean?" The older woman stood anxiously, her hands like pale butterflies flitting in front of her as she moved to the doorway.

The student grinned, "I wouldn't sweat it. I bet it isn't anything serious. He was probably a detective, legit, just like he said."

The secretary returned to her desk. "Well, I would feel silly if this was a big to-do about nothing. I mean, all I actually did was to verify Ginny MacPhearson's attending Weston. That's no papal secret, is it? I didn't even give the year of her graduation. If you don't think it's serious, Holly, maybe we can just keep the call between the two of us?"

"Sure. No prob. I've got a paper to finish by tomorrow. You mind if I knock off early?" The student sauntered to the door, stretching, cracking her neck from side to side.

"You go right ahead, Holly. I realize your first responsibility is to your professors. You slip on out, dear. I'll see you next Thursday, then."

"In your dreams." Holly mumbled, walking into the busy hallway. She headed upstairs for afternoon tea.

———

Gunner replaced the phone.

His palms were sweating.

"Thanks."

He turned and handed the building super a twenty.

As he'd imagined: the paintings matched the photograph from the old copy of 'People Magazine.' It was a series of portraits of Ginny MacPhearson.

Shit.

The perp wasn't a guy, but a woman, a woman obsessed.

New twist.

Hadn't expected a female, let alone a rich, artsy type. Didn't fit the profile. New kink. But no mistaking the obvious. The town house was rife with evidence.

This was so sweet — like finding the address book of the kid and this place scrawled in it. Oh, big mistake, kid. Bigger mistake for your girlfriend! Gunner rubbed his hands together.

The town house was owned by a looker named "Darsen." No first name. Or maybe that was her first name? No matter. The description had been detailed. The super nearly salivated as he spoke of the reclusive woman.

An artist.

Clearly a painter.

Rich.

But not famous.

He'd checked.

What the hell was a woman like this doing in Syracuse? The super didn't have the foggiest. But the super wasn't complaining. She paid her bills, in advance, in cash. Kept up on her dues and tipped him whenever she saw him, which wasn't often enough, as far as he was concerned.

Na, he wasn't letting just anybody into the private homes of his clients, but, if a city servant like Detective Gunner were to insist, especially if his insistence were to be backed up with the proper incentive, the proper paper . . . .

Gunner had dismissed the man the minute he let the detective inside Darsen's place.

Now, Gunner inspected every square inch.

Immaculate taste.

Expensive.

Very.

Oddly new.

Every item, brand new.

Except the clippings.

Picking up an old copy of <u>People</u>, Gunner saw the smiling faces of Ginny MacPhearson and her family peering out. Gunner slipped the magazine under his jacket.

There were other clippings from around the world. MacPhearson got a lot of mileage under his belt. Pretty high profile for the diplomatic corps.

Gunner left the rest. He knew everything he needed to know about Ginny's family.

Sick as it was, if he could find the girl, he'd be able to track down Darsen.

His call to Weston College had confirmed he was on the right track. That and the little hairs arched along his spine. He knew he was about to find his killer.

———

"Manilla, it will be all right. God knows I've got plenty of room for your stuff! Honey, sometimes it's just okay to stop. To be quiet for a while. To slow down and assess the damage, to recover and then to get a game-plan. Look at me. Look at how things are turning around! Haven't we learned anything? Manilla, you are supposed to be with me, under the same roof. This is fate, so, stop fighting it and relax. Please?" Ginny bopped Manilla's head playfully.

"Well, at least you're in a better mood."

"Sweetie, you don't get it, but you will. All my moods are elevated. I'm flying most of the time. You have to forgive the drama. I'm still getting used to this new level of feeling. But it's still me, Manilla. Just me. Slater didn't tell you about this up-side, did she? Well, it's pretty fantastic. Manilla, for the first time in my life I feel that I can protect someone besides myself. That someone is you. Whatever happens, I can protect both of us from now on. I know you. Just take this time to settle down, settle in, paint. The next six months we can pretend you're on sabbatical. Would that make you feel better? It's an early birthday gift from me to you. Stay here. Keep the house together, cook, if you like. But paint. Then, in spring, or maybe even next fall, if you really want to re-enroll at Weston, you can show them the new work. There are fewer distractions here. The light is terrific — and I need you. With me. Even with this new strength, you are still my heart, fool. Got it? Can you relax now?" Ginny put on her coat and boots.

"Thanks, Gin. Not much else I can do. At least you make it sound like a positive arrangement. Okay. I'm going to set up the back room for a studio." Manilla began to unpack brushes.

About to leave, Ginny raced back, turning the painter to face her. "Manilla, if we don't have each other, then we are really alone. Who else would understand?"

"No one, Gin. No one at all."

"I've got to go — got to get this body into the studio before I have to go out. I promise I'll check in with you before I . . ." Ginny let it hang in the air.

"It's cool, Gin. Really. Dance well." Manilla smiled, best she could.

"Someday you'll really believe that." Then, Ginny left.

———

She spun in widening circles across the dance floor.

Her reflection was simply a dervish along the mirrored wall.

Yes, yes, she understood religious fanatics who would use movement to fall into trances. Yes, yes, the not-so-fanatical religions, too. Dance was spirit; dance was prayer.

Faster, faster, her heart barely accelerating, her pulse steady; she could do anything and feel no stress. She came from the pirouette and opened full and high into a stunning leap.

There was no sound as she landed.

"Brava!"

Ginny spun around in the direction of the whisper.

"Don't stop on my account, dear heart. You know how delicious you are when you dance. Please, continue. I am only the humble observer, the privileged, private audience."

Darsen stood not more than three feet away.

"How? Where?" Ginny fell into a seated position. Her steel muscles went limp beneath Darsen's stare.

"How? Come, my pet, surely YOU remember? Ginny, I'm so disappointed. You sadden me with such a callous question. The night of your baptism, darling, the first night of your life, though you didn't know that then. But isn't that how it usually is? Our turning points go unmarked at the moment of their occurrence. It's much, much later that we look back and become aware. Have you become aware my sweet? Have you begun to realize the precious gift I left to you? I must say, you are far more robust than I expected. Your dancing has certainly not suffered!"

Darsen was up close, against her.

Darsen raised the limp dancer in one easy, polished motion. They stood gazing into each other's glare.

All Ginny felt was hate.

It crashed against her heart, raced with her pulse.

Here was the monster who raped her!

Yet, even in the midst of the anger, a single press from the vampire and Ginny felt heat, felt hunger. Darsen still controlled her!

Darsen knew her pull on the girl was clear.

Perfect.

Divine.

Ginny had been worth the wait, all the petty problems, all the mind-numbing details that movement among humans cost. Ginny had even been worth the risky battle with Katherine Slater.

Now, the dancer's futile struggles simply increased her lust.

With controlled hunger, Darsen rubbed her inner thigh high against Ginny, focusing exactly where she knew Ginny would be most open.

Ginny nearly fainted.

The orgasm was violent, immediate, filling every cell of her body, overloading her senses, shattering the light along each snapping synapse.

Her cry thrilled the monster.

"My darling Virginia, don't you understand? Your body is my body. Your mind is filled with hunger for me, your imagination, your dreams, only portals for me to enter. This is a mere taste of what awaits! Come away, now. Come and I'll spare the painter." Darsen slipped her sharp tongue into the dancer's ear.

Manilla.

Manilla.

This brought Ginny from the swoon.

"No!" she screamed, clawing at the vampire.

Shocked at the underestimated strength of Ginny, Darsen lost her embrace. The dancer's body should still be weak, still be transforming.

"What do you mean 'no'? The deed is already accomplished. There is no retreat. Ginny. The only choice left is to choose to save your friend's life."

"I don't need you, Darsen. I don't need what you did to me nor what you can teach me. That it is done. I know how to survive — and Manilla knows how to help me. I do have choices left. I won't become a murderer like you! You'll never get to touch me that way, again. I'll kill us both first. You disgust me!" Ginny tried to sound braver than she felt. She recognized Darsen's surprise at her strength. Perhaps Darsen wasn't as invincible as they'd believed? She'd survived the fire in the loft, but Ginny had broken free, if only momentarily. Darsen wasn't all-powerful.

"I disgust YOU?" Darsen's voice was menacing, "What of the petty creatures you still touch? What of your bestial feasting in the forest? How does that leave you feeling? Do you enjoy eating rodents, killing innocent animals? And, what of the painter? Manilla? Don't tell me she is capable of satisfying your new body? Not with those increased passions! How much do you have to hold back each time you touch her? Afraid if you allow yourself true release you will snap bones and sinew, break the little one's neck with a simple kiss! How often have you run from her simply because the very scent of her incites your lust? She can only be an irritant now, Virginia. If you dare show yourself, your complete hunger revealed, she will shatter. It is the nature of our power. We either suck them dry or we make them one of us. But you, my dear, you already have a consort!" Darsen licked her lips.

"You are NOTHING to me!" Ginny screamed.

"Oh, the lion may lay with the lamb for a brief time, but ultimately, the lamb will pay. Even if I were to take leave of you, I will not, but if I were, and promised to touch nary a hair on the painter's head, it would be only a matter of time. A very short time. You would be forced to kill her or to leave her. So, you see, there really are no more decisions to make. Only lessons remain, Virginia. A universe going back to the dawn of time. Come with me and become what your destiny has ordained you to be!"

Ginny found herself melting in Darsen's arms. Her body responded again and again to the unrelenting touch. She was rising, the orgasm approaching and then breaking like a tide over a breakfront.

When she calmed down, she struggled to get free.

This time, Darsen was not surprised. She simply increased the pressure of her embrace, trapping the dancer to her. "And, if you were able to resist killing the painter, what happens when she ages, as all humans must? What happens as your fame and power increase while hers diminish?" Darsen snarled.

Not wanting to admit defeat, Ginny looked away.

"You haven't thought this through, have you? You know, I could kill you instantly, leave the building and leave you dead. Then, I could hunt her for the pleasure of it. Or, I could leave this instant and before you had time to exit, I could find the painter and finish it altogether."

"You leave her alone!" Ginny clawed at the pallid cheeks of the monster. She left a long, open gash. But, there was no blood. The wound began to heal, even as Ginny watched.

Darsen's laugh was a growl.

"At least I know you have a temper, my sweet! Another facet I had not yet encountered. Interesting! But piteous. You see, you can never surpass your master, Virginia. I am more powerful than you can even comprehend. Don't worry. I won't take your little tantrum to heart, not my heart, anyway!"

Ginny felt the weakness in her knees. She fought to stand upright.

"Ginny, I'm leaving for a little while. Contemplate well what I have revealed. I won't rush your decision, but I am losing patience. Be warned. This time you WILL come to me because you MUST; you must finally realize there are no alternatives. You see that fighting is futile, ridiculous. You ARE mine, wholly and finally sure."

There was a blast of cold, and then Ginny was alone.

———

"MMMM," Florence Kray giggled, coming up for air.

"There's more where that came from." The high school boy pulled her back into his arms, snuggling warm lips in the exposed inch of flesh between the girl's jacket and her hair.

"Yeah, I bet, but I've got to get inside. I told them I was just going to the library. They know it closed over an hour ago. Really, Pete, I have to go in!" Florence pecked at her boyfriend's nose playfully.

"Girl's gotta do what a girl's gotta do. Still on for Saturday? I got tickets this afternoon." The boy bumped his warming crotch into the general proximity of his girlfriend's.

"I'm so jazzed! I cannot believe the band's finally coming to Ithaca! Pete, I really really have to go, now. See you tomorrow!" Florence peeled free.

Pete Cormier whimpered, feigning wounds, then flashed his best football smile. He scooted over the icy walk to his father's car.

Florence waited, watching until the aging Pontiac was out of sight.

The sky above was clear and cold.

Florence took in a final drink of the stars. She could make out Orion, and, if she squinted hard, the Pleiades.

She did not notice the strange mist rising off the lawn, nor how it began to twist itself into a tall, dark column.

It was the light from the Seven Sisters that Florence Kray took to her grave.

———

They'd missed breakfast. The coffee shop was empty. Ginny had the morning paper in her lap. Waiting for Manilla's return from the restroom, she thumbed through the Arts Section.

Ginny put the paper down, glanced about her. Where was Darsen?

She could be anywhere.

Like she had the last time they had come to this place, she could be outside, watching. Even as their coffee cooled, even as Manilla washed her hands, Darsen could be trailing them.

She'd decided not to risk implanting visions of Darsen in Manilla's already overactive imagination. Let old thoughts rule there. For now, if Darsen couldn't feel the pull of Manilla, didn't have the unlocked door of new worry to walk into Manilla's mind. It would be harder for her to find the painter . . . maybe.

Maybe not. It was just easier to buy time with Manilla if she did not yet know Darsen was back. Let her focus on figuring out the altered states of living with a half-vampire — or get lost in some romantic mythology about the mess they were in. Let her have just a bit more freedom before the disclosure. It was all she could give to Manilla.

Ginny let the paper drop to the floor. Headlines screamed: ANIMAL MUTILATIONS BEGIN AGAIN AT WOMEN'S COLLEGE.

Not even the salted release of tears was allowed. The transformation had sucked those from her, finally, as well. Emotion beneath the skin, gritty as sand. Christ, she hated what she was becoming!

Even with the increased physical power, the mind trips, the new passion, the cost was too high! What had gone so wrong?

Manilla cut between empty tables, for the most part oblivious to the latest changes.

"All set?" she smiled.

"Yes, I guess so." Ginny sighed, gazing at the cold coffee and untouched sweet roll in front of her.

Manilla shrugged. How did one get used to living with a vampire? Moments. Moments at a time was the only way to go.

It was like having a recovering alcoholic in the house. Don't think about the next day. Move one step at a time. One foot in front of the other. Tell the truth and don't forget your prayers.

Ginny draped a long arm over her lover.

Walking to the car, Ginny surveyed the street scene. The crowds of college people, the vendors. Darsen could be anywhere, disguised as any one of them. She could be in a doorway, an open window, a rooftop.

Ginny unlocked Manilla's door.

As they pulled away from the curb a flyer stapled to the telephone pole near the sidewalk worked itself free. It was a missing poster for a high school student, a senior named Florence Kray. There were numbers.

They drove past downtown with its pumpkins and Indians and Pilgrim displays. Cornstalks seemed to overflow the storefronts. Manilla wondered where their next Thanksgiving would find them.

Ginny kept her eyes on the road, but broke Manilla's thoughts by asking, "Do you miss New England? Being home, there?"

"What?" Startled from her reverie, Manilla turned to Ginny.

"You know, Manilla, your family there. Do you miss them?"

"Gin, you know I try not to think about it. It's finished. Their decision. Old news. It's probably easier for them this way."

"I don't believe you, Manilla." Ginny kept her eyes straight.

"Ginny, what are you talking about? Why you bringing this up?"

"Well, even if you don't want to actually see them, what about hearing from them? Or even, about them? I mean, I pick up the 'New York Times' and I can pretty much figure out where my parents are, what's going on with my father. That's all I meant."

Manilla scrutinized the dancer carefully.

Ginny was blocking.

This was leading somewhere other than to old family stories.

Ginny began again, "What if something happened to you . . . or to them? You aren't where they think you are, at Weston. How would they know where to reach you — in case of emergency?" Ginny's driving was picking up speed.

"Gin, nobody is hurt. Nobody is going to call for me."

"But in an emergency, they would! Manilla —"

Manilla reached across the stick shift and clutched the dancer's arm.

"Stop the car, Ginny."

Ginny swerved, sending the car into a skid. The car behind them screamed alongside. Its driver shot them the bird as it righted from the skid and slid back onto the road.

Ginny and Manilla sat, shaking, silent. Finally, Ginny spoke, "I wish this was easy."

Manilla looked out the windshield, beyond the car, to the street fractured with patches of ice and sunlight. Cars occasionally pulled from around tight curves. It was the usual morning traffic to town. Houses puffing wood smoke and steam lined the edges of the road. A few truant teenagers lounged around weather-beaten porches. Birds called from the lake. So normal. So regular. All she had to do was to open the door and enter the safety of the landscape.

Ginny reached over and took her hand.

"Gin, I've given up on easy."

"I've been thinking it through more carefully the last few days, Manilla. You should get away. Just for a little while. Get out of this hornet's nest till you can catch your breath, till I can calm down, get my bearings. You know how you love New England at Christmas time!" Ginny was trying to touch all the buttons she'd read in Manilla's mind. Pull out all the shared memories of Manilla's past.

"Ginny, you know, I can't go back there, ever."

"I know, babe. It was just an idea . . . just a passing thought."

Snapping back from the near-accident, from the pastoral scene around them, Manilla turned to face her lover. "Ginny, it's happening, isn't it? It's starting all over again!"

Around them, the sun broke through drifting clouds, dazzling the entire landscape with diamonds and shards of silver. How could the sun shine in such a place?

"I can't . . ." Ginny pressed fists to her eyes. She shook her head. As long as possible, she had to keep the situation out of Manilla's mind, anything to block Darsen's homing instinct. The moment Manilla realized how close Darsen had come, she would be furious. Her hate would draw Darsen like a magnet.

Manilla took another long, slow gaze at Ginny.

All right.

Decision made — don't press.

Ginny's call. In Ginny's time, the dancer would tell her what she needed to know. Another step in re-building their trust. However, the feelings in her gut made Manilla cringe.

"You know you aren't entirely safe around me right now, I . . . need more time . . . to get a handle on the changes . . . the situation. Please don't be angry with me." Ginny dropped her hands from her eyes.

"Gin, I can go to California — to San Diego." Manilla's voice was distant, quiet, already moving away. "I can see Jayne, in San Diego. I'll have to borrow money for the fare."

"God, don't talk like that! Of course there's enough money! Hey, maybe, maybe this will turn out to be a good thing. You're the one who's always saying we shouldn't celebrate Thanksgiving. It's just participation in the genocide, right?" Ginny attempted a smile.

"Yeah, me and my politics. When do you think I should book a flight?" Manilla felt the cool of the morning invade the car. Leaving was the last thing she'd expected to be asked to do. Pull back, regroup, close the ranks: yes, she knew that strategy. Taking sanctuary in each other — hadn't that always gotten them over the bumps? Ginny's transformation didn't alter those facts, not for Manilla, anyway! Together, they had a chance. Together, there was strength and protection. Hadn't Slater warned it would come down to this — always, just to this? Even Slater had enlisted aid, in the end. Why was Ginny sending her off? Apart, anything could happen.

"I don't want this to sound cold, Manilla, but I think we should call the airlines tonight. Get a reservation out as soon as possible." Ginny dropped the facade. Her face was waxen.

Manilla moved as far as she could against the passenger side door.

Decided.

Ginny was not open to arguments or persuasions.

She would have to trust Ginny — or not. But that wasn't an open discussion, either. So, she'd go.

Ginny started the engine.

She couldn't think of anything more to tell Manilla. Further talk would plant the insidious image of Darsen deeper into Manilla's consciousness. That would only goad the vampire into an early strike. However hurtful this silence was, it was better than risking open attack.

As they neared the house, Ginny leaned to Manilla and said, "It isn't because I'm unsure; I do love you, Manilla. Nothing can change that."

A man in a beat-up bomber jacket sat on their front steps.

Her new aspect of "protector" manifesting again, Ginny walked up the path, in front of Manilla. She immediately sensed he was there in connection with Darsen! His coat — his clothes — the scent of the vampire was on him!

Ginny felt her throat go dry. The tiny hairs on the back of her head began to rise. She forced herself to use a civil tone.

"Can we help you?"

"Ms. MacPhearson? Virginia MacPhearson? I was told I might find you here. My name is Kevin Gunner. I'm a detective working out of Syracuse. May I come in and ask you a few questions. please? It's rather urgent." Gunner offered his ID..

It was Manilla who took the badge, scanned it and the detective in a few, careful glances.

"I'm Ginny's . . . room-mate."

Gunner smiled, "So, I see."

He knew Manilla would be there. It had been fairly easy gathering information on the pair at Weston College. Universities and colleges were so lax with their records a high school hacker could have pieced the story together. Made him boil. Senseless. Stupid. Especially a woman's college. Put them all at risk. The killer had probably had as easy a time as he'd had getting information. Gunner shivered, remembering what he'd found in the town house — especially the animal skins . . . then, those paintings . . . all that jungle crap . . . eerie. Sick. He knew Manilla, the roomie, she was a painter, too. He had expected them to be together when he got to the cottage, but he hadn't expected them to look so young. Made him really nervous.

Ginny opened the door, then, turning to the detective, she said, "I don't know how I can help you, Detective Gunner, but, sure, come inside."

Manilla let the man pass.

She followed, behind.

"Just what I'd do!" he grinned to himself.

The women sat on the couch opposite him.

Made him sweat. Had his back to the windows. Hated that position. But they weren't about to trade seating arrangements. He'd expected a posher place. He knew Ginny had money. Still, she was going to school — and, from what he'd dug up, she was supporting the little one, too. He unzipped his leather jacket, then decided against taking it off. They were co-operating, so far, but they were clearly not of the mind to offer him milk and cookies. He took out his note pad.

MacPhearson was the most openly hostile. That was understandable, too. Given her background, nosy strangers were poison. He'd make it fast, then, get right to the point. "Ms. MacPhearson, I know who you are — I mean — who your father is, your family. I know you've had a bit of a rough time, of late, what with the fire in your studio apartment and all — but that's not why I'm here. That doesn't directly concern me."

"What does concern you, directly, Detective?" Manilla leaned forward, uneasy. The cop's manner — she was streetwise enough to know he wasn't acting on a routine investigation. This was about Ginny — maybe why Ginny had wanted her out of town.

Ginny felt Manilla's discomfort. She put her hand on the artist's knee. She didn't give a damn what the Detective thought. If he'd done his homework, he already knew. "Have I broken any laws? Am I in legal trouble?" Ginny asked.

She sensed the man's rising dislike. He had picked up on her discomfort when they'd first met. Maybe he had even felt her amateurish probing, as she'd tried to read him. He knew how to mask his thoughts.

"Cool bitch," Gunner's mind exploded with the image. He tried to hide the mental phrase, to cover with another plastic smile. But the thought kept popping into his mind, unbidden. Something about her gave him the creeps — even with all her good looks. He'd expected, maybe, more warmth — more human connection — grace? Not flowers, okay, but such open hostility? Almost felt like animosity. All his radar said she was connected, but maybe not in the victim-way he'd imagined. The news about Darsen wasn't going to be a surprise.

"You haven't broken any law I know about, Ms. MacPhearson. Let me be up front. I have serious reason to believe you may be in danger. We are investigating an individual in connection with a series of felonies out of Syracuse. I'm sure the officials will be contacting you within the next few days. The investigation got bogged down a bit. I've come a little ahead of the others. I'm being blunt, Ms. MacPhearson, because I am worried. Do you know an artist — a woman painter — who goes by the name 'Darsen'?"

Gunner watched Ginny's eyes. She did not so much as flinch.

It was Manilla who paled. For a moment and she looked directly at Ginny, then, catching herself, she dropped her stare, focused on Gunner's boots.

"Detective," Ginny began, "I do, or did, know a 'Darsen.' She had a studio across the street from me, in Collegetown, before the fire. I haven't seen her since that evening. We aren't exactly close friends. There was no reason to keep up the contact."

Sweat broke on Gunner's face. Ginny MacPhearson's father must be some piece of work because his daughter had inherited ice water in her veins. Shit! This interview was not going the way he'd planned.

"Ma'am, I don't want to scare you, but, if this Darsen does get in touch, would you give me a call? Please? I mean, pronto, soon as you hear from her — if you do hear from her. I'm staying in town for a few days. Here's the number." Gunner scribbled the motel's phone on a business card and handed it to Ginny.

"I'm serious, Ms. MacPhearson. For your own sake. Call me. Don't allow this individual to have any further contact with you. Don't arrange a meeting and don't let her inside this house. She's a dangerous woman. I can't give you anything additional. For that, I apologize. I can't even arrange official police protection, just yet. When the investigation catches up, here, we'll get the locals out. Till then, I'm all you've got. If it makes you feel easier, think of me as sort of an advance guard, okay? I'm just playing out a hunch. But in my line of work, hunches pay off. As long as you and your friend avoid any contact with 'Darsen,' well, just don't worry too much. Now, I'm serious about calling me — day or night. If you have so much as a feeling she might be in the area, you dial that number. Please."

Gunner stood up. He'd revealed a hell of a lot more than he'd intended. Something weird working on him — that blonde girl's stare — the heat in the cottage. His head felt odd, as if someone had spiked his punch. This Ginny, she knew more than she was saying. Meant she was in trouble, and knew it, cucumber act or not. Couldn't put all the pieces in the right places, but he would. Damn straight, he would. He watched as Ginny pocketed the business card. Wondered if that was how her father dismissed people?

Gunner took the hint.

For now, it was enough. Had to be.

He'd scare them off if he pushed.

Tightrope time.

Psychos like Darsen rarely broke their established MOs. These two would be safe. He zipped his jacket. He extended his hand.

Ginny ignored the gesture.

Manilla took it.

He liked the painter. Her grip was firm, but not masculine.

She managed her nerves well. Ginny was in deeper, but Manilla was supporting her lover. That's how it should be. The hand was dry, softer than he'd guessed. Actually, in her own way, she was kinda cute. Hell! He'd been working way too long if even the dykes started looking good.

Ginny watched Gunner as he walked to his car.

From somewhere higher, Darsen watched, too.

———

Night.

Manilla stoked the fire.

Decided — even now that the truth was out — in two days she'd be in California.

Darsen was back, but it was Ginny's show.

Ginny would face the vampire on her own ground — with the detective in the mix, Ginny wouldn't be completely alone. Decided — mostly by Ginny. But Manilla would let it rest. She understood. She was the point of vulnerability. If Ginny was worried about her, Ginny couldn't confront Darsen full throttle. She did understand, as much as could be understood without all the pieces.

Exhausted, they were both moved through the house like ghosts.

Ginny began to pace.

Every night the cold had come sooner.

She needed to feed.

But she needed to stay with Manilla, to protect and watch over Manilla.

Darsen was close.

The vampire knew Ginny would have to leave the cottage to feed. Still early. Neighbors just getting in from work, street sounds regular, even mundane. Maybe it was still safe — safe as it was likely to get.

As if sensing the debate, Manilla looked up from the book she was reading and offered, "Gin, go. Just come back soon."

Ginny came to the couch, leaned over and kissed the dear head. In silence, she grabbed her parka and was out the door.

In silence, she promised to come back quickly.

She meant to keep that promise.

———

Gunner came out of the club, into the alley.

He wasn't drunk.

He wasn't on duty.

So, he wasn't drunk, on duty. End of guilt.

He felt like shit.

Should be staking out the girls' place.

Should be sitting in his rental car, drinking a thermos of coffee and watching the dykes.

But the tall one, the diplomat's kid . . . something about her . . . made his balls freeze. Wasn't just the hoity-toity background, either. He could deal. Had to kiss ass to enough Washington types most of his career, especially the military. He had the calloused lips to prove it — ha ha ha. No, something else got his goat. The way she looked at him . . . those eyes . . .

like she could see . . . all of it. All the bodies, attached and following him . . . asleep, awake, never could shake the bodies . . . .

He pulled near the ashcans.

Out of the light.

Had to piss.

Too much beer. But, it was late. Those girls weren't going to call him anyway. He'd be okay. Just take the fucking whiz, get in the car and start the stake out. Course then if they did frigging call, they couldn't reach him . . . shit. Shit, in Malibu he'd have a cell phone by now. He'd have back-up and three more guys working with him. This was podunk U.S.A. Fucking University town. Who did Cornell think it was? Only reason anybody knew about Ithaca anyway. Okay, so, he'd only wanted a beer, a beer to wash away that awful taste he'd had in his throat after meeting Ginny MacPhearson. Then it had been the papers — they always got to him — then another beer, cause he didn't have a fridge in his motel room — and then the two or three others — cause, what the hell, he hadn't had any dinner and the dyke wouldn't call him. He knew it. They were going to laugh him out of Syracuse when they found out. Nancy would have him by the short hairs. He knew how that'd go. He'd come so fucking close and now the MacPhearson kid was stonewalling him like he'd never been stone-wailed before . . . just like last time . . . a kid holding out information . . . a kid while a killer walked free.

Gunner didn't see the mist begin to enter the alley.

Didn't watch it swirl and rise, changing color from a pure vanilla to deepest black.

Didn't feel the temperature as it began to plummet around him.

His heart . . . .

Something around his heart . . . .

His chest, like somebody was squeezing it, couldn't breathe, his heart . . . .

The side door to the bar smashed open. A woman, leaning heavily on her date, crashed outside. The sounds of a bad local band, rowdy drinkers, all entered the alley at the same time.

"Fuck, honey, it's freeeeezing out here!" The woman pulled her boyfriend after her.

"Hey, what's that?" The man brushed the woman off, leaving her to totter unsteadily on her six-inch wedgies.

"Hey, over there, by the trash — " he moved carefully out of the light under the door. "What the fuck?"

A huge black shadow roared up and over him. His skin turned to goose-bumps where it was exposed to the rushing air. Frigid, like something from a meat freezer. Then, it was gone. But the figure on the ground, by the dumpster and cans, it was still there, moaning.

———

The fireplace had worked its magic. Manilla was curled on the sofa, fighting to stay awake for Ginny. The battle was fruitless. Exhaustion, the rhythmic snapping of the heating wood, the warmth . . . .

Slater stood on the hearth facing her.

Manilla didn't move.

The light shimmered and Katherine Slater stepped from its center, came closer.

This time, Manilla sat up.

The woman smiled, though her face betrayed worry.

"Slater — there's so much I want to ask you. I've been calling." Manilla didn't try to stand, didn't try to touch the anthropologist. She'd learned that much. She waited for Katherine Slater to speak.

"Manilla, you're in grave danger."

"I know. Darsen, she's back."

"She's come for Ginny. Manilla, she will never be satisfied until Ginny is hers, completely. And you are dead. You have to prepare." Slater's form moved in and out of the light from the flames.

So different from the erotic dream. Manilla was ashamed. Her imagination had been working overtime. She blushed now as she faced the real Slater.

Slater's voice was as shimmery as her figure. She spoke again, "Manilla, I am flattered. Don't be embarrassed. We are all innocent in our dreams."

"You could see that? Jesus — " Manilla's blush deepened.

"Sometimes, when you call out to me, when the dream is about me, yes. But only then. Even then, the energy must be exactly right — a kind of frequency or wave — like radio, but more refined," Slater explained.

"Sometimes, you don't hear," Manilla tried to keep the accusation out of her voice.

"Yes, you're right. Sometimes the frequency, the electricity of your energy it's not strong enough. Or, I hear and can't answer, can't get to you. But when the danger is this close, those frequencies change. They clarify and intensify and allow me in." Slater still held her position in front of the fire.

Manilla wished she'd move across from the couch, so the light could play off her face more clearly. Oh, she did love this woman — in ways that had nothing to do with Ginny or anyone else before.

"Manilla, I'm here for this brief time to try to help. The danger is very, very great."

"I don't know what to do. Slater, after you died — after your body died — I started this research to try to find clues to what was happening to Ginny, to what this whole nightmare was rooted in. All the conflicting stories! Christ, you don't know! Everything twists and turns in on itself, or goes off in little sparking directions! Just when I thought I had the answers to some big mysteries — "

Slater's eyes seemed to twinkle golden as she interrupted. "Many mysteries are not meant for human understanding, Manilla."

"But the ring! The power in the ring — your ring! At least the mystery around that! If I don't find out how to control it, I have to destroy it — or hide it where it can't hurt Ginny, at least! I don't want to give it up, Katherine. It's — it's my only connection to you." Manilla's voice broke into a sob.

"Manilla." Slater took a step toward the young woman, but came no closer. "When you need me, I can come to you; that connection is soul to soul, between us. It is not dependent upon the ring."

"Then why did you give it to me? It almost killed Ginny!" Manilla wiped her eyes on her shirt sleeve.

"Manilla, I left the ring for you for the same reason Darsen originally gave it to me. There is great power in that stone. Its power protects the owner from attack — attack by Darsen's kind — my kind — Ginny's kind."

"But Ginny would never — " Manilla sat up straighter, upset at the insinuation.

"Remember that evening? It was early on in Ginny's transformation — a time when she was ravenous and very, very confused. Every cell in her body was changing and screaming for nourishment — for blood. It wasn't Ginny. In that moment, the ring flashed out. It was the power that was corrupting Ginny. The ring repels that power, Manilla. It only works when that power attacks. That night, and only that night, you were fair prey." Slater's voice softened. She knew the effect of the information on Manilla. Then, she went on, "Unfortunately, it is only a defensive weapon. It cannot be used to hunt Darsen down. It will not hurt Ginny in her new identity. She has brought the power under her control. She has nothing to fear from the stone."

"If the ring is so powerful, why hasn't Darsen come looking for it?" Manilla asked.

"I told you. The ring is dangerous to those who would harm the owner. You are the rightful owner, as I was, when she left me with it in the jungle to burn, that first time. She cannot reclaim it. Only you have the power to give it away."

"What if I gave it to Ginny?" Manilla's voice rose with excitement.

"Do you think Darsen would attack Ginny? Manilla, Darsen's seed is in Ginny. Only Ginny's careful pruning of its growth allows Ginny's heart to stay free. Darsen doesn't need to use physical force on her." Again, Slater's voice was quiet.

"Then there isn't anything I can do?" Manilla sank back, her own heart racing.

"No human can ever stop Darsen, Manilla."

"Slater, where did Darsen get this stone?" Manilla felt as if all the wind had been knocked out of her.

"Let me tell you some of what happened to me after the fire, while I was still in the jungle. There isn't much time, but I can give you some rough history that may help you. It took months for my body, even in its transformed state, to heal itself. I existed on whatever small animals I could catch. The myths of vermin heralding the arrival of a vampire, well, those may be rooted in the fact that we can live, when necessary, on small game. What game is more plentiful than rodents? Gradually, as I came to be restored, I had to have bigger prey. Then I learned I could exist and keep most of the cold, the pain, at bay, through the blood of animals between the sizes of monkeys and apes. If I fed on something large, say, a deer, or a bigger primate, I didn't need to feed for a few days. But if I focused only on the smaller animals, I needed to feed more often. I learned the limits of other powers beyond restoration of the body. I learned how to use my night vision and then, how to turn it off, relying upon the other heightened senses. I learned how to communicate, in a rudimentary way, with animals, to 'see' into their minds, minds so vastly different yet as complex as our own. That myth you may have run across, is a truth. We can 'speak' to animals — command them through terror, control them through mental manipulation and fear. Of course, the same principle works on human beings — the highest animals — or so we like to believe. Why it is so easy for Darsen to move through our world? As I healed, I came to cultivate my hate for her. I drew up innumerable plans to begin the hunt to destroy her. But the healing took longer than I expected. My body was a miracle, but it was not magical. During those long, long years I spent there, my loneliness was the far greater pain. I did not seek out the villagers or even the infrequent explorer, however. I was terrified that my hunger would blossom into something like Darsen's. Then, one night, after feeding on a wild boar, I fell asleep in the crook of a tree. You know, from Ginny, how vulnerable we are, our sleep, though dreamless, is total, When I awoke, I was surrounded by women. Indian women."

"Slater, I read about them — they're a tribe — they are connected to legends about red stones, stones that hold souls." Manilla's excitement grew.

"Yes, you have done good research, I knew you would, I saw it in you, even the short time we were Weston. It is the same tribe. I felt no revulsion from them, no fear. In fact, they treated me as if I were a lost cousin. It became abundantly clear to me, they had seen my kind before. They must have known Darsen." Slater's body shifted, shimmering and then growing a bit dimmer. She hurried on, "They were not afraid of me, however. Instead, they took me to their village. They brought me wild animals, mostly monkeys, some small pigs, bound and ready for me to kill. They knew what I needed. Then, they spoke to me of the woman who often visited them. She taught them great magic. She stayed with them and helped them and asked only that they point out their enemies to her."

"God — the missing men from the forest — " Manilla grew pale.

"Yes. They believed when Darsen destroyed their enemies she locked their souls into these red stones, these jewels. She made the women the keeper of these stones. In return, she gave them things they valued, medicinal secrets, information on how to find game. She taught them how to hunt their enemies when she wasn't around, possibly through hypnotism. Sometimes she brought them gold and silver ornaments from Goddess knows where . . . . She became a hero to these women. They awaited her arrival like a second coming. They guarded her stones jealously."

"But, did the stones come from her or did she find them? Why did she want them guarded?" Fully absorbed in the answers to her mysterious questions, Manilla propped herself into a more comfortable position.

"They would not or could not tell me. The stones were souls, they said. They guarded them for their mistress. End of story. I was spared because I resembled their mistress — but more, I was wearing one of the stones — her ring." Slater's energy was fading, going down as low as the fire itself.

"Why didn't she think of looking for you with them — or visit them after the fire?"

"I now know Darsen so thoroughly believed I had been destroyed, there was no need to ask those questions immediately after the fire. I also believe she was sick of the jungle, sick of betrayal, sick of what had happened to her there. She hadn't counted on my refusal of her gift. Manilla, Darsen hates to lose. Anyone or thing. In all the time I spent in the Amazon, she didn't return, once. It was my good luck — or hers. It would have simply meant our showdown would have occurred much earlier. Whatever the reasons, wherever she gets the stones, we know, they do not contain souls — at least not the souls of the people she gives them to. My soul is not on your finger." Slater laughed gently.

"I have to find out what this thing is!" Manilla twirled the ring so the firelight illuminated the gemstone.

"Manilla! I've warned you, there are some mysteries human beings can waste their entire lives upon. Some mysteries are not meant to be found out — not in your dimension. If it helps, think of it as a kind of talisman. Old fashioned magic, if you will. All through the ages there have been power-filled objects people wore or carried for protection. Let this be one. Clearly, Darsen believes in these things enough to give them to her partners. Keep it close. Keep me close." The shimmering shifted and now, only a vague outline of Katherine Slater remained.

"Please, don't go, not yet, I'm not ready to lose you—" Manilla shouted, her arms outstretched.

"You will never lose me. Remember, even if you cannot see me, even if you cannot hear me clearly, I've learned to walk beside you, Manilla. It is our bond." Then, Katherine Slater was gone.

———

The deer moved through the darkness, scared. A young buck, he should have bedded down with the others. But something had spooked him to movement.

Ginny was tracking him. She was careful to keep downwind.

Even with worry about Manilla over her, the thrill of the hunt coursed through her system. Her new senses revelled in it, opening to the life that throbbed in the forest surrounding her. She was part of this meta-existence, as feared and welcomed as any creature who prowled the deep woods. But, this night was different. She wanted to track, to kill the animal. She wanted to be done quickly. She wanted to get back to the house and fall asleep in Manilla's bed, to fall asleep beside the person she felt closest to; she needed Manilla's heart-protection.

The deer broke cover, just as the moon rose from behind the clouds. Awash in the silvery light, the animal seemed unearthly, a spirit loose in the haunted wood.

Ginny moved in, took the vibrant life without a sound. She'd learned well. No pain. No struggle. A least there was that consolation. The best she could offer the animal. And, in deference to Manilla's beliefs, she would utter a short thank-you prayer to the spirit of the beast before she began her long drink.

Indian hunters offered such prayers after each kill. It honored the animal and it cleansed the hunter. Manilla had learned it from her Mohawk friends. Ginny had thought it quaint, once. Now, she believed it necessary.

It was the sound of the twig which made Ginny lift her head from the blood.

A single twig, snapping, off to her left.

Whipping about, face dripping, eyes flashing, fangs still lowered, Ginny faced the intruder.

"Yes, darling. I have been watching for some time, now. I must say you are most impressive. Brava! But such hedonism! And that little prayer at the end — really. You must work on finesse. Sophistication. A touch of panache, a bit more grace. Remember your upbringing — famished as you are, it doesn't look good on a woman of your stature." Darsen moved from the darkness of the trees into the blue moonlight.

Hair sleek as a raven's back, leather impeccable and oily, she seemed carved from night itself. Save for the pale oval face, Darsen was almost invisible. Except to Ginny.

Against her will, she felt Darsen's mind raise her. Move her in a floating arc, deposit her at the vampire's feet.

"Here, let me clean you off. You are much too refined to be seen like this." Darsen reached down and pulled up a handful of fern from beneath the cover of snow. Their smell was green and rooty. Gently, as though wiping chocolate from the face of a child, she cleaned the blood from Ginny's face. One last streak remained along Ginny's upper lip.

Then, Darsen leaned over and licked it from the dancer's flesh.

The touch of that electric tongue caused Ginny to feel weak.

Transformed, strengthened a thousand times over, Darsen was still her mistress. Heat crackled up and down Ginny's spine. Her head was light, her blood-infused system already primed for sleep, kicked into overdrive.

Darsen caught her in her arms.

"It's time we depart. Come, now, no more playing games!" Darsen's honeyed voice filled Ginny's head.

"Darsen, wait, listen! Please! I will stop, I will stop resisting you, but I can't leave now. Not tonight. Manilla's alone. She's waiting. I promised her. She's going to be gone in a couple of days. Then, then I'll do whatever you want me to do. Whatever you ask. As long as Manilla's safe. Please, this last favor!" Ginny was gasping. Her energy was being pulled by the vampire's touch as easily as an infant's breath is pulled by a smothering cat.

Darsen hissed, then pushed the dancer abruptly away.

"One last request? The last? You have pushed me to my limits, Virginia! Take note, my love, you toy with your life here. You toy with the life of your friend! Consider my generosity a wedding gift. Now — leave — before I come to my senses!" Darsen stared at the trembling woman.

Unable to believe her fortune, Ginny needed several seconds to regain control. She shambled off into the snowy wood. She did not look back. She could feel the ruby eyes burning behind her. She believed Darsen. All of it. The finality was branded upon her as surely as that blazing glare. Neither she nor Manilla would be safe if she didn't return to Darsen.

She ran for both of their lives.

Manilla sat up, stared into the dying fire.

The pieces — they were coming together.

"I trust you've been well?"

Manilla slowly turned to the place where the voice seemed to be emerging.

In all her dreams, in all her musings, through the anger and hate and roaring imagination, Manilla had never pictured it would be like this.

Now. In her home.

From right behind her.

"Darsen?" Manilla choked out the name.

"Yes, little one, it is me. I've come to fill your empty evening. I want to show you something wonderful." Darsen's voice was deadly, voluptuous.

Darsen came from the shadows in the corner, came into the golden light of the fireplace, standing exactly where, only moments before, Slater had stood!

Manilla was transfixed. Was this just another layer of her dream?

"No, my pet. You are, indeed, wide awake. Even your wild imagination could not create what you are going to experience. Your dreams, dear, dear Manilla, are pale and puny compared to the dreams you will begin to walk in, tonight. You miss your friend, the esteemed Dr. Slater? Who am I to keep such burning souls apart? Come to me, Manilla, come so I may send you to Katherine Slater."

"Ginny?!" Manilla's lips were numb, heavy. Her entire body cast in stone.

"Oh, you do have a taste for the glorious ones, don't you? I can't fault you for that. Ginny is lost. Just like Slater. Two souls for the price of one, Manilla! Delicious, isn't it? Forgive me if that was indelicate. Too bad, Manilla, you and I have many things in common. This is indeed a waste."

Ginny knew she was close to the lake. She could smell the clay-scent of wet stones, could hear the uneasy bumping of the last of the geese still huddled together near the frozen water. But how far she'd moved up the lake, her blood-muddled mind could not clarify.

Drunk, the deer had made her drunk. She'd been stumbling since leaving the woods. The sleep which hit hardest immediately after feeding was exactly on schedule. It mixed in deadly combination with the spell Darsen had planted in her mind. Drugged, desperate, she spun in circles, clawing at the yellow curtain of light from the street lamps, fighting unseen demons as they nipped at her ankles, tripped her and pushed her in all the wrong directions. Darsen was closer to Manilla . . . Ginny could feel the approach . . . could sense Manilla's terror even as she crashed against the thick walled shield Darsen hid behind. Ginny's probe still too weak to subvert the master.

The only chance was to force herself to stay awake, to push through the rising fog in her brain and make it back to the house . . . the only way.

———

Darsen's mouth parted, the tip of the split-tongue caressed the full lips, flicked in animal abandon, over her pearled fangs.

Manilla could not stop watching. She was aroused. She was revolted.

Darsen wanted her — now — more than anyone had ever wanted her. To be so desired, to be so absolutely thirsted after — necessary unto death — hadn't this always been the core secret of Manilla's heart?

Her first lover, the professor who brought her out, had she said, "If you ever become a necessity, I'll leave you." She'd been good for her word. Then, Katherine Slater — Manilla was still unsure of those feelings — what of Ginny? Ginny needed nothing anymore — nothing she would accept from Manilla, anyway. Her family, her friends — all gone, vanished, she was alone.

Only Darsen remained.

Only Darsen was constant.

Manilla felt Darsen's power playing with her, probing her deeper, making her feel . . . . She began to breathe harder, her muscles tensed, ached with the strain: "NOOO!"

"I beg to differ, sweet one, my darkling." Darsen hissed into Manilla's ear, stroking it softly, calling her name.

Manilla. Ah. An artist's blood — not for many years had she sipped such a vintage. It would fill her with satisfaction and joy. It would rejuvenate her — acting like some vaccine against the diseased and watery drinks she must endure each day. Ah. Manilla as medicine, as sacrament. As sacrifice. She would use the blood for Ginny, too. They would all share in the final act.

Darsen pulled the painter fully into her arms. Stroking the thick, dark curls, she forced Manilla's head back, chuckling, even as she watched the mounting fear in the eyes.

She pressed the demon mouth to Manilla's opened lips, forcing them wider, wide enough to accept her reptilian tongue.

Manilla's mind screamed, her consciousness rebelled even as her body responded.

Such insistence, such heat!

Manilla felt the seduction as it began to roar through her veins.

Darsen's kisses flicked light and burning pain

The scent of moss, of lavender, Manilla's scent, rose, in heady waves up from the warming and fragrant skin. Darsen inhaled deeply, allowing herself total indulgence. It had been so long, so long since such an act filled her with this kind of ritual lust. She needed much more than Manilla's blood.

Bending the half-conscious painter across her lap, exposing the pulsating veins at the neck, Darsen wanted to go slowly, extend the climax, fill both of them with the hideous joy the blood-letting would beget.

Tenderly, Darsen touched the innocent neck; less tenderly, her mouth began the long journey across Manilla's breasts.

Manilla's arm was pushed from the place where it had fallen against Darsen's leg.

The hand splayed out.

The last flames of the fire sputtered. One of them sent just enough light out to reflect in the stone of Manilla's ring.

The refracted light burst out, cutting a line across Darsen's face!

"What?" Darsen, rose, flinging Manilla across the room like a sack of laundry. "No! No! No! Nooo!" The vampire screamed.

Stunned, half-blinded from the fall, Manilla saw that it was as if a razor had been drawn across Darsen's countenance.

Darsen staggered backwards, held her hands to her face. Her body began to shift, to alter.

Manilla remembered . . . in Ginny's loft . . . the beating of the huge, leathery wings, the monstrous transformation. She raised her arms, to defend herself.

In that instant, the stone throbbed with light. The beam broke from its center forcing the hell spawn backwards, screeching!

Too late. Her hands blocking her vision, she'd misjudged the distance. Hungry for the dry and changing fuel the monster's body was becoming, the fire licked out of the hearth. Darsen's screams turned to gasps as she beat at the engulfing flames.

The only way of escape was past the fire, behind her.

Before Manilla could raise the ring a third time, the shattering of the lake front windows filled the room, followed by the freezing night air. The fire roared out, over the hearth for a second, then died.

Up and down the snowy street, dogs began to howl.

———

They stood on the shore beneath the frozen stares of the stars.

Beyond, the lake shown like a snow-encrusted jewel: dark, sparkling, dangerous.

Ginny held Manilla's hand tightly.

Around them, houses glowed amber and gold. Families were deep into holiday planning. People were tucked safe for the night. The neighborhood was quiet and ignorant.

"Manilla, I am so sorry — " Ginny hugged her lover hard, as if to press Manilla into her own body.

From the fold of Ginny's embrace, Manilla whispered, "I know. I wish you weren't. That only makes it sadder. We're okay, Gin. We're okay."

"But for how long?" Ginny answered.

Manilla moved away from Ginny, looking back out over the lake. In her pocket, she twirled the Slater's ring. "Gin?"

"Yes?"

"Something Slater said to me didn't really sink in till now. I've been thinking." Ginny stared hard at Manilla, feeling the words before they were wholly formed in Manilla's mind, seeing the images breaking there. The power was increasing. They both knew it was increasing within her.

"Slater said Darsen would never be destroyed by a human being."

Ginny swallowed hard, feeling the frost in the air, feeling that outside cold as surely as the one that grew in her nightly, "No. I can't."

"Gin, this is our life. That's all there is for me. Period. Our life. Without you there is only death; fast or slow, it will come for me. Darsen's hunting me, she will continue to hunt me — even if you left, for good, even if you left tonight, it wouldn't change."

Ginny turned, taking Manilla's face between her hands. She looked deeply into her lover's eyes and asked, "You knew?"

"I know you, Gin. I know what you'd promise if you thought it might save me. Listen to me now. Hear me out so there can never be a doubt that it is MY choice, MY request — please?"

Ginny dropped her hands, pulling away, trying to halt the mounting dread. "You don't know what you're asking me to do! Manilla, you don't understand. There are so many levels — just the pain. We don't even know — the worst of it!"

"But I DO know. From Slater. From watching and being with you — now, even from Darsen. Most of it. There's more to learn, of course, but, it's like Slater said, there will always be another mystery — another piece. Some pieces we maybe will never find. I believe in her — her connection to me. To us both. I think I understand why she said what she did. She couldn't tell me to do it, but she knew, when I was ready, I'd understand the deep meaning. I'm ready, Ginny. It's more than just me. It will affect you, too — that's the hardest part of all. But if we don't, more people are going to be hurt. It's my choice to ask. So, I'm asking for this most intense favor, Gin. Please." Barely brushing a golden hair, Manilla touched the dancer gently on the cheek.

Ginny closed her eyes at the touch. Manilla's finger burned as it grazed against her. The immediate, total response was terrifying. Yes, this too, part of the argument. Manilla would always be in danger — not just from Darsen, but from her, too.

"Manilla, you can't take responsibility for something without rules. We don't know what's out there, who's out there. We don't even know where she's hiding. Tonight, it may seem right but what if tomorrow we get some more — pieces? What if that detective shows up and he and his department have hunted Darsen down? It will be too late to — "

"Ginny, she's killing children."

"She's always killed children." Ginny stared up at the stars, wished they were both somewhere else.

Manilla stood behind the dancer, wrapped both arms around Ginny's slender waist. She rested her head against Ginny's back, whispering, "I know. That's why we have to stop her — we have to do whatever we can to stop her — because we do know what she does. You can't do it alone. You don't have to do it alone. I have the ring, I have Slater's . . . insights. We have Detective Gunner. It's a start, Ginny. Beyond the knowing, it's also, I'll admit, revenge — for what she did to Slater and what she did to you. Even if she didn't kill kids, for me, it would be enough."

"Darling, I don't know if I can — if it will work. What if, something goes wrong?"

Manilla didn't reply. She only held on. She could feel Ginny's breathing, even through the thick coat. It matched her own.

How odd, so very different, coming from opposite directions all their lives, but now, so perfectly fitted together.

Ginny was her life.

All ways. From the first, she'd known. Unwavering, never lost.

"Ginny, it has to work. You never were Darsen's. It will work because you are MY heart, MY blood."

"Manilla." Ginny sighed. It was true.

They were. Blood.

Gently, beneath the starry witness, Virginia MacPhearson turned and unbuttoned Manilla's jacket. Without words, she cradled the painter's face in her hands; then, she whispered only that Manilla must look away, must lower her eyes, must concentrate only on what was passing between them, concentrate solely upon her kiss.

———

Gunner awoke, gasping.

The hospital room smelled of disinfectant, of burnt metal — probably from all the machines in the room — of lilies. He couldn't figure out the lilies.

Fingers.

Fast as the smells registered, followed the sudden inability to breathe. Fingers cutting around his wide throat, cutting off all his air!

Survival training kicked in. He suddenly realized whoever had him could snap his neck if he continued to thrash. He forced himself to push back the panic.

The hands slid away.

His vision cleared.

Only the night lights shone in his room. Empty beds on either side. None of the machines hooked up to him, so it seemed, nothing giving off enough light, anyway, for him to see who was there.

Then, the second wave of scents — this one fast and frightening — very, very familiar.

Gunner smelled blood.

"Christ, it's you!" he coughed.

"So, we meet, face-to-face. You came so close, Detective, closer than any of your Keystone Cop friends from Syracuse. Bravo! But it doesn't pay to be this good, not in your profession." Darsen caressed the grizzled cheek.

He tried to pull away.

This time, her touch blistered his chin.

He tried not to scream.

His heart hammered in terror.

Even in the pain, something about her moved him. He found himself stirring to her animal sexuality. It sickened and drew him at the same time.

"Oh Detective Gunner, you are a man of wit and intelligence. You know, I don't find many of your race to be so entertaining. The bravest are usually dullards, the most brilliant, usually weak. You are balanced, a quality — which puts you at the point of calamity."

Darsen stretched her hands like claws, purred out the final syllables.

"Fuck you, bitch!" Gunner spat.

"No thanks, I've given that activity up, at least with the males of your species. But I am flattered. Still, not enough to get you out of this sticky situation. While you are a charmer, detective, and quite the Boy Scout to have tracked me so closely, you made serious errors in your assessment of the past. These mistakes have left you here, in my hands. Would you like to know? Of course you would — another fatal human flaw: curiosity. Well, because I know you will keep this secret, I will fill you in, detective.

"There were patterns between what happened in Syracuse, patterns linking it with California — but the murders in Malibu, simply an odd twist of fate. You forgot that on the West Coast drama permeates everything. It wasn't me, detective. I would never have associated with such moronic rabble — that low-life cult, please! And the Hollywood scene — so bourgeois! Mass murders are not my style — so much needless waste. So banal. Empty displays of power. You inadvertently came across the handiwork of one of my younger cousins. Poor sap. He HAS succumbed to Tinsel Town. Boring. In any case, it was a dandy leap of a connection you pieced together. Not many men have such intuition about blood. Too bad it has taken a turn for the worst. Too bad you won't have a chance to hone your talents."

"Filthy whore!" Gunner gasped as her blade-sharp nails raked his calf muscles.

He couldn't scream. She'd done something to his throat. He couldn't press the nurse's call button, his body was paralyzed. Her touch had turned him to a mass of nerve endings and quivering jelly.

"You know, detective, you shouldn't judge me so harshly. I put that poor teenager out of his misery, really. Saved him from a horrible AIDs end. Didn't your coroner share that tidbit with you? And I did a public service — the boy was passing on the plague to all his gentlemen friends. Every night, out there on the street, detective. He acquired the disease long before our meeting. And those men — well — it was their own poor choices that netted them those gruesome ends, was it not? I didn't create a single one of these situations. I simply move through the sad comedy you call society. Like all predators, I do my job. I just do it exceptionally well — much like you, detective. Much like you. See, we are kin, after all. I cull the gene pool — and you, you, too, put away the sick spore."

Gunner's tears were openly flowing. He hated her for making him weep.

The paralysis seemed to intensify, rather than dull, the pain.

"Why don't you beg, detective? Call for your God or your mother?" Darsen stroked closer to his groin, drawing blood.

"Fuck you, you bitch! You've left a trail, Darsen. You aren't so smart, after all. I found you. The Syracuse PD will find you. No more hide and seek. Time's coming for the end of your line. The others don't know, yet, what you are, but they will. They have all the evidence to see what you've done. They'll never let up, now, Darsen. This is the twentieth century; it's only a matter of time. You can't run twenty-four hours a day. Even you, you have to stop, to rest. They've got you, lady. You're toast. You're history!" Even as he grunted out the words, Gunner knew it was futile.

"You know, just for a second there, you had me going, detective. Good for you! Hmmmm, let me ponder this for a moment . . . maybe I should reconsider. Would it be more noble to let you live? More of a challenge for me, knowing you're out there — so you could spread the word to my enemies and strike further fear into their already quaking hearts? Hmmm . . . ."

Darsen climbed atop the bed and then began moving over the prone man. "Unfortunately, you've caught me at the end of a really bad month." She licked her lips. "Time's up! Buzzzzz. You lose! Sorry. All those other scenarios are too cliche. You know, detective, too Malibu!" She was fully astride his heaving chest, "And so, I must bid thee adieu, sweet Gunner. Adieu."

EPILOGUE

The figures move under the bridges.
Light spills on soft faces, tender bodies.
Under the bridges.
In the doorways of closed storefronts.
Atop roofs; in back alleys; at the edges of
    parking lots.
It is dark.
It is cool.
It is humid.
It is rainy or foggy or dead-on clear outside.
They shiver, they sweat, they laugh and curse and
    are quiet when the big cars purr up closer,
    nearer to the light.
They break ranks, strike poses, call the predators in.
They separate out, the younger, the sick, the
    weaker ones.
 Under amber floods or pools of cool blue.
They move out, each one, alone, in his place,
    waiting to be chosen.
Just like that.
Exactly.
Like that.

ABOUT THE AUTHOR

Karen Marie Christa Minns is the Gemini-born, 1956
author of "Virago," 1990, — a two time Lambda Award
Nominee for Best Sci-fi/Fantasy and Best First Novel, and
"Calling Rain," 1991. Her poetry and short stories have
appeared in such collections as "Daughters of Darkness,"
Cleis Press and the "Herotica" series, Plume/Penguin
Press. Minns' paintings have been exhibited both in the
U.S. and Europe.